D0190415

LAST MAN OUT
by Donald Honig

It is February, 1946, in New York. The sensational baseball rookie Harvey Tippen has just signed on with the Dodgers. Everything is going great until fate throws a sharp curve. A gorgeous, young society heiress is found brutally murdered, and Tippen, who was her last lover, is now tops on the suspect list. Agonizing over a secret he is afraid to confess, Tippen is caught between cops looking for a quick conviction and a Dodger ownership seeking to sweep the scandal under the carpet. It looks like Tippen's diamond future is over before it's begun when baseball reporter Joe Tinker sends the game into extra innings. But nothing can prepare Tinker for what awaits him at the end of this twisted trail of desire as he hunts for the truth and tries to persuade the police that a vital piece in the puzzle has been overlooked. Ringing with authenticity, this mystery-thriller is as rich in nostalgic magic as it is in spellbinding suspense.

Coming from Dutton Books

THE PLOT
TO KILL
JACKIE
ROBINSON

Donald Honig

A SIGNET BOOK

SIGNET
Published by the Penguin Group
Penguin Books USA Inc., 375 Hudson Street,
New York, New York 10014, U.S.A.
Penguin Books Ltd, 27 Wrights Lane,
London W8 5TZ, England
Penguin Books Australia Ltd, Ringwood,
Victoria, Australia
Penguin Books Canada Ltd, 10 Alcorn Avenue,
Toronto, Ontario, Canada M4V 3B2
Penguin Books (N.Z.) Ltd, 182–190 Wairau Road,
Auckland 10, New Zealand

Penguin Books Ltd, Registered Offices:
Harmondsworth, Middlesex, England

First published by Signet, an imprint of New American Library,
a division of Penguin Books USA Inc. Previously published
in a Dutton edition.

First Signet Printing, May, 1993
10 9 8 7 6 5 4 3 2 1

PUBLISHER'S NOTE
This is a work of fiction. Names, characters, places, and incidents either
are the product of the author's imagination or are used fictitiously.

For Cathy
"A Thousand Skies"

1

New York City. November 1946.

"That was a pistol shot," Tinker said.

"How can you tell?" Sally asked.

"Lady, I spent three years in the Pacific. Believe me, I know a pistol shot when I hear one."

"Aren't you curious, then? It wasn't very far away."

No, Tinker thought, it wasn't. In fact, it had been pretty damned close.

"I'm not in the least curious," he said, drawing the bedcovers up around his ears, nestling with a luxurious sense of detachment. Not so long ago gunshots had been fearsome adjuncts to his life, and one that sounded suddenly in the night, as this one had, could cause a lot of tension and uneasy speculation and maybe some panic. Combat tended to personalize circumstances and situations; New York City was splendidly the opposite. A gunshot in one of the world's most cultured and sophisticated cities could be casually ignored. By Tinker anyway.

Sally rose next to him in the bed and rested on one elbow, staring at the window. The streetlight downstairs on Christopher Street delineated her bare back, the soft contours of her shoulders and the slimness of her arm. Her brunette hair, unpinned at bedtime, hung below her faintly jutting shoulder blades. Risen in bed, she was not clutching the covers to her breasts, as most women he knew would have done. Tinker did not care for excessive modesty.

"What do you think it was?" she asked. In deference to the hour, and maybe as well to the gunshot, she was whispering.

"A thirty-eight," he said indifferently.

"I didn't mean that."

"A murder, a suicide, a holdup. Russian roulette. How the hell should I know?"

The November night was balmy, the window partly open, and through it came a sudden eruption of loud, excited voices. Lying motionless on his pillow, Tinker pursed his lips and squinted, trying to get a reading. He heard panic, consternation, and then anger and profanity, all of it punctuated by an abrupt, toneless screaming that broke off as quickly as it had begun. One voice broke through the clamor: *"Get 'im! Hold 'im!"* There was another loud clash of indistinguishable voices, ending with a shrill, semihysterical, *"Kick him in the balls!"*

Sally spun around.

"That was a woman!"

"And a tactician," Tinker said.

8

Then there was another voice, loud and blunt, and though its utterances were not clear, Tinker knew the law had arrived. A thin siren, growing louder and more urgent as it poured through the canyons of dark urban concrete, foretold the approach of more law.

"Why can't you live in Queens," Tinker said, "like normal people. Nothing happens in Queens. You can sleep through the night there."

Sally threw back the covers and went to the window.

"Shit, Joe," she said, "it's right across the street."

"It'll be right in this room if they happen to look up. For Christ's sake, crouch down at least."

She lowered her slim naked body until her chin was level with the windowsill, her fingertips resting lightly on the sill like a tentative typist's.

"What a circus," she said. "They've got a man pinned to the sidewalk. One guy is sitting on his chest and another one is on his legs."

The siren came rushing into Christopher Street with ear-piercing shrillness, then abated to a low moronic drone.

"It's turning into a block party," Sally said. "People are running from all directions. Maybe you ought to get down there."

"Why?"

"You're a newspaperman."

"Currently under suspension, without pay. And anyway, I'm a sportswriter."

"Jesus, Joe, two cops just ran into the building with their guns drawn."

"You'd better get your head down."

"A car from the *Daily Mirror* just pulled up. Maybe we ought to call the paper and tell them to get somebody down here."

"Screw the paper."

"It might be a good story."

"Then cover it yourself."

"I write society news, sweetheart."

"Maybe this involves some bluebloods."

"Not in that building," she said with some distaste. "Anyway, anything sordid repels me."

"Oh?"

"Watch your tongue, Tinker."

"I was very careful with it," he said.

"You're disgusting," she said mildly, then turned around in her crouch at the window and added, "in an entertaining way. What are you doing?"

He was standing, bare-chested, buckling his trousers.

"You told me to go down there. I'm going down there." He wasn't going to be able to sleep, and they had already screwed for several hours; so in the absence of one or the other, he saw no reason to remain in bed.

He slipped his shirt on, worked his fingers quickly up along the buttons, then stuffed it into his trousers. He pushed his bare feet into the pair of loafers on the bedside floor, then picked up his corduroy jacket and slung it over his shoulder, holding it by one finger through the cloth loop inside the collar.

"Hurry," Sally said. "I want to know what happened."

By the time Tinker reached the street three deep flights below, two more green-and-white NYPD prowl cars had arrived and were positioned in the middle of the street, all doors hurled wide like semaphoric signals of urgency. The impersonal monotones coming from the police radios in the empty cars sounded eerily autonomous.

The crowd of onlookers, several in bathrobes, had been pressed into a horseshoe shape by the police and were fanned out from the tenement's entrance into the street and behind the prowl cars and around back to the entrance, like a church crowd waiting for newlyweds to emerge.

The people near one side of the entrance broke aside as two policemen, one of them belligerently ordering them to "move the fuck out of the way," hustled a black man toward one of the cars. The man was short, muscular, the pomade in his wavy hair glistening in the streetlight. He was scowling, his eyes so hot that whoever they made contact with turned quickly aside. Tinker noted that the man's tieless white shirt was silk and that his sausage-thick fingers were gaudily ringed and that his polished black shoes were of expensive leather, were indeed more than just a man's churchgoing best, not that today was Sunday or that this looked to be much of a churchgoer either. The man's arms were behind his back, joined at the wrists by a pair of handcuffs. Tinker noticed that the back of the white shirt was darkly smudged and he assumed this was the man Sally had seen pinned to the sidewalk listening to some woman urge that he be given one in the nuts. When they reached the prowl car the man was shoved through the door, landing awkwardly on his side and wriggling about on the seat to right himself.

One cop got in the back with the prisoner, another slid behind the wheel, and doors slammed. The crowd, fascinated by the sight of a handcuffed man, gave way as the car began moving slowly, siren rising; and then the car went wailing into the night. The fading siren seemed to be picked up by another shrill night-call as an ambulance from St. Vincent's turned into the street from Seventh Avenue and lunged to a halt in the space just vacated. A pair of white-jacketed attendants with intently impassive faces got out and went to the rear of the vehicle. They threw open a pair of heavy-handled wide-swinging doors, jerked out a stretcher, and hurried with it through the crowd into the building. A knot of people bunched behind the ambulance and stared soberly into it.

One of the *Daily Mirror* reporters emerged

from the tenement, stood framed in the lighted foyer for a moment, then walked down the four brownstone steps. He was wearing a tan raincoat and a fedora and was holding a small notebook in his hand. Tinker recognized him: Morrie Jacobs, police reporter.

"Morrie," Tinker said, approaching him.

"Hello, Joe. What are you up to?"

"I live across the street."

Tinker took him by the arm, guided him away from the crowd, and quietly asked what was going on.

"Guy got shot in there," Morrie said.

"Dead?"

"Extremely. They haven't got it sorted out yet. They're questioning the girl, or trying to."

"What girl?" Tinker asked.

"The one whose apartment it is. She seems to be in a state of shock. They can't get a word out of her. She just sits there staring. Colored girl. About nineteen. I caught just a glimpse of her." Morrie lowered his voice. "A real piece."

"Lovers' quarrel?"

"I wouldn't think so."

"Who's the guy they dragged out?"

"Say, are you covering this, Tinker? What the hell am I telling you all this for?"

"Because I'm asking you. If I was covering it, would I be standing here asking you what happened?"

Morrie smiled. "I heard about the stunt you pulled in Boston. Got yourself canned, huh?"

"Not canned, just suspended for a while. So what's this anyway—just a shooting between some coloreds?"

"I didn't say that, Tinker."

"I can see why Hearst pays you guys bottom dollar—you're so tentative."

"The cop on the beat says the guy they took away was her pimp."

"Sounds like a heartwarming story," Tinker said. "Snowball prostitute, snowball pimp, dead customer. It could be your first Pulitzer."

Another prowl car came rushing to the scene as if in pursuit of its own siren wail. The car skidded to a halt with crunching suddenness, so abruptly its brakes let out barely more than a yelp. A stocky, bull-necked policeman bolted from the passenger side and rushed toward the tenement, his face grim, flushed, as though he had been holding his breath for the past minute.

"McReynolds," Morrie said. "Precinct captain."

"He looks like somebody put a finger up his ass."

"You bet."

"What the hell's going on here, Morrie?" Tinker asked.

"The dead customer is a white man."

"But more than just a white man."

"You're sharpening up, Joe. Yeah, it's a top-line detective named Harry Wilson. One of the most decorated cops on the force."

"What was he doing in there? Who shot him?"

"That's all I got, Tinker," Morrie said. His partner came out of the building now, carrying a flashbulb camera. Together, the *Daily Mirror* men got into their car and drove away.

Tinker drifted back into the crowd and stood with his arms folded, staring moodily up at the tenement, which stood sheathed in an intricate-looking network of rusty fire escapes. The action was behind the drawn shades of a second-floor front apartment, where he could see silhouetted figures passing back and forth in the lighted window behind the iron rungs of a fire ladder.

Tinker felt a twinge of envy. Writing sports was enjoyable, often exciting, but it was never anything like this. In sports a life or death situation—fourth down and one, bases loaded in the bottom of the ninth of a tie game—was strictly a metaphor. This was the real thing. Bullets, blood. A dead man. A murderer. Three years as a fighting Marine in the Pacific had been—in retrospect, of course—an exhilarating experience, the thin patina of time passed now making it seem like something it surely was not at the time. But the truth was, everything seemed tame since he had come home.

By this time a steady stream of people was moving in and out of the tenement—more reporters and photographers (Tinker recognized men from the *Journal-American*, the *Post*, the *Sun*, the *World-Telegram*), scene-of-the-crime people from the medical examiner's office, some grim-faced top brass from the Department. It was after 2 A.M. now but the crowd was still in the street and there were still faces at most of the windows that gave upon the scene. It was known now that there was a dead body in that second-floor apartment, and those familiar with the building had let it be known that there was also a young, attractive black girl who sold her body for cash up there. So, patiently, doggedly, the crowd was waiting.

Then one of the uniformed policemen came out of the building and started snapping at the crowd in a voice edged with the kind of nastiness a subordinate will employ when giving orders in the proximity of a superior, telling the onlookers to move aside and not crowd, gesturing irritably with his billy, the leather loop at the top tossing from side to side like a tassel, the expression on his face suggesting it wouldn't have taken much provocation to make that billy rise and cleave somebody's skull. "Keep it that way," he said when he had provided clear access from the front door to the vehicles in the street.

From where he stood, Tinker could see the lower half of the narrow staircase inside the tenement. Watching it, he saw a pair of black shoes appear in a hurry as if they were dancing on the plain wooden steps, then the navy-blue trousers, and then the policeman, brass buttons and silver shield, visored hat, anonymous face.

They all looked alike, Tinker thought, and that was because a city kid growing up made it a point never to look a cop in the face. The policeman opened the front door with its peeling gold-leaf street number and made sure it stayed open, which it did, its spring having long since ceased to react.

Then Tinker saw the white trouser legs appear, taking one cautious, mistrustful step after another. Behind the attendant came the stretcher, tilted up into the hands of the second attendant, its burden covered with what looked like a sheet of black canvas, buckled tightly to the sides of the stretcher.

When they reached the foot of the stairs, the attendants moved with processional deliberation toward the front door. A self-conscious silence fell over the people in the street when the attendants and their laden stretcher appeared.

The girl appeared on the staircase a moment later. One uniformed cop was walking in front of her, another next to her holding her arm, another behind her. She was short, maybe five-two, and seemed even smaller compared to the uniformed officers around her. She was wearing a dark mouton coat that seemed to engulf her. Morrie had said she was a woman worth looking at, but because of the coat's bulk Tinker couldn't tell, though there was surely nothing wrong with her legs.

Tinker had never been attracted to black women. He had never taken one into the rack with him, had never even been curious, though such curiosity was by itself foolishness since anatomically they were no different from white women or any other women; hence the validity of the old schoolyard wisdom that "in the dark they're all alike." But this one of course was not. Along with the lurid aura of prostitution, she was freshly involved in a murder—had maybe even pulled the trigger herself—and not just any murder, but one resounding enough to bring some of the Department's heaviest weights scuttling to the scene.

Her face was expressionless. Her eyes remained downcast as she was led from the building, raising but once for a furtive glance at the stretcher that was being lifted into the ambulance, and in that brief unguarded moment Tinker caught a glimpse of wretched torment, and when her eyes lowered again he noted that they fell fully shut for several seconds.

She was almost to the police car when a man suddenly came charging out of the crowd toward her. He was thin, light-haired, wearing a half-zipped blue jacket cinched at the waist by gray elastic—the kind of jacket worn by members of tavern-sponsored softball teams. His pale, plain-featured face was furiously contorted, and as he dove for the girl he began screaming, his voice a frenzy of grief and rage.

"Fuckin' black nigger bitch, you killed him!"

The cop to the right of her blocked him with a shoulder, throwing him backward. The man rebounded quickly, though, and rushed forward again. This time the cop hit him flush on the jaw, knocking him to the sidewalk.

"Get the fuck outa here!" another cop roared, running up and grabbing the man by the collar and sliding him back across the concrete so violently the man's feet jerked upward for a moment and Tinker saw the soles of his shoes, saw where a nub of pink gum was stuck to one of them.

"Fuckin' black nigger bitch!" the man screamed in a voice pitched near to frenzy, looking both lunatic and ludicrous as he was being dragged backward across the sidewalk.

The girl glanced coldly at him as she got into the police car. The few blacks in the crowd began drifting away.

When the man was released by the cop he got to his feet, passively accepted a shove from the bluecoat and retreated to a place a few feet beyond the crowd's perimeter. His eyes flooded with tears that he seemed adamant about not shedding. He looked up at the second-floor apartment, then at the car into which the girl had disappeared, then menacingly, with unspent fury, at the onlookers, who were watching him with wary curiosity, uncertain about this unexpected coda to the night's events.

When the precinct captain came hurrying from the tenement, followed by his driver, one of the cops looked around and in a voice loud and mean with authority said, "All right. It's all over. Break it up. Go home."

The crowd began to disperse. The departures of the ambulance and police and press cars left behind an exaggerated sense of emptiness and finality.

Impelled by a prickly curiosity, Tinker watched the man who had created the scene, who was still standing in place, looking abandoned by the crowd, which had melted off in ones and twos. He was standing just outside the pool of streetlight, solitary and sullen, staring at nothing, still within the coils of his fury. Then he swung slowly around and began walking with tedious deliberation toward Seventh Avenue.

Tinker looked up at Sally's window. She was still there, wearing a robe now. She gestured to him to come back upstairs. He shook his head, jabbing a finger toward the departing man and beginning to follow him. They pantomimed to each other, she with raised, questioning palms, he with a placating hand. Then he made a short, sweeping gesture: Go back to bed.

It was not easy to follow someone who was barely moving. Once the man stopped completely, in mid-step, covered his eyes with his hand, remained like that for almost a half minute, then lowered his hand and began walking again, passing a row of garbage cans with lids askew and sides variously dented and caved in.

At the corner the man stopped, standing in

the light from the windows of an all-night United Cigar store. He looked around, first to his left, then to his right, as if to get his bearings and come to some decision. Then he walked again, along Seventh Avenue.

Tinker paused, wondering whether to go on. Curiosity was a hellish fidget to have at three o'clock in the morning. Then he thought: *Fuck it.* His newspaperman's nostrils were flaring. Even though he only wrote sports—the toy department of a newspaper, Cannon said, though Tinker didn't think Jimmy was being belittling but rather was implying some moral purity, the magic and mystery of toys—and even though he was for the moment cold-storaged by the paper, Tinker still felt an allegiance to the profession at large.

When he reached the corner, Tinker saw the man standing in the middle of the block staring into a bar, neon Rheingold and Schaefer signs glowing in the window, their sizzling tubes casting a lurid light upon the sidewalk. The man slowly unzipped his jacket, then went into the bar.

It wasn't a Village bar; that is, it was a bar that happened to be in Greenwich Village but that had never possessed any bohemian appeal. It was a neighborhood drop-in, where members of father-son unions stopped on the way home from another laboring day to observe another mile further from the cradle, another nearer the box.

The man was sitting at a far table against the wall, near the kitchen door. Hands in his lap, he was staring vacantly at the raw tabletop with its decades of stains and dents. His shoulders were slightly hunched, giving him a chilled look.

The bartender, leaning on the bar with his forearms, looked at Tinker when he walked in, then turned away. Two bulky middle-aged men were bottom-spread on splay-legged wooden stools, and they weren't showing any interest either. If they were consciously doing anything, it was avoiding looking at themselves in the backbar mirror.

The anguish looked pinched and mean in the man's thin face. The eyes remained fixed in lifeless concentration on the tabletop for a full thirty seconds after Tinker had slipped into the chair opposite, then finally rose and cast a flat, morbidly uninterested scrutiny on him.

"I saw what happened back there," Tinker said. "That cop had no right to do that."

There was a bruise on the man's jaw, colored by a few pinpoints of blood where the skin had broken slightly. He was wearing a white shirt with a narrow, patterned tie. Why a man would wear a tie with that tavern-team jacket was beyond Tinker, though having grown up in Queens it wasn't the first time he had seen the fashion. The name "Quentin" was stitched in white thread across the small breast pocket, which was closed with a zipper.

"He really clipped you," Tinker said, trying to sound both indignant and sympathetic. And I'll bet, he added to himself, it wasn't the first time that face has been punched. I'll bet it's been punched soundly and consistently for years. There was something offensively malcontent about it, a sullen nastiness that seemed innate. When you saw a face like that in a movie, you knew the character was going to be shot away in the first fifteen minutes and remain unmourned throughout the rest of the movie.

"You feeling better?" Tinker asked.

"I would have killed that black nigger bitch," Quentin said. His voice was without inflection.

"Why?"

Quentin looked stonily at Tinker for a moment, then slid his eyes so that they were gazing over Tinker's shoulder and out the window at Seventh Avenue.

"We were sitting here," he said. "Right at this table. I had two whiskeys and he had a beer, which he didn't even finish. He'd just come in from his tour and we met here for a drink. 'Don't go up there,' I told him. I told him to forget it, to write it off, that it was no good. But he wouldn't listen. He said she was expecting him. I told him I'd wait here. Give him an hour or so. I had another whiskey. Then somebody came in and said there'd been a shooting around the corner. I knew right away. I knew just what it was. Those goddamned niggers killed him."

"I know," Tinker said.

"How do you know?" Quentin asked, a sudden sharpness in his eyes as they made a quick lateral shift. "Who the hell are you anyway?"

"I came in for a drink. You want a drink?"

"No," Quentin said, covering his eyes with his hand. He sobbed quietly, his shoulders shaking fitfully. Once upon a time Tinker would have been embarrassed by a man crying, but he had seen it too many times in the Pacific to think it anything but natural.

"Christ," Quentin said, his voice sodden with grief, "I can't believe he's gone." He shook his head, his hand still hiding his eyes.

Tinker got up and went to the bar and ordered two straight whiskeys. The old remedy. Never fixed anything, but never hurt either. When he returned to the table, Quentin had composed himself. Tinker put the thick-bottomed shot glass down in front of him and Quentin picked it up, tossed the whiskey down in a gulp, then gripped the solid little glass tightly in his fist.

"Just a few hours ago," Quentin said, "we were sitting here. And now he's gone."

"It can happen fast. Were you in the war?"

"Yeah."

"It can happen awfully fast. He was a friend of yours, huh?"

"He was my brother."

"Oh, shit. I'm sorry. Really sorry."

"Those black bastards killed him."

"What was he doing up there?" Tinker asked, but a sharp little glance warned him away from that.

Tinker sipped his whiskey now, frowning at the hand resting on the other side of the table, the fingers wrapped tightly around the shot glass.

"He have a family?" Tinker asked.

"Just me."

"Older brother?"

"Say, why are you asking so many questions? You sound like a goddamned chaplain." The pugnacity was back in the thin face, accentuating the petulance, the eyes suddenly hardened, looking as though they had been screwed into their sockets. "You a fuckin' chaplain?"

"I'm a newspaperman."

"Big fuckin' deal. So go write a story."

"I'm not doing this story," Tinker said. "I'm a sportswriter."

The face across the table turned from pugnacity to skepticism to curiosity.

"Yeah? A sportswriter? Then you must've heard of him. Harry Wilson."

"He went to Newtown High out in Queens?"

"That's right."

"I'll be goddamned," Tinker said. "I went to Newtown. Harry was a legend out there. Baseball, track, basketball."

Into Tinker's mind came the corridor outside the gymnasium, where the trophy cases were. There, under glass, for generations of students to muse on and try to emulate, were the ribbons, medals, cups, and plaques won by Harry Wilson, class of 1920.

"He was the greatest athlete Newtown ever had," Tinker said.

"Newtown? He was the greatest athlete to ever come out of Queens, maybe out of New York City. Baseball. That was his game. He played minor-league ball and was a cinch for the majors. Everybody said so. I wanted to see him with the Dodgers. He could've made it too," Quentin said, banging the table with his fist and glaring at Tinker as though Tinker had tried to dispute him. "Sometimes," Quentin went on, both expression and voice softening, "I'd be out at Ebbets Field and I'd look down at the grass and imagine Harry standing there, in a Dodgers uniform. I could see him."

He's seeing it now, Tinker thought, noting what was now a look of aching memory in Quentin's face.

"He could've played his whole career with that team," Quentin said. "His whole career. And he was good enough. That was the pity of it. How many guys ... How many could have done it? But he quit," Quentin said, adding tonelessly, "he wanted to be a cop."

That brought memory lane to a sudden dead end, jolting the conversation back to the present. Harry had become a cop all right, and tonight had become a dead one, if being a cop had had anything to do with his being shot, and it probably did. What the hell was a cop doing up there with a black prostitute? Either shaking her down or trying to use his badge as a punched ticket for a free piece of tail. One way or another, he had got himself shot dead, either by the girl or by that pimp who'd been hustled out of the tenement. And now what about those showcases of pride and glory back at the old high school? Would they drape them in crepe or discreetly slip Harry and his triumphs down to the boiler room? A hero suddenly sordidly dead could be a troublesome exhibit.

"Killing cops in cold blood," Quentin muttered. "They're going to take over if we don't stop them."

"Who?" Tinker asked.

"The niggers. Do you know how many of them there are? A hell of a lot more than people realize."

"Where?"

"Here," Quentin said, tapping the tabletop with his finger, "in this country. Do you know that when the census takers go up to Harlem the spooks there hide the kids in the closet so we won't know how many of them there are? That's a fact. And how about down South? There's millions of them down there. Nobody ever counts them. And what about in Philadelphia and St. Louis and Chicago? And Detroit? What about Detroit?"

Shit, Tinker thought. This guy has got windmills going around inside his head. Is that what the shock of sudden tragedy does? Your brother is killed and you sit and rave about niggers hiding in closets? Well, Tinker thought, fuck him. A locomotive goes off the tracks, you just let it go until it runs into something it can't get through.

"They're out to take everything we've got," Quentin said, his thin malcontent's face earnest and dogged. "They're even coming into baseball, for Christ's sake, with that black son of a bitch the Dodgers got up in Montreal. They'll be in our jobs, our neighborhoods, our homes. It's changing ... everything's changing. Somebody better do something before it's too late."

Your keen, infallible newspaperman's instincts, Tinker thought. You followed him, you sat down with him, in a dump you normally wouldn't be caught dead in. You even bought the asshole a drink.

Quentin seemed to notice for the first time the shot glass clenched in his fist. He moved his hand up and down as if hefting a weight.

"You're not going to throw that, are you?" Tinker asked.

Quentin closed his fingers more tightly around the glass, long, slender fingers, the kind that people believed concert pianists had to have. He rested the hand on the edge of the table. "He was a damned fool," he said quietly, as if muttering into some haze of old, old memory. "In so many ways. He was too good. He brought it on himself. That goddamned fuckin'

Angel. I hope she burns. I hope they all burn."
Then his expression, which had been lost and
abstract, tightened once more, as though his
mind had refocused. "Look," he said, scowling
at Tinker, "I don't need your sympathy. I can
manage. Why don't you take a walk?"

Jesus yes, Tinker thought as he pushed his
chair back and got slowly to his feet. This guy
must have a lot of experience in getting the shit
punched out of him.

2

The big laugh in the *News* sports department was that Tinker had been suspended indefinitely without pay and nobody knew what he had done. They only knew what he had not done, which was cover games six and seven of the World Series in St. Louis, as he had been assigned to do. Probably as near an unforgivable offense as it was possible for a sportswriter to commit.

"It wasn't any of their business what I was doing," he said to Kelly, the old rewrite man who worked in the city room.

They were sitting in a red leather booth in a coffee shop downstairs from the paper on Forty-second Street, having breakfast. It was eight o'clock in the morning. Tinker was glad for the company; he wasn't looking forward to going upstairs.

"As I recollect," Kelly said, "you told 'em a quart of bourbon got stuck to your right hand and you couldn't shake it free."

That was the simplest and best excuse, the

one that most honored the old tradition, one that people could understand, and once you had understanding you were halfway toward forgiveness. Young sportswriter back from the wars, covering his first World Series, overdoes it by a large margin, gets drunk in his hotel room and misses the last two games of the Series.

"But I didn't believe that entirely," Kelly said. "Because you know who told me you were a hell of a drinker?"

"Who?"

Kelly leaned forward until his vest buttons were touching the edge of the table and his moist blue eyes livened under his feathery white eyebrows. He was about to pronounce a venerated name.

"The Babe."

"You're kidding. The Babe said that?"

"Remember that night after the writers' dinner, we were all sitting upstairs at Shor's? Well, the Babe said to me later, 'The kid can really hold it.' "

Well, goddamn, that was one hell of a tribute, because the Babe wasn't just the all-time home run blaster, they said he was the all-time boozer too.

"Didn't think he even noticed me," Tinker said.

Kelly leaned back, squeezing off a knowing wink.

"The Babe notices everything," he said. "Don't sell him short."

They'd be selling him short soon enough, Tinker thought. The Babe had just come out of French Hospital and word was they'd found a malignant growth on the left side of his neck and that things didn't look too good. The news had depressed Tinker. He couldn't imagine a failing, unhealthy Babe Ruth, much less a world without Babe Ruth. What kind of world would that be?

Maybe an interview with the Babe, Tinker thought. Maybe that would get him back in good graces, if he did a really touching, poignant piece, approaching the illness by implication. He thought it over for a moment, then rejected it. His other idea was better.

"It was a woman," Kelly said.

"What?" Tinker asked, his reverie interrupted.

"That kept you in Boston. It had to have been a broad."

"What are you, working for one of the columnists or something?"

Kelly made a face. "The columnists aren't interested in you."

"They would be, if they knew what I knew."

"What do you know, Joseph?" Kelly asked with a touch of good-natured disdain.

"Listen, Kelly, if I'm a lousy newspaperman it's only because I'm an exemplary human being."

32

"I'll reserve judgment until I hear your story."

"My story is—I know how to keep a secret."

"Jesus H. Pulitzer," Kelly said, "if they were all like you we'd be putting out a blank edition every day."

"Who'd know the difference, Kelly, as long as they kept the pictures?"

"Don't knock it, laddie," Kelly said, shaking an admonishing finger. "We got two million circulation, biggest in America."

"That's the key word right there, Kelly," Tinker said, pulling a cigarette from his pack and sliding it between his lips. He slapped his chest with his hands, then found his matches in his shirt pocket. He lit the cigarette, frowning for a moment, as people were apt to do on the first puff. "Circulation. The *Times* and the *Herald-Tribune* have *readers*. We got circulation."

"Who cares what they do with it after they plunk down their two cents?"

"Do you think they ever meet in the middle?"

"Who's that?"

"The guy who opens the paper from the back and starts reading the sports and the guy who opens it from the front and starts reading the news."

"Why don't you watch them next time," Kelly said, "and tell me." He slipped a small silver flask from an inside jacket pocket, unscrewed the cap and poured a quick stream into his coffee, then put the flask away.

"In your coffee?" Tinker said. "I never saw you do that before."

"There's a lot of things in this heaven and earth you never saw, Horatio." Kelly stirred the mixture with his spoon for a moment, then started sipping.

And some of the best things I ever did, Tinker thought, I can't even talk about. One adventure that was going to have to remain decently interred was the one that occurred in Boston after the fifth game of the World Series, and as a matter of fact kept occurring during the next few days, not concluding until the morning of the seventh game, which crack sportswriter Tinker didn't even know was on until he heard the play-by-play coming from a radio in a bar he was sitting in just off Kenmore Square. Let's see, he had thought, if that's the seventh game then there must have been a sixth, both played in St. Louis—after one day out for travel—and I'm still in Boston. I'm a sportswriter, an alleged baseball specialist, for the biggest-circulation paper in the United States and I'm sitting with sore nuts and a headache in a bar in Boston while the seventh game of the World Series is being played in St. Louis.

He wondered what kind of story to concoct for the paper. Since they weren't going to believe anything he came up with anyway, he decided on the simplest, most basic story: he had been on a bender.

It was all because an elevator stalled between

floors of the Kenmore Hotel on the morning of the fifth game. The occupants were the uniformed operator, who was both exasperated and embarrassed by their midair suspension; Tinker; and a trim, regal-looking thirtyish blonde wearing a pale-blue dress and navy-blue bolero jacket, from whom emanated a subtle perfume that dissipated all thoughts of baseball.

"I'm sorry," the operator muttered, futilely working his stop-go lever. "It should start up again momentarily."

"As long as I'm at the ballpark by game time," Tinker said, wanting to sound lighthearted and unconcerned. Game time was still four hours in the future.

The woman said nothing. She was staring straight ahead, in poised concentration, as though reading something on the elevator door. She was apparently a woman adept at concealing the irritations of inconvenience.

"You going to the ball game?" Tinker asked.

"No," she said, continuing to stare straight ahead. His question had glanced off of her as a breeze off a palisade. She remained motionless. Tinker kept sidling looks at her that were accompanied by a wry smile more admiring than flirtatious. He knew what that seemingly infinite self-possession was: breeding. You didn't have to possess it yourself to recognize it. He imagined her being able to walk through a roomful of admiring men and make eye contact with none. She knew he was staring at her, but she remained coolly indifferent. Those long lashes seemed to work no more than twice a minute. Her lips lay softly together, the lower slightly more full.

When Tinker stepped back and lounged against the wall and crossed his arms she turned her head and looked at him, briefly but by no means casually. His smile did not falter and he assumed that in her few moments of impassive staring this woman of impeccable breeding had read him to the core—to her own satisfaction anyway (Tinker did not consider himself a subtle man). A few moments of polite, uninhibited appraisal, and then she turned away.

"Anything we can do?" Tinker asked the operator.

"We're doing it," the man said, then let out a sigh of resignation.

After about five minutes of suspension in the shaft high above the Kenmore lobby, the elevator began descending again. When they reached the crowded lobby, Tinker followed the woman out and then caught up to her.

"I'd say that after that ordeal you need a cup of coffee," he said.

She stopped, tilted her head to one side and studied him with one faint blonde eyebrow slightly arched.

"Thank you," she said.

They threaded their way through the lobby's busy, festive World Series animation. For Tinker it was a sea of familiar faces: Commissioner Chandler with his broad politician's grin; league presidents Harridge and Frick; various club executives; managers, scouts, coaches, old-time players, all gathered together for baseball's culminating event. And of course journalists to burn. Tinker's people, all of them.

"Are you a ballplayer?" she asked when they had taken a booth in the coffee shop.

"No ma'am," he said.

"You look like a ballplayer."

"Where I come from, that's flattery."

She smiled faintly, studying him most candidly.

"What are you doing in Boston?" he asked.

"Nothing. And you?"

"Business."

"I see."

That breeding again, he thought. Shows all the time. It won't allow inquisitiveness. And the deepest blue eyes. Forget hints and clues from them. They weren't going to give away anything. Eyes that had read Byron, Keats, and Shelley at an expensive private school, that closed and listened dreamily to Chopin études.

"I'll bet Mata Hari had eyes like that," he said.

"Is that also flattery, where you come from?"

"I'm not sure. I never heard anybody say it there. Listen, my name is Joe Tinker."

"I'm Judy Millwood."

She was wearing white gloves and he was trying, without being obvious about it, to see if he could read a wedding ring under them.

"How long are you staying in town?" she asked.

"I'm not sure. What about you?"

"I haven't decided," she said, watching him inquiringly with those blue eyes. Tinker knew she was deciding now.

The waitress placed two cups of coffee between them.

"It's going to be quiet around here tonight," he said. "This place is going to empty out. Everybody's catching the train for St. Louis. The Series picks up there the day after tomorrow."

"I know."

"Hell of a train ride. Twenty-four hours."

"How tiresome."

"Listen," he said, "if we're both going to be here this evening in a quiet hotel, why don't we have dinner together?"

She lifted her cup for a moment, sipped, replaced it soundlessly on the saucer, and said, "That might be nice."

"I'll be back here after the game and then give you a call."

He already had it worked out. Tinker the tactician. Instead of heading for South Station with the rest of the crowd after the game, he'd come back here, have dinner, and then guide this lovely creature through realms of ecstasy. Then tomorrow he'd grab a plane for St. Louis and catch up with the World Series. It wouldn't be too difficult to contrive a story to cover it. Maybe use the one he'd heard one old-timer hand out after missing a train in Detroit: he'd gone to the men's room after the game, had slipped on the pissed-over floor, had struck his head on the urinal and had lain there for hours. Could resurrect that one, or try for an original. They'd bitch about paying for a plane ticket, but then that would be that.

So Tinker sat in the Fenway press box that afternoon daydreaming about Judy Millwood sans clothing, sans breeding, sans everything, and watched the Red Sox punch out an orderly 6–3 win, and not even Ted Williams, who could manage only one single in five tries, could get beneath his first layer of interest. When the game was over and 35,000 Red Sox rooters were streaming contentedly down the ramps to the street, he wrote his game story, dispatched it to New York, and headed back to the hotel.

He found Judy Millwood sitting in a red leather chair in the lobby, legs crossed, chin raised, eyes watching the twirl of the revolving door, and when the door finally spun Tinker into the lobby she gave him a smile at once inviting and mischievous.

They went to the lounge and had a drink, sitting at a table not much bigger than a waiter's tray. Whenever she sipped from her Gibson she watched him over the rim of the glass, a sly, almost wanton play in her eyes. Tinker put his hand over hers, feeling the wedding band under the white glove, but now it was no more than a scrap of information for a momentary curiosity. Securely irrelevant.

Mrs. Millwood said she had had a late lunch and was not interested in dinner. He told her he wasn't hungry either, and she said yes, she could see he had eaten, which he didn't appreciate until later when they were lying in bed and he glanced at the white shirt he had thrown to the floor and noticed the mustard from one of his several ballpark hot dogs.

They went directly from the lounge to his room. She had said, "I think your room would be preferable, don't you?" He wasn't sure why, but agreed that absolutely it would be. They stood apart like strangers in the ascending elevator, each gazing passively at the floor numbers being illuminated in the brass plate above them. Then they walked along the carpeted corridor to his room, still wordless. He inserted his room key into the lock, spun the tumblers, opened the door, and showed her in with an outstretched hand. She looked at him with an amused smile.

She undressed with her back to the bureau mirror, while he sat on the bed and leaned back on his elbows and watched, enjoying the fore and aft view. She had strong, athletic legs, a full henna-colored muff, a flat stomach, and a pair of very womanly, heavy-bottomed breasts. Nude (as she was for the next two days), she had a way of coming up on her toes when she walked across the room that was saucy and girlishly whimsical.

She suggested they first take a shower, and it was Tinker's most erotic ever. She kept soaping him between the legs and swirling her fingers about in the lubricious lather until he felt his temples were going to blow out on him. He was in throbbing, steel-rod extension and knew exactly what he wanted to do.

He put his hands on her hips, turned her around and told her to bend over and flatten her hands at the corners of the bathtub. Then, with the shower water racing vigorously against him, he crowded against her rear end and thrust himself in. She quivered and groaned and kept gasping as he ran himself back and forth. It took him less than two minutes to deliver and during the final moments she kept murmuring, "Oh my God."

Later, in bed, she languidly told him she was starved for sex. Tinker told her she was now in the land of plenty. Her husband was twenty-five years older than she, she said, and although he was still impressively virile for a man his age, he traveled a lot, kept late hours when he was home, and evinced little interest in her body when they were together. "Then you're a pinky ring," Tinker told her. "What's that?" she asked. "An ornament for him. Something for show."

She gave Tinker everything that night: her fingers, her mouth, and whatever contortions her body was capable of. And he responded. While awaiting restoration between his legs, he draped her legs over his shoulders and swung his tongue into her for several hours while she machine-gunned orgasms and clutched fistfuls of his hair. When she spoke in exhausted reverence of his technique he told her its origins were too sacred to be spoken of.

It wasn't until four o'clock in the morning, when they had awakened from brief naps, that he found out she was the wife of Senator Millwood. Morris Cameron Millwood. Midwest Republican. Tall, stiff-backed, white-haired, ecclesiastically distinguished and fervently conservative. She had married the Senator two and a half years ago, about a year after he'd become a widower. She had been working in his Washington office.

"You'd been having an affair with him, huh?" Tinker asked.

"Uh-huh," she said, nestling against him. But she was not, she insisted, promiscuous. This was the first time, she said, that she had ever "suspended my fidelity" to "Cam." Tinker was impressed by "suspended my fidelity." Boy, if that didn't show breeding. Or was it just political circumlocution?

Cam's politically adroit advisers suggested the Senator make appearances at that All-American jamboree known as the World Series, wave, shake hands, pose with Williams and Musial, spout a couple of baseball-wise quotes, look like a regular guy, even though the Senator didn't know the difference between a baseball and a cue ball.

Tinker figured he'd catch a late-morning plane to St. Louis. Then late-afternoon. Then early-evening. By then it was already early evening and they had spent the entire day in bed, shouting away the chambermaids, ordering food and booze from room service (she retreated discreetly to the can when the waiter appeared). He finally confessed to himself that he was going to miss the rest of the Series, because she was staying on in Boston for another few days, ostensibly visiting old college friends—the Senator had gone on to the Midwest after the Series' fourth game.

To salve his conscience, he told himself that he could still hop a plane out on the morning of the sixth game, then grab a taxi to Sportsman's Park and hit the press box by the second inning. Only he knew he wouldn't. That was movie stuff, and he'd been told a long time ago not to believe any movies about newspapermen because they were usually romanticized bullshit and could cost you perspective, the advice coming from boozy chain-smoking old-timers who tried to talk in "Front Page" dialogue.

So it was a decision between the World Series and that hot clinging body with its caressing fingers and steamy insatiable lips which never failed to ethereally whisper, "Oh, Tink, Tink," when she was being buffeted by yet another surge of ecstasy. That breeding. He loved it. No woman had ever called him Tink. Under any circumstances.

Tinker stayed in Boston, in the hotel, in his room, in bed, behind drawn blinds, drinking straight bourbon and fornicating unto debilitation, while out in St. Louis the Cardinals won game six and pushed the Series into a deciding game.

When he awoke on the morning of the seventh game, half a continent from where he was supposed to be, she was already showered and dressed, transformed back into the woman he had first met in the stalled elevator, cool, aloof, and unattainable. She walked to the bed with its crushed and twisted sheets and covers, held out her white-gloved hand to him, and lightly touched his wearily raised fingers.

"Good-bye, Joe," she said. "If you ever speak of this to anyone, I will be most disillusioned."

He gave her his promise, and after she was gone he thought how romantically sad it was: a woman worth giving up the seventh game of the World Series for, and maybe even his job too—and the whole sweet, lovely story to be hushed forever.

Sally had insisted he dress up—"You have to look nice when you're being contrite," she said, to which he responded, "I don't feel in the least contrite," which she had expected him to say— so Tinker was uncharacteristically well dressed when he walked into the sports department after breakfasting with Kelly. He was wearing his suit, the one he had bought in Robert Hall's when he came out of the Marines. It was light brown, with white pinstripes. His maroon and yellow polka-dot tie was held in place by a narrow clasp. Sally had arranged a white handkerchief in his breast pocket so that it was three-pointed, like a stand-up napkin on a restaurant table. The suit did give him an air of sobriety and dependability, he had to admit, though some of that was no doubt relative, a contrast to his customary informality, which his boss sometimes remarked on. "I cover the Dodgers, Scotty, not the Yankees," Tinker had told him.

Actually, Tinker wasn't concerned about being cold-storaged for a while. The baseball season was over, and it was the only sport worth writing about, with the best working weather. You could freeze your gonads covering football, and basketball was a game of uninteresting perimeters and smelly gymnasiums. Nor was he worried about employment; there were a half dozen other sports departments around New York where he would be welcome. He was regarded as the sharpest of the young writers. Hadn't Runyon himself, larynx eaten away by cancer, pushed a scribbled note across the table to him at Lindy's one night that said *Don't take any crap, kid. You don't have to.*? And the suspension had given him the excuse to plead poverty and move in with Sally.

So he walked into the sports department that morning with the casual self-confidence of a man in control of his situation, completely at ease with himself. He was tall, sandy-haired, limber, with the rangy build of a crack center fielder. His was an urban face, with nonchalant guile and unforced irreverence apparent in his friendly good looks.

The big, glass-walled room was quiet except for the chatter of the AP wire and the soft rat-a-tat from the typewriter of Scotty's secretary. The boss's office, behind its panes of glass, was empty. Ike, the gray-haired old black porter, was emptying wastebaskets into an oversized gray-canvas bin that he pushed around on casters.

Tinker went to his desk, shuffled through the stack of mail on it, patted it condescendingly, and walked across to where two of his colleagues were in conversation at a desk. Fred Mason, a paunchy man with curly black hair, small black mustache, and a Phi Beta Kappa key on a gold chain looped across his vest, had been hastily switched during the World Series from interviews and analysis to covering the action when Tinker disappeared after the fifth game. The other man was Jimmy Edgers, who covered boxing and the racetracks. He was a stick of a man who always wore a fedora in the office, his vest clutching his narrow torso as tightly as a girdle. His small eyes looked pale, almost sightless behind the misted lenses of his silver-rimmed glasses. Jimmy Edgers had been around. He claimed to have been in the room with Bat Masterson at the *Morning Telegraph* on the evening in 1921 when the old gunfighter-turned-sportswriter keeled over his rolltop desk with a heart attack after doing a column on the Lew Tendler-Rocky Kansas fight.

"You been reinstated, Joe?" Mason asked.

"Not yet," Tinker said.

"You going to plead your case with Scotty?" Edgers asked in his quiet skeptic's voice.

"What makes you think so?" Tinker asked.

"The suit."

"It bespeaks repentance," Mason said.

"He's not in yet, huh?" Tinker asked, looking at Scott's office.

"We were just talking about your team, Joe," Mason said.

"The Brooks?"

"Discussing the big question: Are they or are they not going to bring him up?"

"Robinson?" Tinker asked. "Sure they're bringing him up."

"Not everyone thinks he's ready," Edgers said.

"The man batted three forty-nine," Tinker said. "He's twenty-seven years old. If he's not ready now, forget it."

"I called Rickey the other day," Mason said, "and I asked him: 'Are the Dodgers bringing Jackie Robinson to the major leagues in 1947?'"

"Sure," Tinker said, "he's going to tell you that over the phone."

"Shit, I knew he wasn't going to give me a direct answer. That old windbag wouldn't know how to give a direct answer."

"He tells you what he wants you to know," Edgers said. "I've known Branch for a quarter century. You've got to know how to decode him."

"I can't see him starting the whole thing," Mason said, "signing Negroes and all that, if he has no intention of bringing them up."

"So what did he say?" Tinker asked. He noticed that Ike, the porter, had paused in his basket-emptying and was listening, and not furtively either, but was standing there and listening, as though he were in the conversation, head cocked, attentive. Ike had never paused to listen before, not to clubhouse gossip, not to inside stories, not even to some of the risqué tales passed around about Joe Louis and white women. Ike was listening now.

"He said," Mason said, "that the Dodgers' 1947 roster was yet to be determined."

"He's full of shit," Edgers said. "He knows what he's going to do." His thin lips barely parted as he spoke, like a second-rate ventriloquist's.

"It's a very delicate situation," Mason said. "This is no ordinary rookie. There could be hell to pay. The old man could be opening a Pandora's box. Right on his own club, to begin with,

with all those Southern boys—Walker, Higbe, Casey, Reese."

"I say he's already made up his mind," Tinker said. "Especially with the year Robinson had. He tore up the International League. I saw him play over in Jersey City a few times. He's the best second baseman in baseball right now."

"I wouldn't want to go into print with that opinion," Edgers said. "But I agree, the man is a hell of a player."

"It could tear the game apart," Mason said. "I've spoken to a lot of players, Union and Confederate both. Off the record. There's a lot of strong feeling about this."

"Against," Edgers said.

"Definitely against."

Tinker heard the casters rolling on the hard floor; old Ike was pushing his bin away.

"And there'll be a lot of hard feeling in the stands," Mason said. "And all of the other club owners are opposed. And believe me, boys, it behooves me to say there will also be some discouragement from the fourth estate. Rickey's playing a lone hand."

Tinker saw Scott coming along the corridor from the elevator. The sports editor was a compact man, in a blue serge suit, red tie, dark hair brushed back and gleaming. He was carrying a gray houndstooth overcoat over his arm. Serious face, with incipient jowls spelling the onset of middle age. All business, this fellow, with parade-ground stride and comportment. Just the editor to stiff with a two-day bat in the middle of a World Series. But inside that refrigerator lived a man with a grudging understanding of the world, of its temptations, of its frailer souls, and with a professional's appreciation of a reporter who could write a snappy game account and get athletes to confide in him.

"Good morning, Joe," Scott said as he walked in, then nodded to Mason and Edgers.

Tinker winked at the other two and followed the sports editor.

As soon as he entered his office Scott removed his jacket, stuck a wooden hanger into the armholes and hung it on a nail, then opened his collar and dropped his tie knot and drew and exhaled what sounded like his first serene breath of the day. It made Tinker wonder why the man bothered dressing so neatly to begin with. For whom? The people he rode down from the Bronx with on the subway? The elevator man? Tinker suspected his boss was henpecked.

"You ought to mess up your hair too, Scotty," he said.

"What are you talking about?" Scott said, sliding in behind his desk and slipping into the corner of his mouth the day's first Robt. Burns panatela. He struck a wooden match against the side of his swivel chair, flamed the cigar, and took several puffs. Then he frowned at his mail; it was stacked in two piles on a broad green desk blotter blotched with what looked like Rorschach test patterns.

Tinker sat down on the wooden folding chair next to the desk.

"You going to a funeral?" Scott asked. He sounded tougher with the cigar in his mouth. He unbuttoned his cuffs and rolled them back twice. He had heavy forearms, thick wrists. You wouldn't want to take a shot from that fist, Tinker thought.

"You're all dressed up," Scott said. "You look like you're going to a funeral. I'll bet this is the first time since you came out of the Marines that your pants match your jacket."

"I've got an idea for a story."

"You're under suspension."

"Scotty, I've been standing in the corner like a good boy for nearly a month."

"Look, Tinkerbell," Scott said, the cigar batting up and down in his mouth as he spoke, "it took me some fancy footwork to keep you from being shitcanned totally. There were more than a few people around here offering to chip in toward your severance pay."

"We're gonna outlast them all, Scotty. You and me."

What was it—twelve, thirteen months ago?—that his picture had been on the back page, shaking hands with the publisher, with a beaming Scotty standing nearby, over the caption NEWS WELCOMES MARINE HERO BACK TO SPORTS DEPT. First day back on the job. The bastards had made him go home and put the uniform back on for the picture, and don't forget those medals either, Joseph. Purple Heart and Bronze Star. Those medals probably were the difference between being fired and being suspended. You don't fire a hero that easily, not so soon after the war anyway.

"What's the story?" Scott asked.

"Are you really interested?"

"Joseph, please don't fuck around with me. Not first thing in the morning."

"You heard about that cop that was shot last night? Harry Wilson? Well, he's out of my old neighborhood in Queens. Just about the greatest schoolboy athlete they ever had. All-everything at Newtown High, then went into minor-league ball, but gave it up to go on the Force. Go back, recall some of his athletic exploits, talk to some old friends, teammates, dig up a few old photos. It could make a nice story."

"It could," Scott said noncommittally. He grunted. "Guy winds up shot dead in bed with a colored prostitute."

"Was he in bed with her?"

Scott shrugged. "I don't know." He leaned back against his yielding swivel chair, locking his fingers together behind his head, the cigar angled out for a moment like FDR's cigarette holder. "Christ," he said, "but they're going to fry those two coloreds."

"It's a big story right now. And right up my alley."

Scott smiled cordially. "But you're under suspension, Joe."

"Oh, horseshit, Scotty. It'll give you a chance to run that picture again: 'News welcomes back Marine hero yet again.' "

Scott pulled the cigar from his mouth and examined it thoughtfully, then said, "Former top schoolboy athlete who meets a sordid, still not fully explained end. Yeah. Not bad."

"Make a nice feature for the Sunday sports section."

"No kidding, Joe?" Scott said archly. Then, "All right, run with it. Dig up people who knew him as a kid, when he was a star. Game-winning home runs, that sort of thing. I want him painted as pure as you can. If he was screwing darkies in the wilds of Queens in 1918, I don't want to hear about it."

"Then I'm back on the payroll?"

"Yes, Joseph," Scott said with exaggerated magnanimity. "I'll notify the proper authorities. I'm going to cover your tail again—for the last time. Now, buzz on out."

3

It was indeed a big story at the moment, made to order for the unblushing front pages of the *News*, *Mirror*, and *Journal-American*. HERO COP SAVAGELY SLAIN. HERO COP SLAIN IN SIN DEN. D.A. PROMISES SWIFT JUSTICE. And there were photos of Harry Wilson lying face down on the bare wooden floor, arms reaching out over his head, the blood on the floor making it look as though his face were casting a shadow. Fully dressed too, Tinker noted, putting quietus to the story that Harry was plugged while in bed with the girl, Angel.

Tinker, not a man to let ironies pass unremarked, appreciated the name. Angel. Angel Smith. Probably a phony name. The neighbors had known about Angel all right, with some of the quotes no doubt tidied up a bit.

"I always wondered about her. She didn't seem to have a regular job."

"She seemed to have a lot of male visitors, especially in the evening and late at night."

"She kept to herself. If you said hello to her,

she'd answer. Otherwise, she never said anything."

"Men. Lots of men. Always white men. The guy they took away last night was the only colored I ever saw there."

Most interesting of all, Tinker thought, were the comments of Mr. Arturo Valvolio, the janitor, "whose habit it was to sit outside on a chair on fair-weathered evenings." According to Mr. Valvolio, the deceased had been a fairly regular visitor of Miss Smith's. Did the sharp-eyed janitor know the deceased was a police officer? *"I did not."* Did he have any inkling as to Miss Smith's source of income? *"I do not pry into the tenants' lives."* Miss Smith had been living there about six months, paid her rent on time, caused no trouble, and that was good enough for Mr. Valvolio. What about Mr. Rush, the alleged panderer? "I don't know nothing about panderers," said Mr. Valvolio.

Tony Marino was covering the story for the *News*. They called him "Dago" when he first joined the paper, but his response, a cool, condescending smile, soon put a stop to it. He was the son of immigrant parents, had worked his way through CCNY during the Depression, gone through OCS during the war, emerged a lieutenant in the infantry, and returned to the old country via Anzio. Just over thirty years old, he'd played semipro football in Queens and Brooklyn before the war. Sturdy through the chest and shoulders, Tony was slowly going to fat, especially in the middle. A big man, with short curly black hair that had retreated almost to the middle of his head, he was considered something of an intellectual, a guy who could quote Aquinas, Plato, Virgil, Socrates, Dante, and other intimidating forces of nature.

Tinker found Tony upstairs in the library, sitting at a gray metal table leafing through bound copies of the *Daily News* that went all the way back to Day One.

"What was he doing there?" Tinker asked, sitting in a hard metal folding chair opposite Tony.

"They don't know," Tony said, slowly turning the large leaves of a volume from the mid-thirties.

"Or won't say."

"They're not happy about it," Tony said, watching the pages.

"They trying to smoke-screen, you think?"

"They won't smoke-screen me."

"It's got to be one of three things," Tinker said. "He balled her and wouldn't pay, he was trying to shake her down, he was there to make a pinch."

"Scratch the last one. It wasn't Harry's style to run in prostitutes. That would have been a waste of his time; he was one of the best detectives on the Force. Shake her down? He had a reputation as an honest cop."

"How'd an honest cop become a detective?"

"Don't be cynical, Tinker."

"Then he balled her and wouldn't pay."

Tony's urbane composure remained undisturbed, but he sighed. Still not looking up, he said, "Joe, you've been around. Do you think a pimp and his lady would kill a New York City detective for *that*? A sportswriter maybe, but not a cop."

"Sportswriters do not patronize prostitutes," Tinker said with mock indignation.

"No, they're too busy covering the World Series."

"I'll ignore that. Look, maybe they didn't know he was a cop."

"Cops aren't shy about letting you know they're cops. And anyway, it wasn't the first time he was there, according to the janitor."

"What about the two coloreds? What's their story?"

"From what I hear, neither one has so far said a word."

"She could be afraid of the pimp," Tinker said.

"More than of the electric chair?" Tony asked.

"Momentarily, yes. The pimp is still more of a reality."

Tony looked across the table thoughtfully for a moment, then looked down again and resumed his slow, methodical turning of the bound-up old tabloid pages. That was Tony, slow and methodical, letting his intelligence out by cautious degrees, as though he had it strung on a tight leash.

"Looking for anything special?" Tinker asked.

"Not really. Just trying to get the feel of the way it was. You can get that from old newspapers with greater fidelity than anywhere else. The ads, the prices, the pictures, the styles, the haircuts. Yesterday in still life. A book knows what's going to happen tomorrow. A newspaper doesn't. Life is definitive. Until the next edition. Why are you interested in this case, Tinker?"

"Which one of them shot him?"

"They've got her prints on the gun."

"*She* did it?"

"Apparently."

"He wasn't shot with his service revolver, was he?"

"No," Tony said, swinging his face slowly from side to side as he examined each page. "He was shot in the back of the head with a Colt thirty-eight-caliber Super Automatic from about five feet away. The room was in a slight state of disarray, leading to speculation there might have been a brief brawl before the shooting. Rush's face was marked, but no one is sure whether the bruises came from Detective Wilson's fists or from the people who tackled him when he came running out of the building."

"Those bruises must look like caresses compared to what they've put on him now."

"It's true that a Negro pimp involved in the murder of a New York City cop is not in the tenderest of hands, but those guys are professionals, Joe. They can work a man over and never leave a mark. I asked you why you're interested in the case."

"Wilson came from my old neighborhood. He was a great schoolboy athlete and Scott wants me to do a story from that angle."

"I thought you were on the restricted list."

"I've been pardoned, as of today."

"Pardoned," Tony asked, "or paroled?"

"Probably the latter," Tinker said.

4

A man is known by the company he keeps. Shopworn old saying, Quentin thought, and essentially empty. A man would be better known by the secrets he keeps.

The Department would see to the funeral, Quentin was assured. It would be an inspector's funeral. And of course a limousine would transport the bereaved brother to and fro. If I attend, Quentin said. That rattled them a bit, the two bulky big-brass cops and the padre. A padre in brass-buttoned blue coat and garrison cap, the clerical collar the only telltale. The padre said, You're in terrible distress. We understand. Quentin looked him defiantly in the eye. I don't have to attend if I choose not to. The padre nodded with understanding that was benign and infuriating, his pink, freshly shaven under-chin bunching over the collar for a moment.

No, Quentin said, there is no one else. No aunts or uncles or cousins. Only me. My parents died during the war, while I was in Europe. First my mother, then my father. The padre said, That must have been terribly distressing. Yes, Quentin said. Especially losing my father. I miss him. The brass and the padre exchanged glances and coughed discreetly into closed hands. There's just me, Quentin said. I'm his only relative. The only one. He looked at them, his eyes going from face to face, as though swearing them to some sort of oath.

Standing behind the white lace curtains of a downstairs window, Quentin watched them leave in a black sedan driven by a police officer who had waited outside. Then he went upstairs to his room, his old room, the one he had grown up in, where for years the aging newspaper clippings of Harry's exploits had been tacked to the walls. From this window he looked down into backyards, at clotheslines shivering stiffly in the November wind, at cold brown grass.

He left the room, crossed the upstairs hallway and stood in what had been his parents' bedroom. It was bare. When he'd come home after the war he had called a furniture dealer and sold everything, the bedroom set, chairs, lamps, mirrors, right down to the shag throw rugs. Harry, living alone in his small apartment in Manhattan's West Eighties, hadn't wanted any of it. (Nor, though Quentin offered, any of the money either. That was Harry.) But Harry was surprised when he learned that Quentin was selling it all. I thought you were sentimental, Quent. Not about furniture, Quentin said. A man couldn't be sentimental about everything. Quentin's languishing nostalgia was reserved not for things he could touch but rather for those he could feel inside himself and summon when needed. He had taken these guardian memories with him to Europe and they had helped sustain him, get him through the tension and the fighting, from Normandy and the Bulge and finally across the Rhine into Germany, through the malevolent streets of Aachen and Leipzig. It was as though memories, being insubstantial and timeless and indestructible, could cast him in some invisible armor and protect him from German onslaught and from the deathly cold of an alien winter. He had seen other people's streets and homes and playgrounds blown to hell, sent piecemeal into the thundering air, gone forever.

When he came home Quentin's Capstone, his corner of Queens, was still there, unchanged, as though remembering had preserved it. Unlike its sister boroughs, Queens was most characterized by side streets and plain frame houses fronted by stout little hedges and hawthorn bushes and guarded by the modest formality of wooden or wrought-iron fences and gates. Many of the fields where Harry had played baseball so spectacularly around the time of the War—the other one—were still there, stretched between those clusters of houses which themselves were built on what had once been meadows and pastures belonging to the dairy farms that had covered large tracts of the county.

But something disquieting and unsettling was happening. Already one of those fields, the one that lay on Calder Avenue, a bumpy-surfaced street that meandered through the north side of town, was gone. Cleared and leveled and gone forever. The government had thrown up several hundred Quonset huts to house some of the veterans who had emerged from the service as husbands and fathers and who were strapped for living space. And now there were strangers shopping on Grant Avenue on Saturday afternoons, and drinking in the Stumble Inn, the Merries, the Hamlet, Paddy's, and the other taverns on the avenue and the side streets. People whom Quentin didn't know, people who had never heard of Harry.

He had asked Harry to move back to the old house. They had been talking about it in that bar in Greenwich Village when Harry slid his chair back from the table, stood up, and said, I'm going over there now.

So Quentin had never got his answer, though he didn't think Harry would have moved back. Harry, after all, had not lived there for over twenty years. It was Quentin's home, the place he had grown up in, left in 1942 to go to war, come back to in 1945 to find dead and empty and waiting, totally his.

He went back upstairs, sullenly in search of solace. He stood in painful indecision for a moment, then went to his room. From the closet floor he lifted a small cardboard box and placed it on his bed. He pulled away the linen cloth that covered it and gazed down at the collection within. Here, lovingly accumulated, were the ticket stubs and the scorecards from every game he had ever attended at Ebbets Field. Many of the earlier ones had a note attached that read *Went with Harry*, or *Harry took me*. Each represented a day of warm, sweet sunshine long vanished. Sometimes, on winter nights, when the dark grandstands of Ebbets Field were cold and empty and there was snow on the grass, he would take out his collection of mementos and slide his fingers through them as if trying to evoke the old sunshine with its sights and sounds of baseball.

He gazed moodily at a manila folder in the box. He hadn't looked inside it in years, since before the war. It contained Harry's "major-league record" as compiled yearly (beginning in 1924) by Quentin. Making his entries in the neatly ruled columns on a piece of paper, Quentin had determined each year what Harry had achieved while playing for the Brooklyn Dodgers: how many doubles, triples, home runs, runs batted in, batting average, etc., with league-leading statistics denoted by a carefully drawn asterisk. When he opened the folder now and looked at the page of numbers, Quentin had an odd mixture of feelings—embarrassment at having so assiduously tracked a fantasy career, and regret that the career had been just that, fantasy. He looked at one of the bottom figures:

lifetime batting average, .351. He closed the folder and dropped it back into the box.

On the wall was tacked an aerial photograph of Ebbets Field, clipped from an old magazine. Staring at it with narrowed, remembering eyes, he recalled that day in the mid-1930s when Harry had stopped by with some news.

"I pulled a few strings," Harry said, "and guess where I got you a job."

Quentin waited.

"Ebbets Field," Harry said, smiling at Quentin's slow, wordless elation. "It's on the turnstiles. You work there until about the third inning, then you get a half a buck and can watch the rest of the game from the bleachers."

"I'll be able to see every game," Quentin said.

"And get paid for it."

"Listen," Quentin said, "maybe it can lead to something. Maybe I can work myself up to a real job with the team."

"Like manager," Harry said with a laugh.

"If I get to manage the Dodgers, then you're coming back to play for me."

"I don't think so," Harry said, patting the slight thickness that had formed around his middle.

The job did lead to something; the following year Quentin was hired to work with the grounds crew. Now he was on the field before and after every game, working hard but feeling privileged. He was up close to the players but seldom spoke to any of them, content to watch and listen, enthralled by the crack of the bat, the sound of leather snapping a thrown ball out of the air, the pregame banter in the dugout, the clack of spiked shoes on concrete. Soon he felt he knew the shape of the field's every grass blade and was familiar with every nook and cranny in all of Ebbets Field. But the job didn't last—nothing ever seemed to last for him—and after several disputes with the head grounds-keeper, Quentin was fired, and thereafter whenever he wanted to watch his beloved team he had to buy a ticket, the stub of which he added to his collection.

He went back downstairs to the kitchen, where they had been sitting at the oilcloth-covered table. He picked up the three pint bottles of Rheingold and dropped them into the garbage bag. He put the three tall V-shaped stemmed glasses in the sink; the padre's was still three-quarters full and Quentin emptied it down the drain.

He went into the front room, where the windows looked out over the small lawn (his parents always called it the garden, though they never grew anything in it), which was defined on three sides by the hedges with their small, ovate leaves, trimmed by next-door neighbor Mr. Gustafson, who did it as a favor because Quentin would not and because Mr. Gustafson didn't want unsightly hedges growing next to his own lovingly tended home. Quentin sat down in the easy chair with the big armrests that looked like bedrolls.

Condolences and funeral arrangements did not quite cover all the reasons for the visit. They wanted to know what light, if any, Quentin could shed on Harry's being in that apartment. Even the fat-chinned padre had seemed interested. It seemed odd, Quentin was told. It seemed unusual. There didn't seem to be any satisfactory explanation. People were "speculating." "Wildly speculating." So are you, Quentin thought, never mentioning having been with Harry just before, staring back at them, defying them to guess how much he knew, with surly perverseness almost wanting them to know he wasn't going to talk. And they probably did feel that he knew a hell of a lot more than he was letting on, these two good old cops of thirty years' experience, with their still-life interrogator eyes that seemed able to read right through to the back of your head, with their tough-guy bellies and their half-curled bone-breaker fists and their uncharitable Irish faces veined and road-mapped with broken capillaries. I don't know, Quentin told them. When you tell a world-hardened son of a bitch that you don't know and he continues to stare right at you with eyes that seem incapable of blinking, you are not being believed. But what were they going to do about it? He was the bereaved brother. The padre didn't have the same kind of eyes, nor the same manner of poised disbelief, but he was shrewd enough to pick up the subtleties of tension. Then finally Quentin said, It doesn't matter. Which could have meant, My brother is dead and he and I are both beyond caring; or it could have meant, You're not going to find out anything from me. So the last look from those two sets of cold pebbly eyes told him that some good old police instincts were being grudgingly suppressed. A cop doesn't want to hear that you don't know, when his instincts, through which his pride lives, tell him otherwise. Nevertheless, they deferred to the occasion.

You threw shit on the family, Harry, that's what you did. Part of you I understood and loved and worshiped, part I didn't and rejected. Oh Christ, Quentin thought, covering his eyes, the air in his lungs thickening. His sobs choked him for a moment, the tears flooding his eyes. One hand rolled into a fist and pounded hatefully at the armrest.

His glance fell on the sports magazine that lay open on the reading table next to him. The strong black face looked out at him, bold and defiant. Beneath it was a picture of Robinson in a Montreal uniform sliding home, terrifically inanimate in an explosion of dust, and next to that another picture of organized baseball's first black player completing one of his powerful, muscle-locked swings at home plate. IS HE COMING TO THE BIG LEAGUES? ran across the top of the double-page spread, and beneath, in smaller letters: JACKIE IS READY. IS BASEBALL?

Quentin didn't understand it. Why? What did they need them for? And it wasn't going to be just this one, either. If he made it there would be others. They'd come flooding in, just like they always did, from all over, and once they were in how were you going to get them out? And the more of them there were, the fewer white players there would be, because how many self-respecting white men would stay in the game, on the same field with them? It would be the old pattern, like in a neighborhood: as soon as "they" began moving in, people began moving out. Only this time the neighborhood was Baseball. The big leagues. Where Harry should have been. But instead of Harry, *they* were going to be there. And of course the grandstands would be filled with them too. You wouldn't be able to go to a major-league baseball game anymore. The death of baseball meant the death of summer, and people were sitting complacently and letting it happen, letting themselves be deluded, because they didn't realize how many of *them* there were and that once the tide began to flow it would be unstoppable.

And he knew all about this Robinson too. College man and a troublemaker. Been booted out of the army for causing a row about not wanting to sit in the back of a goddamned bus down in Texas somewhere. An aggressive, belligerent

5

The offices of the *Long Island Courier* were in Long Island City, facing the elevated train, at the foot of the Queens side of the Fifty-ninth Street bridge. Sitting in the morgue, Tinker could hear the trains clattering in and out of the Queens Plaza station, the sound coming like a soft crumbling rumble by the time it had passed through the city room's windows and drifted down the corridor to the morgue.

Elevated trains. One of the great old sights and sounds of a city. Tinker missed them; the Third Avenue was the last one left in Manhattan. When they tore down the Sixth Avenue El in the late thirties, the scrap iron was supposedly sold to Japan. When the Eighth Avenue El was demolished, the old rails and girders and pillars were melted down for munitions by the government, leading some apocryphal soldier in the Pacific to write home, "Ma, they're shooting at me with the Sixth Avenue El and I'm firing back with the Eighth." It would be nice, Tinker thought, to think that the piece of Jap shrapnel that burned into his shoulder like a branding iron was a chunk of the old Sixth Avenue El, preferably from around midtown.

"Figured your paper would have whatever you needed," said Murphy, keeper of the morgue files, an old-timer with garters on his sleeves and silver-rimmed glasses with frames the size of checkerboard squares.

"Nah," Tinker said, turning over the yellowed clippings from the manila folder Murphy had brought him. "They only have pictures there."

"You're kidding."

" 'New York's Picture Newspaper,' " Tinker said, shrugging.

Murphy thought about it for a moment, then said again, "You're kidding."

Tinker glanced at him with a sly smile.

"The stuff we've got on him only covers his police career."

"I can tell you why," Murphy said. "Because Captain Patterson didn't start up the *News* until 1919, and most of your man's schoolboy heroics were furled up by that time."

Tinker looked up from the table. Murphy was sitting on a tall iron stool, gartered arms crossed, the stub of a dead cigar in the corner of his mouth like a rusted bolt.

"I never realized it, Murph," Tinker said. "Me and the *Daily News* are about the same age. We started out together. But I guess the paper's worth a hell of a lot more than I am."

"Except nobody's ever going to buy *you* for

two cents, are they, kid?" Murphy asked with a slow, wise old Irish wink.

"I hope not."

"You any relation to the ballplayer?"

"Nope."

"Same name. Joe Tinker. Tinker to Evers to Chance. I used to go up to the Polo Grounds years ago, saw them play many a time."

"Any good?"

"I'll say," Murphy said emphatically. "Quick as rabbits. You've got nothing like them today."

"Atta boy, Murph."

The clippings told Tinker just how good and how esteemed a ballplayer Harry Wilson had been, playing for Newtown High and then in amateur leagues around Queens. It wasn't just the exploits, it was that after a while the game stories were personalized, with headlines like HARRY HITS TWO and HARRY LEADS GAELS TO VICTORY. No need, apparently, to tell the sporting folk of Queens and Long Island in 1917 and 1918 who "Harry" was.

And good-looking the hero had been too. A big, laughing smile, the smile of a winner. Full head of black hair standing up and leaning every which way. One picture in particular caught Tinker's eye. Harry's team had just clinched the Queens Unity League championship and there was the hero and several teammates and a little kid not holding but grabbing Harry around the waist, wrapping him with both arms. Harry's little brother, though Tinker did not need the caption to tell him that. He studied the boy's face; the boy was eight, maybe nine years old, and while there was no longer any sign of the boy in the man, the man surely was limned and prophesied in the boy. Amid the elated faces of youthful triumph, this one was intense, unsmiling, almost surly as it peered back at the camera, as though experiencing some mordant vindication. Despite the old newsprint photo's poor quality, Tinker could see Quentin's fingers bunching up the wool of Harry's uniform where they were clutching.

"Jeez, you can see it," Tinker said. "This kid really loved his brother."

"You *should* love your brother," Murphy said soberly.

Peter Nelson was in his mid-sixties, burly, the sleeves of his zippered windbreaker barely able to contain his biceps. The old gym teacher and coach was moon-faced, almost hairless, carrying a generous paunch. His voice was a resonant baritone, a weapon, Tinker imagined, that must have intimidated students as much as his physique had.

Tinker found him sitting on a wooden bench outside the cavernous trolley carbarn in the center of Capstone. It looked like an old boys' hangout around here, with trolleys clanking in day and night and a candy and cigar shack nearby and a bar across the street. A painted metal sign bolted to a black crowbar that was imbedded in a heavy concrete pedestal announced that this was a Hack Stand, though nobody could remember the last time a hack had come and stood there. The big yard adjacent to the carbarn held a scattering of empty trolleys, some of them the latest models, which had leather seats and cruised at a lower decibel level.

"There's talk," Peter Nelson said, his Rodin-sized hands resting on his kneecaps, "of tearing up the tracks and the cobblestones and replacing the trolleys with buses. Jesus, I'd hate to see that. There's nothing like the sound of a trolley car going by in the night. It's an *urban* sound, you see. Clanky, mechanical. It's got the same meaning to us as a train whistle to a country kid."

"Progress, Mr. Nelson," Tinker said.

"Changes, changes," Nelson said, shaking his big dome of a head. "I don't like 'em. Leave things as they are. We've been managing just fine." He pulled a cloth cap from his jacket pocket and covered his bald head with it, adjusting the cap front and back with his fingers. "Gettin' chilly," he said. "Look, you're a veteran," he said, eyeing the small gold discharge button Tinker wore on his lapel. "You weren't out there fighting for changes, were you? You were fighting to keep things as they were."

Damn right, Tinker thought. I was fighting against the biggest change of them all—becoming dead.

"You see," Nelson said, "that was Harry's problem. He changed. Instead of sticking to baseball and working his way up to the big leagues, as in my opinion he could have done, he gave it up to become a cop. Gave it up completely. Wouldn't even play on the Department team. They had a good team too. Used to play the Sanitation Department an annual game at Queens Park. But he gave it up completely. See what it got him. Poor kid. Jesus, I went upstairs and cried when I heard about it."

"When was the last time you'd seen him?"

"Oh, Christ, not for years. Before the war. Thirty-five, thirty-six. In there sometime. A team reunion. I was surprised to see him, because he'd dropped out of touch even before that, when his marriage went to hell. We'd always been like that," Nelson said, lifting one of his anvil hands and crossing the first two fingers.

"How good a ballplayer was he?" Tinker asked. An obligatory question, answered exactly as he knew it would be, with superlatives for Harry's hitting, running, throwing, fielding. Tinker sat back and let the old coach spin through the spirals of time, to when Harry Wilson, dead these few days from a bullet fired into his head under sordid circumstances, when this same Harry was young and limitless and ripping long hits into outfield gaps and running out home runs on those unfenced ball fields with "blinding speed." Bat meets ball, a generation ago, and a memory impervious to time is shaped and embossed. Baseball memories, Tinker had learned, were long and keen.

"A fellow from the Cardinals came around," Nelson said. "Rickey was just starting to build up the farm system in those years, and they signed Harry to a contract. They came around to me first and asked about him. Not what kind of ballplayer he was—they already knew that—but what kind of kid. Rickey was always interested in a guy's character. 'You're getting the best,' I told the scout. 'A straight arrow. You'd be proud to call him your son.' Harry went out to the Midwest somewhere and smashed away at about three-thirty. Helluva hitter. Held that bat back and steady, then strode into the pitch, and wham! But he came home that first year and I could tell he wasn't happy playing pro ball. He came around to my house one afternoon and we sat on my back porch watching the leaves fall and he said he didn't think he was going to make baseball his career. It was the traveling, you see, being away from home. Harry was a real homebody type. All he ever wanted was a wife and family and steady work. You know, the sort of everyday, unexceptional life-style that nobody ever seems to get," Nelson said, chuckling sardonically.

"Evidently he was a hell of a cop," Tinker said.

"Well, on the one hand, it didn't make a lot of sense, the way he kept putting his life on the line and collaring all those guys and getting all those decorations and stuff. But on the other hand, I think that was probably the athlete in him, the competitor. You give an athlete like Harry a job and he's going to try and do it the best he can, better than anybody else. But, oh boy," Nelson said, shaking his head, "there were times when I'd open the paper and couldn't believe what I was reading. Like that time about a dozen years ago when he chased some dago holdup man down a BMT subway tunnel and shot the son of a bitch dead on the tracks. I said to my wife, 'Is this the same kid I had at Newtown who always called me sir and mister?' "

"He liked being a cop, huh?"

"That's what he wanted to be," Nelson said. "I guess the thing was, he wanted to do something *interesting*. Here was a kid who gave up pro ball, a good shot at the big leagues; he wasn't going to do that to take a job in Woolworth's. You're around athletes all the time, you know what they're like. An athlete's got hot pokers up his ass; he fidgets his way through life until he becomes a lard-ass like me and has got to sit still."

"Why'd his marriage break up?"

"You got me there, kiddo. He married a hell of a girl too. Nice-looking, with a good head on her shoulders. They seemed like the perfect couple, the kind you put on a magazine cover to advertise America."

A trolley car, with Capstone its terminus, came turning in off Grant Avenue and clanked slowly into the carbarn's massive darkness, red-orange sparks sizzling from where its pole touched the overhead cable.

"Can you imagine?" Nelson said, watching it with affection and a certain wistfulness. "They want to replace 'em with buses. 'Bustitution,' they call it. Why can't they just leave things as they are?"

Tinker found Cornelius Fletcher at work down at the industrial end of Capstone, a neighborhood of light industry housed in the same kind of soul-sucking brick buildings one found in used-up New England textile towns, block after block of them, interrupted only by an empty lot overgrown with country graveyard weeds and littered with windblown newspapers, rotting cardboard boxes, and occasional pieces of abandoned furniture. Connie Fletcher had been the star pitcher for the Capstone Gaels, winners of the Queens Unity League championship in 1919 and, according to one of the clips Tinker had fished out of the *Courier*'s morgue, Harry's closest friend.

Tinker and Fletcher sat on the edge of the corrugated-iron loading platform behind the bottling plant of Kimball Farms, distributor of dairy products throughout the Borough of Queens. A plant foreman now after twenty-two years of muscle-building milk deliveries to mom-and-pop grocery stores, Fletcher was waiting for the trucks to return with their rattling cases of empties. He was a swarthy man, with knots of black curly hair that rolled across his forehead when he turned his head. He was wearing coveralls, with a long leather apron over them, and combat boots that dangled above the concrete floor where the trucks backed up and dropped their tailboards onto the platform. Tinker liked the smell of the place, a farm-fresh commingling of milk, cream, butter. A row of heavy iron milk containers with round lids like leaden hubcaps stood against the wall next to him and Fletcher.

Good old Harry, Fletcher said. Yeah. It was too bad. Real shock. Couldn't believe it when he read about it in the paper. Brought back the old times. Great times, of course. Kid athletes winning a championship together. What a ballplayer, that Harry. And such a modest kid. They were a rowdy bunch. You know how it is. But not Harry. Harry was a real gentleman. Levelheaded. Mature. A very settling influence, not by what he said but by the way he conducted himself.

Shit, Tinker thought, I'm doing a story about a Boy Scout, an All-American bore. Didn't young Harry ever get drunk and piss in the street or kick a dog?

Fletcher reached toward the wall and picked up an empty, unwashed milk bottle and held it in his hand with a strong man's almost awkward affinity for a key part of his work world, running his fingers up along the raised Kimball Farms lettering on the side of the bottle and then along the narrowing neck, which flared into a wide opening.

"You won't be seeing these fuckers around too much longer," Fletcher said, turning the bottle around in his hand. "Everybody's going to be switching over to cardboard containers before you know it."

"Probably be better," Tinker said.

"A lot of people in there," Fletcher said, pushing his thumb over his shoulder, "don't think so. They're worried about their jobs. The people who unload the empties, put them in the washing machines. You know how it is. Something new comes in, something old goes out."

"What about Harry's brother?" Tinker asked.

"Quentin? That little cocksucker. You know him?"

"Not really."

"I haven't thought of Quentin Wilson in years," Fletcher said. "You want to know about him?"

"It might help."

"The sun rose and set on Harry, as far as he was concerned. Idolized him. I'd say Quent was about eight or nine years younger. He was always at the games. Batboy. Very serious kid. Never smiled, never laughed. I knew him growing up—I was still living in Capstone then. Nobody liked him. I mean, he didn't let you like him. It was almost as if he didn't want you to. You know the type? When he had something to say, it was nasty and snide. A real little prick, that kid."

"Was he athletic?"

"No," Fletcher said. "He wanted to be an actor."

"An actor?"

Fletcher shrugged, as though this were a mystery too abstruse for comment.

"Did he do any acting?" Tinker asked.

"Now and then, as far as I heard. He was on the radio a few times, on some show. I don't know, I never followed it. And I think he had a small part in one or two shows on Broadway."

"That's interesting."

"He's not interesting," Fletcher said. "He's a shit. I think he's probably a very frustrated guy. You know, growing up in Harry's shadow and all. He's a baseball nut, I'll tell you that about him. I mean really a fanatic. One of those guys who knows every player on every team, memorizes batting averages, knows all the records. You know the type. Brooklyn Dodgers fan, I remember that. Took it all to heart. You know the type. Two brothers couldn't have been more different. Harry always looked out for him. I guess he knew the kid was a shit, but what the hell. And I can tell you, the only thing that stopped Quentin from having his beans handed to him every day and twice on Sunday was because he was Harry's brother. People tolerated him or looked the other way, or pretended not to hear. But he always had something snotty to say, like he was begging for it."

"He must be taking this hard," Tinker said. "This business with Harry."

"Christ," Fletcher said, "I can imagine. Listen, what really happened there? With Harry, I mean. Nobody seems to know, or if they do, they're not saying. I can't believe he was in there screwing that nigger. Although between you and me, Harry had a weakness for that sort."

"For prostitutes?"

"No, for colored. Now, don't put this in the paper, you hear? But Harry was always sort of open-minded about people. He always used to say, 'Give them a chance. Everybody's entitled to a fair chance.' Live and let live, you know," Fletcher said with a self-conscious chuckle. "That was Harry. But listen, keep it to yourself."

"Sure," Tinker said.

"He'd probably be very happy over this guy Robinson. 'Give him a chance,' he'd say. What do you think, the Dodgers gonna bring him up?"

"There's the possibility."

"Well, I know a hell of a lot of people who'll never go to Ebbets Field again if they do. Real Dodgers fans too. People got feelings, you know."

6

Tinker took the subway back from Queens and got off at Sixth Avenue and Forty-second. He could have stayed on and gone back to the Village, back to Sally's. She was probably home now, waiting for him. An exceedingly patient and tolerant woman, which was surprising, because clearly she didn't have to be. With her beautiful and intelligent face, her rhythmic sensuality, her Smith girl poise and self-confidence, she did not have to put up with any man's nonsense.

But she put up with Tinker's, not that his derelictions involved much more than a soul-satisfying bender and twenty-four-hour disappearing act every so often. But these were episodes of pure booze and escape. Tinker had not bedded another woman since checking his duffel bag in Sally's apartment. Living rent-free with a woman of this caliber entailed certain obligations and he felt proud of himself for having so far abided by them. A man who recognizes his own frailties can induce pride whenever he wants simply through the exertion of self-discipline.

He knew that he had great latitude with her and that it was due only partly to his wayward charm and the multiple skills he brought to bed with him. Her brother, Alex, two years older than she—Tinker's age exactly, in fact—had also been a Marine in the Pacific. Alex had not come home, not even in a coffin. He had been blown to pieces while running across the volcanic ash of Iwo Jima, where Tinker had earned his Purple Heart and won his Bronze Star. ("No big deal," he said. "All I did was let the air out of a Jap machine gunner.") Haunted by her dead brother, still not reconciled to his death, Sally sometimes wept quietly when she had drunk too much white wine, and would take Tinker's hand in hers and hold it tightly.

He had found her working at the paper when he returned from the war. She was writing society news. He thought a society writer for this newspaper was pure conceit, a silk tie on a blue work shirt. But the publisher thought it added tone, something to counterbalance the three-inch headlines, the graphically featured rape and slaughter stories, and the general hokum and pablum that entertained a couple of million New Yorkers every day.

Tinker walked across Forty-second Street, heading for the *News* building, his normally crisp, swaggering wiseacre's strides slowed to those of a contemplator. He shouldered unmindfully through the crowds in the cool November evening, passing the library's stately walls. He crossed Fifth Avenue in the tidal flow released by the green light. How many was it supposedly passed this intersection per daylight hour? Fifteen thousand? Thirty thousand?

Men wearing cloth caps and half aprons with enormous pouch-like pockets for storing coins were hawking the evening papers from the corner shacks, and thumbs and forefingers were reducing the fresh stacks as people bought their papers and then hurried on toward Grand Central to catch trains for Connecticut. This goddamned city, Tinker thought somberly, became very impersonal at this hour, when people were in a hurry. Looking straight down the canyon, the view carried across the East River into Queens, where Tinker's old friends and neighbors were easing into a night in the beer gardens, or the bowling alleys, or the movies, or around the living-room radio, while back over his shoulder a few blocks Broadway was gearing up for another round of *Born Yesterday* and *Annie Get Your Gun* and God knew what else; Tinker was not a man for the theater, couldn't name more than two or three shows despite all the times he walked under those marquees or drank with the stars themselves, who liked to infiltrate the sporting fraternity at Shor's or Lindy's.

Scott was gone when Tinker walked into the sports department. Jimmy Edgers was there, as usual. The thin man with the fedora and the narrow mouth and the vest and the misty eyeglasses was always there, not so much coming early as staying late. Probably lonely, Tinker thought once, and then forgot it. Loneliness was a man's own business. A man was lonely because he wanted to be; if not, then he was dangerous. So leave it be.

Tommy Curry was there too. Assistant sports editor. Just about thirty years old and already beginning to spread in the middle. He always wore an unbuttoned vest, as if striving for the formal and the hardworking image at the same time. When they'd played the *Daily Mirror* sports staff in a softball game in Central Park, Tommy'd got hit in the nuts with a grounder and been carried off to the shade where he lay on the grass and admitted he didn't know how to play ball. Hell of an admission for a sportswriter to make.

A cliché is coming, Tinker thought as he watched Tommy turn around and see him.

"So the prodigal has returned," Tommy said. "Scotty told me you're back. How's that Wilson story?"

"The guy was a fucking bore. Makes Gehrig look like the Marx Brothers."

"You mean he was a nice kid."

"Yeah. A nice, boring kid."

"Well, that's what you want. It makes it a great story, when you consider what ultimately happened to him."

"Any more word on that?" Tinker asked.

Edgers stirred in his chair. He took a last, long drag on the runty bit of cigarette in his fingers, then reached across the desk and stubbed it out in the ashtray.

"The Department," he said, "either does not know or would prefer not to. They've got two chunks of dark meat they can fry, and by so doing they know they'll get the guilty party plus a dividend. So they seemed satisfied."

"Still bothers me," Tinker said.

"Why should it?" Tommy asked.

"That's it—it shouldn't."

Tinker checked his desk. Nothing there except a message that Sally had called, twice.

"You get any pictures?" Tommy asked. "We've got to have some pictures."

"The *Courier* thinks they might have some. Their files are all fucked up, but they're gonna rummage."

The telephone rang and Edgers reached out and lifted the receiver. Tinker wandered across the office, trying to decide what to do. The options were these: sit and breeze with the guys; call Sally, which meant going home; or go downstairs to the White Rose for a sandwich or over to the Pen and Pencil for a real dinner, which he would then have to work into his cheat sheet somehow.

Edgers was on the phone for a minute or two—listening, mostly—before replacing the receiver.

"They all make sure to call here on their way to the booby hatch," he said, leaning back in his chair, the fluorescent lights catching his lenses for a moment.

"What was it?" Tommy asked.

"Some guy railing against Robinson coming up next year. Says it would be a calamity and that the press has an obligation to say so. Says the niggers—his word—are taking over the country and somebody better stop 'em. Says we'd better hurry, too, before they start outnumbering us. Tom," Edgers said whimsically, "did you know that the people in Harlem hide their kids when the census takers come around so we won't know how many of them there really are?"

"The guy on the phone just said that?" Tinker asked.

"Swear to God."

"What else did he say?"

Edgers grunted. "He said that if Jackie ever takes the field in Brooklyn his life won't be worth two cents."

Tommy Curry, going through a file cabinet, his back to them, said, "Robinson received plenty of death threats all summer. One of the Montreal writers told me."

"Were they taken seriously?" Tinker asked, staring at the telephone Edgers had just hung up.

"You always take those things seriously," Tommy said, pushing the drawer shut.

Tinker asked Edgers, "What'd this guy on the phone sound like?"

"Sound like?" Edgers pushed out his underlip for a moment. "Rational. But tense. I'd say he sounded very tense."

7

To Sally, it seemed like an entirely new situation and she didn't quite know how to handle it. The ice cream–cool young lady out of Smith College, from the genteel, conservative southern New Hampshire family, was, for the first time since Tinker had known her, uncertain. She was delighted, of course, she said, that he had been reinstated. But then she became quiet.

Tinker had come straight home from the office and now they were having dinner in an Italian restaurant on Thompson Street, entered by going down a flight of stairs. Shrimp marinara with a plate of spaghetti on the side, both of them. White wine, of course, for Sally; Seven-Up for Tinker, the ordering of which always seemed to offend the small restaurant's lone waiter, a large man with a granite Mussolini bald head, who when he called the order from the table to the open-doored kitchen always concluded by raising his voice and disdainfully crying out, "An' wahn Seven-Up!" Sally covered her smile and Tinker refused to be mortified.

Someday he would rock the son-of-a-bitch waiter and order a glass of wine with his shrimp. Red.

Midway through the meal Sally came around to voicing what was on her mind.

"Now that you have income again, will you be staying on?"

"If I'm invited to," he said.

"Okay."

"Is that what's bothering you?"

"Nothing is bothering me," she said unconvincingly, twirling her fork slowly into her spaghetti. She could come up with an almost symmetrical forkful of the stuff, which Tinker never could. He had to eat spaghetti by getting under the dangling strands with a wide-open mouth.

She remained reticent on the subject of his staying, leaving it to him to work out. She had never lived with a man before. Taking him in, when he had been suspended and unable to meet his rent, had had samaritan overtones, even though he had been seeing her for six months. But now the situation had changed. Under these circumstances, there was in her mind, he realized, a question of morality.

"That's it, then," he said, after delivering himself of this judgment.

"Something like that," she admitted.

"That's a mighty thin line your morality stands behind. You want me to leave?"

"No. I want you to stay. But there's one condition."

"Oh yeah?"

"It's not unreasonable, Joe. Now you're going to have money again, be out on assignments, roaming around. No other women."

"The thought never entered my head."

"It's not your head I'm worried about."

Given the directness and the simplicity of the facts, and the almost classic structure, the Harry Wilson story should have been a walk around the block. The problem was—and Tinker admitted it to himself—he had little interest in it, or in his assigned end of it anyway. He was more interested in knowing why Harry had been in the building across the street, and what had happened there. What he was writing was the "toy department" side of the story. Even though this was his normal beat, he felt demeaned.

He was sitting at the bedroom window now, elbows on the sill, face resting in hands, gazing moodily across an empty, untroubled Christopher Street at the building where Harry had been shot. The shades in the dark second-floor apartment were drawn. In due time it would be rented again; maybe a family would move in, maybe a small child would play on the floor where Harry Wilson was shot dead.

Tinker was wearing shorts and had a towel draped around his shoulders to ward off the chill. Behind him, Sally lay asleep in the bed-covers they had churned into lumpish disarray. If ever proof was needed that a human being possessed differing compartments that were sealed off one from the other, she could embody it. Proper, almost aloof at times, she underwent transformation when she got into bed, from Miss Gentility into a clawing, writhing, panting, biting hellcat of passion. The bed's big, heavy wrought-iron headboard slammed against the wall like a ponderous metronome until he couldn't help wondering what the people on the other side might be thinking, and how they reconciled all this vigorous action with the polite, neatly tailored young woman they encountered in the hallway.

The night was chilly. Autumn was turning surly, especially after dark, the season being muscled aside by the first hoary gusts of blind blundering winter. Pages of newspapers glided down the center of the street, chased along by the wind blowing in off the river. They were followed by dead leaves, which he could hear making ticking sounds as they scraped and bounded toward Seventh Avenue.

He could remember how he had tried to alleviate the tedium of those Pacific islands during the war: replaying in his mind some of the bitterly tense Dodgers-Cardinals games of the summer of '41. Or recalling the accumulating wonder of Joe D.'s hitting streak. Or seeing again the Louis-Conn fight, the one that people said Billy should have won. He'd close his eyes and write the stories in his head, with brilliant leads of course, and he'd think that writing sports was the most blessed occupation a man could ever hope to aspire to. The World Series. Army–Notre Dame. Friday nights at the Garden, standing in the teeming lobby with Cannon, Runyon, Granny Rice, and the other writers, watching the Broadway crowd coming in, the show people, the rackets guys wearing glittering blondes on their arms, the politicos, maybe some of the ornaments of past occasions like Dempsey or Mickey Walker, with a couple of tough New York detectives leaning against the wall with their arms folded, watching it all with almost predatory interest. New York's own Milky Way. There were guys in his outfit who couldn't wait to get back to their farms in Iowa or the open ranges of the West or lakes in Wisconsin or small towns in Oregon or South Carolina, to traditions of murmurous tranquility. But the hell with cowshit and nature and Main Street, he'd think. He yearned to hear thirty thousand people howling as Reiser stole home or Williams bashed one into the Stadium's third tier. He wanted to see Willie Pep after fifteen rounds without a mark on him, the lethal suddenness of a Sugar Ray left hook, and then get in front of a typewriter still emotionally drenched from what he had seen and machine-gun it into graphically descriptive prose that would freeze the moment forever.

And now he was back, despite his peccadilloes one of the bright young boys of the profession, and yet disquieted by gnawings of dissatisfaction that were growing and becoming more frequent. Harry Wilson's triumphant boyhood should have come singing out of the typewriter. But Tinker was thinking instead of that phone call Jimmy Edgers had taken earlier in the evening: had it been from Quentin Wilson? Jesus, but it had sounded like it, the same irrational, moronic idea. And what had Quentin muttered the other night in the bar? *"That goddamned fuckin' Angel."* Little brother had damned well known who big brother had gone to see. Should have asked him who Angel was, Tinker thought. Sure, like he would have told you.

So Harry had gone around the corner to take the spread from a black hooker.

Harry had no prejudices. Didn't the milkman say it?

So what? A lot of guys like to change their luck now and then.

And Quentin hated blacks. Right?

So?

So maybe nothing. So maybe just that.

Tinker went to bed.

8

Tinker was at Stillman's Gym when the telephone call came for him.

"You here?" Rocco, an ex-pug with a punch-squashed face, asked him, leaning out of the phone booth, one hand covering the mouthpiece.

Tinker pondered for a moment, turning away from the ring and looking at Rocco. Lou Stillman's almost parodic sidewalks-of-New-York voice—the guy must gargle with pebbles every morning, somebody once said—was rasping into his stem microphone, announcing to the dozen or so spectators that climbing into Ring One to spar was "the Puerto Rican Phantom . . ."

Tinker gave it another moment's thought. He wasn't supposed to be here, which meant somebody was looking for him. He was supposed to be back out in Queens, sifting through the sweet, unoffending sands of Harry Wilson's boyhood. Two days removed from the shit list and already he was fucking off. But he'd heard that morning that the Rock was coming up to Stillman's for some ring work and Tinker could never resist the Rock. Graziano hadn't appeared yet, but it was all right. Tinker liked this airless, perspiration-drenched, liniment-whiffed place with its rows of folding chairs lined up before the two adjacent rings. When he came through the old turnstile at the head of the long staircase leading up from the Eighth Avenue sidewalk, he felt peculiarly at home, listening to the fighters in the ring grunting and exchanging leather, their sneakers rubbing on the resin-covered ring floor.

"I'm here," he said, walking over to the booth and taking the phone from Rocco, exchanging places with the fog-brained old club fighter and sitting down inside the booth. "Yeah," he said into the phone.

"Joe? It's Tony Marino. I've been calling around, looking for you."

"Why'd you call here? I'm supposed to be in Queens."

"I don't know where you're supposed to be."

"Well, you never reached me here. Okay?"

"Are you still interested in the Wilson case?"

"What've you got?"

"Something that might intrigue you," the police reporter said. "You ever hear of Floyd Haberman?"

"No."

"He's a top-drawer criminal lawyer. He's been retained to defend Angel."

"By who?"

"He's not saying."

"It's got to be Rush. Pimps sometimes have a lot of money."

"If Rush is retaining him," Tony said, "why is he defending Angel? And anyway, from the looks of things, Rush can't afford a lawyer and will be getting a public defender."

"Haberman, I take it, is expensive."

"Very."

"So how do you figure it?" Tinker asked, watching through the fold-up glass door as Graziano walked in, surrounded by a coterie of ginzos wearing oversized pearl-gray fedoras. Rocky was hatless.

"I can't figure it yet. Just letting you know about it. You seemed interested."

"Yeah, I am. Thanks, Tony," Tinker said, watching Graziano and some ex-pug greeting each other by throwing up their hands in time-honored defensive postures, then laughing and wrapping their arms around each other.

"One other thing that might interest you," Tony said. "I got this from a contact down at Centre Street. This won't be in the papers, but Quentin Wilson—that's Harry's brother—was in a brawl last night in an apartment up on Amsterdam. Seems he got worked over."

"By who?" Tinker asked, turning away from the Rock's reception and frowning into the mouthpiece.

"Some Negro."

"What the hell was he doing in a Negro's apartment?"

"The apartment's occupant is a Miss Ettie Pearson."

"Negro?"

"Yes. Her friend was bashing Quentin around and some neighbors heard the commotion and called the cops. They came and pulled him out of there, and when they found out he was Harry's brother they decided to bury the thing."

"They didn't want Harry's name in the paper again," Tinker said.

"Especially associated with this kind of episode."

"So what was Quentin doing there?"

"Nobody knows."

"You talk to this Pearson lady?"

"No. I can't. It was told to me in confidence. The whole thing is off the record. I just thought you'd be interested."

"Very strange," Tinker said, trying to imagine what in hell Quentin was doing in the apartment of a Negro woman on Amsterdam Avenue. "What time did this happen?"

"Around five o'clock."

And that belligerent, threatening, anti-Negro phone call had come to the sports department when? Six-thirty, a quarter to seven? It had to have been Quentin, smarting from his pasting at the hands of some black buckaroo.

"Tony, I appreciate this," Tinker said.

"Remember, the business with Harry's brother is off the record. The department is very touchy about the whole thing."

With good reason, Tinker suspected.

9

Before the war Elmer Cregar had been a practicing middleweight, a club fighter around New York who had been good enough to head the card at Ridgewood Grove, Jamaica Arena, and other small arenas, and occasionally to get a main event in places like Providence and Holyoke. Sometimes he fought as often as three times a month, because he pleased the crowd and the matchmakers knew him as a "money's worth" attraction who usually went the distance and who, win or lose, was never dull.

Born in the Washington Heights section of upper Manhattan, Elmer had begun boxing professionally when he was eighteen years old and was able to get booked for four- and six-round preliminaries because a crowd from his neighborhood always came to see him and the arenas came to count on them. That sort of following always gave a local fighter the edge over the out-of-towner, and not just in bookings but in close decisions too.

Elmer slammed his way through three dozen

fights, winning most of them, until he was handed his first big opportunity, in the winter of 1940. It was the pivotal, stepping-stone fight that most career club fighters eventually looked back on wistfully. This was a semifinal in St. Nicholas Arena in New York, next to the Garden the city's most prestigious ring. A good showing could mean a main event at St. Nick's or a semifinal at the Garden. Elmer trained hard at Stillman's and forwent booze and women for the several weeks leading up to the fight, which he went into so confident that he booked a table at Dinty Moore's for a victory celebration.

His vociferous followers filled St. Nick's that night, calling for blood. But after two rounds it became apparent that the ladder to the top was going to be too steep for Elmer. He was clearly outmatched by his opponent, a sleek black from Philadelphia with a relentless jab that made Elmer's defense look porous and a right hand that landed like a brick.

Frustrated, furious, Elmer began thumbing and hitting low, to finger-shaking warnings from the referee. Then in the third round that right hand from Philadelphia whistled over his glove from eight inches away and Elmer vaguely remembered lying on his back and gazing at the roof of St. Nicholas Arena, so relaxed that his every bone felt like it was resting on a velvet pillow, his thoughts trying to swim together like opposing waters and not connecting.

No longer regarded as a fighter with a future

but still well liked on the circuit of small, smoky arenas that enlivened Saturday nights in New York and New England, Elmer became a trial horse, the raw meat that those kids with the feathery toes and piston elbows had to consume on their way toward being ranked.

The dream of a championship belt was hard to dislodge, and Elmer went on pursuing it, abetted by his neighborhood friends, to whom he was the real thing, who remembered him as the most savage and merciless street brawler in Washington Heights before he'd gone into the punch-for-pay business. And then he had what amounted to an epiphanic experience and the dream stopped. Just before he was drafted, in February 1942, he took his girlfriend to the Garden on fight night. The main event was Tony Zale and Billy Conn and for twelve hellish rounds Elmer's mesmerized eyes watched the skilled ferocity of both men. The professional inside him was proud and admiring, but the rest of him ached with biting envy. After the fight, sitting in the lounge at the Hotel Taft, the girlfriend, with a wry smile and brainless disdain, told him, "You wouldn't have lasted thirty seconds with either one of them." He threw a glass of Scotch and water in her face. But the wisecrack remained deadly; it shredded the last veils of illusion he had about himself.

When he was discharged in 1945, Elmer, who had boxed some exhibitions in England during the war, tried to resume his career. He worked himself into excellent shape and ran off a string of victories over soft opposition in tank towns. He was winning, but he knew it didn't mean anything, that all he was doing was waiting for the few starchings that would end it once and for all. Then he was booked to top the card at Ridgewood Grove, the small, venerable arena that stood next to the Myrtle Avenue El on the Brooklyn-Queens line, where a generation of headliners had got their start.

He was sitting alone in the dressing room several hours before fight time when a couple of B-movie characters in tight-fitting knee-length overcoats walked in. They were wearing fedoras with brims that looked like they could slice your throat. They said they would give him two hundred dollars if he would flop. One hundred now, the rest later. No, he said. He wanted all of it in hand now. The boys in the hats exchanged glances, and then one of them handed Elmer a couple of tightly folded C-notes, which felt good. The patronizing pat on the cheek didn't.

He took several flops, here and there, and then his manager dropped him and then the matchmakers dropped him, especially after a smart-ass *Daily News* sportswriter named Tinker had written how a "certain journeyman middleweight had irrigated half the gardens in Brooklyn with his latest splash."

Elmer's next series of knockouts came at various bars and dance halls around Brooklyn and Queens, where he was hired as a bouncer. After

doing some heavy damage to a few mildly ob-
streperous customers, he was cautioned by his
employer just to "stun" them. But Elmer
couldn't find it in his soul to pull a punch just
to give some loudmouth a break, and after one
of his victims returned at 5 A.M. and lobbed a
hand grenade through the window of the empty
bar, it was necessary to seek work elsewhere.
One club owner found out that his bouncer's
presence was actually counterproductive, that
some of the customers were unnerved by Elmer's arms-crossed, restlessly gazing stance
against the wall, and were going elsewhere.

In November 1947 Elmer was working in
Jackson Heights in a club called the Blue Harbor, a place illuminated with dim blue lighting
that pitched diagonally forward from the high
walls in soft, smoke-clouded columns. The
music came from a bandstand in the rear.

Elmer looked up one evening—it was early on
a weekday night, with only a handful of people
at the bar and none at the tables—and frowned
at the man who had just walked in. Then he
smiled listlessly, the kind of smile the wise guys
remembered seeing just before the flashpoint
moment when a sudden fist from nowhere
landed with professional impact and accuracy
and ended their evening. He remained sitting
at the circular bar, motionless, waiting to be
discovered. It didn't take long.

He could tell from the way Quentin walked
toward him that this was no chance meeting,

could tell from the businesslike stride and the little lift of the head, as though an appointment were being kept. Elmer smirked, maliciously amused by the sight of his old army buddy. The son of a bitch, nicely dressed in an olive-green suit, still exuded that unshatterable self-possession, that intense inner wiring that Elmer always found baffling because there never seemed anything to account for it, which in Elmer's world meant something physical. Elmer, who saw the world in brutally defined simplicities, could not account for this son of a bitch. A guy that skinny should not have been so sarcastic, so provocative, should have been taught that a long time ago. But the son of a bitch seemed impervious, refused to pull in his ground no matter what. Elmer had seen him punched out a number of times when they were in England waiting for Eisenhower's Crusade to begin, but it never seemed to hurt, or at least the guy never showed it. Blood, cuts, loosened teeth, barrages of punches landing on a face that never changed its expression. Some of the men in the company told Elmer they didn't understand why he bothered with that miserable bastard. The reason was simple, Elmer told them: you had to stay on the good side of a guy like that, because get into combat and the son of a bitch was capable of shooting you in the back.

"How'd you find me?" Elmer asked when Quentin had seated himself on the adjoining bar stool. There had been no handshake.

"Why?" Quentin asked. "Are you in hiding?"

"No."

"There's something I want to find out, I find it out."

Elmer smiled thinly, maliciously amused by Quentin's attempt at tough-guy suavity. Quentin had always been like that. If there was anything behind it, Elmer never discerned it. Maybe there was nothing. Probably why the son of a bitch wanted to be an actor. Elmer had heard it said they were people born essentially without personalities and that the profession was designed to fill the vacuum, for a few hours at a time anyway. Elmer had known a few and they had seemed like that, a bit different each time, as if trying to fill or appease another area of the vacuum.

Quentin's appearance had struck a rare light-hearted chord within Elmer. The rock-fisted bouncer ("I'm a protective custodian," he told Quentin) introduced him to the bartenders and to several of the waitresses as "Quentin Wilson, the actor." The name meant nothing, of course, but they were impressed nevertheless. After all, Elmer had been a celebrity himself and certainly must know one when he saw one. They glanced curiously at the actor's scratched chin, puffy lip, slightly discolored eye, but made no comment. And it was in fact this evidence of yet another beating having been administered to that insolent face that provoked Elmer's levity. The war may have changed a lot of things, but not everything: Quentin Wilson was still taking his lickings.

Quentin said he wanted to talk privately, and Elmer took the request seriously, for in his life private talks were often meaningful, freighted with privileged information and interesting propositions. His most recent private talk had taken place a few weeks ago, when two old friends from prewar days had dropped by and told him of a blessed opportunity that was his for the taking. It involved a factory on Greenpoint Avenue in Queens, a dinky office, a couple of bookkeepers, and a payroll that would be as easy as lifting an apple from a tree. They could use another man. Just for the sake of conversation, Elmer said, what could this other man expect to take home with him? Around two thousand dollars, he was told. No, he told them. Armed robbery should be worth more than that. A few days later he congratulated himself on his decision. The boys got the payroll out of the building all right, but in their haste to get away they ran their car into a steel utility pole a block away and were too battered to attempt an escape.

Elmer, however, remained open to private talks. He didn't mind working as a bouncer; he was keenly aware of the tension he created when he moved with his fixed surly expression through the crowd. He liked muscling people, liked it even more if somebody was foolish enough to try to unload on him. It was dangerous to swing at a pro, and it was futile; you weren't going to hit him, and the moment you realized the abrupt ease with which you had been blocked you knew it was too late for apology. An express-train fist into the midsection scissored you and then you were being hustled through the door. A nice job for an ex-pug, but definitely with limited prospects.

The musicians hadn't set up yet and the rear of the Blue Harbor was just fine for a private talk. The two former army buddies slipped into an empty booth, sitting across the table from each other.

"Working in a dump like this," Quentin said, "you must be hard up. You're not fighting anymore, are you?"

"No."

"You knock out some drunken slob, it doesn't go in the record books."

Elmer felt a short, sharp rise of malice, just a spurt of it, causing an involuntary curling of his fingers and forcing a tight, insinuating smile.

"And what have you been up to?" he asked.

"I've been thinking."

"Didn't go back to acting?"

"I will when I'm ready. There are other things right now."

"What do you want, Quentin?"

"Over there," Quentin said with a quick toss of the head, as if Europe was in the next room, "you used to talk about getting a stake and doing something for yourself when you got back."

"So?"

"So, you were my buddy over there. We went through a lot of tight spots together and now I want to do something for you. I remember you telling me more than once that you had associated with some pretty hard guys before the war, and I used to tell myself, 'This man has been around. He knows how to get things done.'"

"What the fuck do you want, Quentin?"

"Elmer, you don't want to spend the rest of your life as a guard dog in dumps like this, do you?"

"Get to the point."

"The point is—we can help each other."

"How?"

"I want you to pull the trigger on somebody."

Noting that Elmer's first reaction was bemusement rather than shock or indignation gave Quentin a positive feeling.

"What am I?" Elmer asked. "Murder Incorporated? You were one of the best shots in the battalion. Why don't you do it yourself?"

"I don't have the stomach for it," Quentin said with cool directness, sensing that such an admission was disarming to a man like Elmer Cregar. And indeed, Elmer stared guardedly at Quentin for several moments, almost as if wondering whether he hadn't already been subtly lured into a trap.

"You were a goddamned good shot yourself," Quentin said.

"Not as good as those Missouri farmboys we had."

"Except that they shit their pants when things got hot. I want somebody whose trigger finger is going to be as cool as his eye."

Elmer felt the need to minimize this conversation, trying first with his slow, malicious smile, then saying, "What happened—somebody steal your girl?"

"This isn't something petty, Elmer," Quentin said as if delivering a mild reprimand. "The fact is, I've never met the man in question. But that doesn't matter, because he himself isn't important. It's what he represents."

Quentin wanted a trigger pulled on somebody he had never met. Because the man "represented" something. Elmer felt a discomfiting ambivalence: he was skeptical and curious. Skeptical because he had never heard anything like this before, and curious for the same reason. A clenched fist sent sharply to the point of a chin was as complex as the world of Elmer Cregar ever became.

"Somebody has got to do something to stop them, to turn them around," Quentin said. "Somebody has to draw the line."

"Who are you talking about?"

"The niggers."

Elmer said nothing, but felt the unease and resentment a man feels when he knows he is being accurately read. The fact was plainly in Quentin's blandly staring face. Elmer wet his lips with the tip of his tongue, as if tasting the words he was sullenly resisting speaking.

Quentin glanced over his shoulder, as if these, more than any others, were the words he did not want overheard. Elmer peered warily through the hazy blue light toward the bar, where several men were sitting like statues. His eyes moved sharply back as Quentin confronted him once more.

"Five thousand dollars," Quentin said.

The words, the amount, seemed to rush to the back of Elmer's mind and lodge there. Five grand. More than he had ever seen for a main event, more than he had ever possessed at one time in his life. It would take him a year to earn that working in this dump.

"You want me to drop some nigger for five thousand dollars?" he said.

"You drop the right one and they'll all feel it. That's the point of it—for them all to feel it, every black bastard one of them. I want to strike the fear of God into them."

For a moment Quentin's intensity made Elmer self-conscious of his own prejudices. But only for a moment.

"One of them has broken out of the pack," Quentin said. "If we don't stop him the pack will begin to follow. Every last one of them. And there's more of them than you think, more than anybody realizes. They start breaking loose and they'll run in every direction; this won't be our country anymore. But shoot the one in front and the others will stop in their tracks. The message will be clear."

"You really got five grand to burn, Quentin?"

"I don't want you to think of this just in terms of money. It's more than that."

"Listen, Quentin, for all I know you could be cracked. You wouldn't be the first."

"You'll get half when we agree, half when it's done. Plus, I'll pay your expenses. You're going to have to travel to get it done."

"Travel?"

"South, in the spring."

"I don't get this. Who the hell are you thinking about?"

"Robinson."

"Who the fuck is Robinson?" Elmer asked.

"Don't you follow baseball?"

"Oh. That Robinson."

"A college nigger. You know the kind. And the Brooklyn Dodgers are going to bring him up next year. People are saying the move hasn't been decided yet, but I know better. I follow baseball; I know what's going on. It's going to happen, unless somebody stops it, and somebody had better stop it, because this black son of a bitch is becoming a symbol for all of them. They're already dancing in the streets in Harlem."

"Well, I can see your point," Elmer said. "But it's a risky thing."

"That's why you're getting five thousand dollars."

"Which ain't worth shit if you get caught."

"Or if you miss," Quentin said. His voice carried a cordially threatening note that annoyed Elmer for a moment. "But I'm not worried about you," Quentin went on. "I saw you in action. You know how to survive."

"Oh, yeah. I knew how to survive all right—by not taking dumb chances. The heroes, they're still over there, six feet under."

"That's right. But you knew the secret, Elmer. Surviving is a secret that only certain people know."

"Well, I'll have to figure this out. You just don't walk up to a guy and bang him down."

"You'll figure it out. You're a combat veteran. This will be pure chickenshit compared to what you did over there."

"Leave out the horseshit, Quentin. Who else knows about this?"

"Nobody."

"Keep it that way."

"Of course."

"Anyway, it's still just talk. I haven't absolutely agreed."

"But I want you to agree. Before I leave this table. Look, there's really not that much to worry about. Once it happens, there'll be a million suspects. Every Southern cracker will have talked about doing it themselves. All you have to do is get it over with and get back to New York and count your money."

Elmer smiled enigmatically, and Quentin could see that the ex-boxer's mind had taken a quantum leap ahead, all the way to the satisfying feel of money in his hands. Then Elmer frowned. "Fifties," he said. "I'll want it all in fifties."

"Of course," Quentin said.

10

It occurred to Tinker as he walked along Amsterdam Avenue, the address and apartment number of Miss Ettie Pearson fixed in his mind, that he had never been inside the apartment of a colored person. Well, he thought, not so remarkable. There had been zero Negroes in Capstone when he grew up there, and as far as he knew there were still zero Negroes there. A neighborhood of Poles, Italians, a scattering of Irish, some Jews.

"We'll never have niggers here, and I'll tell you why," his father had once told him. "For one thing, it's only one- and two-family houses here, and nobody would sell to them. It's sort of a code, you see? An unwritten law. You know where you get them? Where you got apartment houses. That's where they come in. You got some Jew landlord who lives in Great Neck who don't give a fuck who he rents to. That's how they get in. The next thing you know, there's piles of shit in the street. But I'll tell you how we saved Capstone."

That story went back to the 1920s, when the Independent Subway was being dug. Originally, according to Tinker's father, who had hung around the Democratic clubhouse in those days, the subway was supposed to come through Capstone. But the local pols fought against it, afraid that a subway hookup with Manhattan would mean high-rise apartment buildings—the big boxes always followed the subway, the pols claimed, citing dire examples in Brooklyn and the Bronx—and apartment houses meant "all sorts of people." So the subway sped past Capstone, and the neighborhood, already hemmed in on three sides by cemeteries and thus impeded from expansion, remained lily white. "We knew how to do things in those days," Tinker's father said.

Growing up, the only time Tinker ever saw a Negro was when one happened to be a helper on a truck delivering to one of the stores on Grant Avenue. So he grew up in helpless thrall to the stereotypes: "they" had uncommonly thick skulls, had natural rhythm, had dicks as long as pythons. His father believed it, his friends all believed it. And the way Henry Armstrong could take punches and the way Bojangles danced on the screen in the darkness of the Capstone Theater did nothing to disabuse him of the stereotypes. But Tinker never thought one way or another about it. There was no reason to, not when all the other stereotypes, the ones in front of him, seemed—on superficial observation—to fit into place: the Poles were dim-witted and heavy-fisted, the Dagos were loud and coarse and talked with their hands, the Jews (who seemed to own every other store on the avenue) were cheap, the Irish drank too much, and the only Chinaman in town ran a laundry and lived with his family in back of his store. Even the neighborhood's most conspicuous German, who ran the delicatessen that stayed open until midnight, was drawn increasingly into stereotype as war neared. He was a big-shouldered, mean-eyed bull of a man with a size 18 neck, a close-cropped cannonball head, a sinister gold-toothed smile, and a Doberman named Rienzi. They said he held Bund meetings in the back of the store during which he wore a swastika armband and gave the Nazi salute, none of which seemed to disturb too many people in the generally anti-Semitic neighborhood until war with Germany broke out, and then one night some Legionnaires, oiled up after a card party at the Legion Hall, marched into the deli and knocked the shit out of the perceived Nazi, smashed the angled windows of the meat showcase, knocked over the bread and cake stand, brained Rienzi with a bottle of Canada Dry ginger ale, and marched out with a roar of patriotic fervor.

Stereotypes, Tinker thought as he watched the addresses on the buildings on Amsterdam. No group, race, or profession was free of them. Newspapermen? Boozers, soft-hearted cynics, disreputably virtuous, charmingly irresponsible.

The entrance to the building where Ettie Pearson lived was around the corner from Amsterdam. A small, marble-floored foyer went up two steps and led to a broad, red-carpeted lobby furnished with brown brocade chairs and a plain, backless mahogany bench in the middle. Tinker let himself into the automatic elevator, punched the sixth-floor button and took the brief, weightless flight up the shaft.

As he walked along the sixth-floor corridor, Tinker wondered what the hell Quentin had been doing there. Did both Wilson brothers, despite Quentin's bluntly stated antipathy, have some kind of quirky affinity for Negro women?

Tinker rapped on the door at the end of the corridor. He waited. He had no idea of what he was going to say; the curiosity that had impelled him uptown from Stillman's seemed to have left his mind in suspension, as if curiosity by itself was its own explanation.

From behind the door a woman's voice asked who it was.

"Joe Tinker, *Daily News*," he said quietly, as though imparting something in confidence. Always undersell it. People were impressed when a newspaperman came to their door; identify yourself without any hint of self-importance and the impression went still deeper.

The door opened a crack and Tinker was staring at Ettie Pearson. She was a handsome woman, aged anywhere from late thirties to late forties. She was light-skinned, with as much Caucasian as Negroid in her features. Her light brown hair was neatly coiffed, each strand looking as though it had been laid in place by hand. She was wearing a yellow blouse, collar up, open at the throat. One of the fingers that held the door aside wore a large ruby ring. Her dark eyes held Tinker with a wariness that seemed hardened, self-protective.

"What do you want?" she asked.

"I'd like to talk to you."

She waited. Tinker ran his mind for a moment.

"About Harry Wilson," he said.

"Why?"

"I'm doing a story about him."

Her expression changed, a frown mirroring her uncertainty. She was contemplating him— not so much Tinker personally, but who he was, where he was from. Then the corners of her mouth pressed in for a moment. She gave a barely perceptible shrug.

"Why not?" she said quietly, as if to herself, opening the door the rest of the way.

Tinker glanced around as he entered the living room. It was tastefully furnished—sofa, armchairs, coffee table. Maroon carpeting covered the floor. A set of small Japanese prints hung on the wall. A baby grand stood near the window, its top down, bare and shiny.

Ettie Pearson was very trim in her yellow

blouse and dark brown knee-length skirt. She had good legs and she certainly looked alluring in her high heels. He didn't think she was a hooker, though he had to admit he was not an expert in these matters. Or maybe she was, after all. Maybe that's why Quentin had come here, to bang this very attractive colored woman, and then had not paid her and been knocked around by the man Tinker sensed was sitting on the other side of the living-room wall, in the bedroom (why else was that door open about eight inches?). And that could have been exactly what happened to Harry—knocked off a piece and then refused to settle up; only Harry wasn't so lucky, with Angel or her pimp shooting him in the head . . . No, Tinker told himself. You don't shoot a New York City detective for that. Lay off the pedestrian speculation.

"May I?" he said, pointing to one of the chairs.

"Of course," she said. She had just closed the door.

He sat down and crossed his legs, noticing that the toe of his brown shoe was scuffed almost white. Walking on concrete.

"Why are you writing a story about Harry?" Ettie Pearson asked. She had moved across the room and was standing in front of the piano, arms folded, the window behind her. She seemed quite self-possessed. He could see he wasn't going to be able to bullshit or unduly impress this woman. Tinker was uncomfortable

123

with people who were not unduly impressed by his being a newspaperman. Status was one of the compensations of the job; along with free tickets and flexible hours, it made the negligible salary tolerable.

"My editor's idea," Tinker said. "Harry is news right now and they want a story about him. And it isn't just because of his unfortunate death, but because he was also quite a school-boy athlete back when."

"I didn't know him then."

"Just when did you meet him?"

"I met Harry in 1926."

Tinker could feel the surprise registering in his face.

"That long ago?" he asked.

"Oh yes," she said with evident satisfaction, almost as if hoping to shock him.

"How'd you meet him?"

"What has any of that to do with your story?"

"Well, we have to accumulate all the facts in order to write a complete, well-rounded piece."

"I see."

Tinker found her steady, skeptical stare unnerving.

"Well, I don't think those facts are anyone's business, Mr. Tinker," she said.

"It would help."

"Help whom? Help what?"

The man appeared silently, from the room on the other side of the wall. Tinker sensed him before turning around and actually seeing him.

The man was big and bulky, broad in the chest, heavy in the middle. He was wearing a green flannel shirt and a black suit jacket and tan chino trousers. Hands as large as first baseman's mitts hung at his sides. There was a curious formality about the man. Ettie made brief introductions. The man's name was Charley.

Charley gazed sternly at Ettie, a moist, poignant pain in his eyes, and Tinker could sense something compelling and ineffable passing between these two people standing on opposite sides of the room.

"Tell him," Charley said quietly, then repeated the words several times, his rumbly voice growing in volume and feeling. *"Tell him. Tell him!"*

She stared at first quizzically at him, and then with depths of feeling that Tinker saw but knew immediately he could never understand. He did feel certain that the man's passionate insistence was out of character, a coming loose of old, pent-up frustrations.

"Secrets," Charley said, his voice lowering, pronouncing the word almost with contempt. "Hiding. As if there was shame in it. There's been enough secrets, enough hiding. To what good? It's not a secret anyway," he said. "Tell him."

She studied him for several moments, then smiled faintly, and turned back to Tinker.

"There was never any shame in it, Mr. Tinker," she said. "Or if there was, it should have been felt in the world around us, not by us. But sometimes they can make you feel it, when you're alone, when you feel surrounded. You don't understand what I'm talking about, do you?"

"No, ma'am. But if you tell me, I'll try."

"I'll tell you what you want to know, but I don't think they'll want the story in the newspaper."

"Why shouldn't they?"

"They've painted Harry as some kind of hero. 'The Department's most highly decorated detective, gunned down.' I don't think they'll want to hear anything that besmirches his name," she said with a pungency that was flat and bitter.

"Nobody seems to know what he was doing there," Tinker said.

"No, they don't."

"Do you?"

"Yes."

"Will you tell me?"

"Perhaps we'll get to it."

Tinker pondered that for a moment.

"You had a long relationship with him, didn't you?" he said.

"Yes."

"A close relationship."

"Very."

"And you don't care if people know?" Tinker asked, then realized to his momentary dismay that he had misstepped slightly, that he had in a way offered an opinion.

Ettie Pearson remained motionless, seemingly with calculation, as though posture were a statement, arms folded, staring at Tinker with a steadiness that approached defiance, or was perhaps simply unrepentant pride. Whatever it was, it was being braced by a disconcerting candor, the last thing, Tinker thought, you'd expect to put a newspaperman off his ease.

"We met at Lenox Avenue and 142nd Street," she said. "That's where I worked. I was a dancer. Do you remember the Cotton Club, Mr. Tinker?"

"I've heard of it, of course."

"Well, if you were a young colored girl up from South Carolina with music in your feet, the Cotton Club was the place to kick it out. Watching Ethel Waters standing on that stage singing 'Dinah' or 'Stormy Weather,' knowing that you were a part of it, however small, made you feel important. And what else does a young person want? It seemed that all of high-flyin' white downtown came up to the Cotton Club in those days; you'd see the cars parked outside, the Rolls-Royces and the Cadillacs and the Stutzes and whatnot. Not just anybody could get a table there; you had to be in the know. Colored couldn't get in there, except if they were light enough to pass. But only colored could work there. So that audience, the men in their tuxedos and the ladies in their silks and furs and feathers, sitting there drinking champagne and Prohibition gin, would be looking at the Old South plantation cabin and the rows of fake cotton bushes set up on the stage and think they were seeing the real thing, some good old Deep South nigger livin'.

"But I'll tell you what was real. As far as I was concerned, there was only one real thing that ever came into the Cotton Club. It was that policeman. He started coming in after midnight, when his tour was over. He'd stand off to the side somewhere, inconspicuous, a drink in his hand, and watch. Of course at first I didn't know he was a policeman; naturally he didn't stand there drinking in uniform. But when I found out he was a cop, I thought it meant trouble. You see, the place was owned by Owney Madden, the gangster . . ."

"He drove around in a bullet-proof Duesenberg," Tinker said.

"So they said. But it shows you how naive I was in those years. The last person who was going to cause trouble in a place like that was a young policeman, not with all the payoffs that were going higher up. But I soon realized what he was doing there: he was watching me. And that's all he did for a couple of weeks—watch. You damn well know it when a man's standing out there with his eyes set on you. You come to *feel* it. At first I said to myself, 'I know what he wants.' But then I wasn't so sure, because somewhere along the night he'd disappear. But then after a few weeks, maybe a month, he sent word back to the dressing room asking if I'd meet him for a drink when I got off work. Normally I would have said no, because you know what it's all about. But I said to myself, he can't be too bad if he's been standing there all this time before asking. I guess I was a little bit intrigued. You can understand that. And anyway, my instincts told me he was all right, and a girl who's alone learns to guide herself by that.

"And I wasn't wrong either. Harry Wilson was the finest man I ever met. And I can tell you, it was reassuring for a colored woman to meet a white man who was that tough and that strong and find him a perfect gentleman. And a policeman, too, no less.

"I knew he was married. He told me that the first night. He said his marriage wasn't a happy one. Otherwise, he said, he wouldn't be sitting and having a drink with me. I didn't realize until I'd gone home that night what he had said: that a happily married man wouldn't be seeing another woman. Mr. Tinker, you don't know how refreshing that sounded.

"I don't think that it was because of me that Harry left his wife, but you can never be sure. He simply said one day that they weren't happy and that he was leaving her. That was Harry: an announcement that a decision had been taken and then the book was closed, no looking back. We took an apartment together on 112th Street, not far from the park. We knew exactly what we were doing. Falling in love may be beautiful, Mr. Tinker, but it's never been a passport out of the real world. Have you ever been in love, Mr. Tinker?" she asked him.

The unexpectedness of the question made him stir uncomfortably in his chair. "I'm not sure," he said, still trying to assimilate the fact of a white man living with a black woman. The worldly young sportswriter had to admit that he had never heard of *that* before.

"It wasn't easy," she said. "Not then, not now. But even worse then. We kept to ourselves, which wasn't hard to do, since most people preferred to avoid us. But we were content and so nothing else seemed to matter. At least not to Harry. But I knew better. I knew a little bit more about these things than he did. Harry believed in people, you see, despite the fact that his job kept showing him the worst side of them. But that was his nature. That kind of innocence was endearing, but it wasn't very reassuring.

"Then I became pregnant. It was around that time that some people in the Department found out who Harry was living with. They told him, off the record of course, that he had better end it, or else he was dead on the Force; he'd never get anywhere. Now, Harry loved me. I knew that. But he loved his job too, and he was a very ambitious man. He used to say that someday he was going to be commissioner. He was so strong about it, so self-confident, you had to believe him. He would have stayed with me, but I knew that would be wrong, because I knew they would have drawn a line under his name and that would be that. Eventually he would start brooding about all that might have been, while I was getting older and not turning any lighter. Love is wonderful, Mr. Tinker, until it starts getting in the way of a man's dream. Then it starts to seem like competition."

"Yes, ma'am," Tinker said, wondering why he was agreeing with this particular suggestion.

"So I made the decision for him," she said. "I took my pregnant belly and moved back up to a small apartment in Harlem. Harry moved out to Queens. We still saw each other, on the sly now, because he'd told whoever had been so worried about his purity that it was all over. There were times when he wanted to come back, but I told him no, because, you see, most of the time what he talked about was what he was doing on the Force, about the commendations he had received and the promotions he was going to get. That was where his heart was; his passion, you might say, and I recognized it, and I understood. Does your woman understand you, Mr. Tinker?"

"I think she tries," he said.

"Don't make it difficult for her," she said, smiling self-consciously at her well-intended advice. The smile lingered for a moment, then faded back into old memories. "Harry was crazy about that baby. I can tell you that. But

Lord, it was tough for him. He was the only father in New York, he'd say, who couldn't take his baby outside for a walk. Couldn't take her to the park. Couldn't take her to the circus."

Ettie Pearson sat down now, on the sofa opposite Tinker, an expression of tired, wistful resignation on her face, and like some chemical dye, it suddenly revealed time, age. Charley remained standing, hugely immobile, staring at her expressionlessly.

"Angel," Tinker said. "Angel was the baby." But all the vast revelation told him was that the scope of his ignorance had multiplied: a door opening into further darkness.

"Harry scraped together some money," she said, "and bought me a small beauty parlor on upper Madison. This was during the Depression and we got it for a song. I worked hard and built it up. Then I bought a bigger place. We've got six chairs now and doing very nicely, and I'm able to take time off whenever I want. But during those early years I had to be there all the time, and I couldn't always keep an eye on Angel. Maybe that was the reason I began losing her. Maybe there was no reason. Maybe she was just an attractive Negro girl growing up in New York with a working mother and a father who came around less and less because there was no way he could fit into her life. So she learned how to lie when she was a child, telling the other children that her father was dead. And learned how to keep a lot of things to herself, not even asking questions when she was still too young to be able to figure things out for herself. I guess that was a bad sign, and I guess I missed it. I'll take my share of the blame, Mr. Tinker.

"She was almost sixteen years old before I found out what she was doing, what she'd been doing for two years. I told Harry. I had to. It just ate him up. He knew how absolutely awful and sordid and dangerous it was. He talked to her, he pleaded. She just listened, and then went her way. He knew he had no leverage with her; that had been lost. Angel was Angel, and there was nothing we could do about it. Sometimes I didn't see or hear from her for weeks. But I think the worst thing that ever happened to her was getting caught in the riots."

"Riots?" he asked.

"In 1943, the race riots, so called."

"I was in the South Pacific at the time," he said. "But I know what happened."

"She got caught right in the middle. It went on for days. Carloads of white men were driving into Harlem from all over the city to fight, like there was an army to enlist in, as though it had suddenly become legal to hunt down Negroes and smash them around. Some of the police weren't much better. Lord but she was out there and saw it all—Negro heads being bashed by clubs clutched in white fists, Negro heads being broken against the curbs; Negroes being pounded around and thrown through plate-glass windows; blood and screams and the kind of fury that tells you that it isn't strictly of the moment but that it has been festering just under the surface for a long, long time and isn't just showing itself to you now but is also warning you that it's always there, waiting for you, and that this is what it looks like. She had nightmares for months, and no wonder. When I saw the pictures in the papers of those battered, broken people, covered with blood, I had to tell myself: she saw that."

She fell silent for several moments, during which Tinker felt himself contending with a mass of details that refused to shape themselves into any sort of portrait.

"What was Harry doing there that night?" he asked.

"He visited her every so often. Still trying to talk her out of what she was doing, trying to steer her into a better life."

"How did she feel about him?"

"I suppose she cared about him. But he had forfeited a lot. An awful lot."

"But he was her father, didn't she love him?" Tinker asked, suddenly playing advocate for the dead Harry Wilson, as though Harry's hovering ghost were waiting for the answer.

"Children love their parents," Ettie said, "and then sometimes forget that they do."

I'll think about that one later, Tinker told himself, then asked, "Did she shoot him?"

Ettie moved her head vaguely from side to

side, her eyes shutting softly for a moment in an expression of the deepest unknowing.

"I don't understand my little girl, Mr. Tinker. Nor have I for a long time."

"You hired the lawyer, didn't you?"

"Yes, for all the good it's going to do. 'I'll try to keep her out of the electric chair'—that's as encouraging as it gets. The tragedy of our lives, Mr. Tinker, if you care to print it in your paper, is that we—Harry and I—allowed ourselves to feel threatened, self-conscious, even ashamed, I suppose. And for doing what? We tried to abide. We stood in the shadows with our heads bowed, tried to hide ourselves away as best we could. Maybe that's what we're paying for today—having been afraid. So you write what you want, Mr. Tinker, and let's see if it can make things any worse."

Tinker had been hit with more than he bargained for and was having trouble assimilating it. For one thing, Harry Wilson suddenly was not the dullard he seemed to have been. Tinker much preferred this new Harry: standing in the shadows of a Harlem club night after night, drink in hand, falling in love with a Negro woman, a dancer. And then cheating on his wife, and then leaving her and moving in with the Negro woman, ex-dancer now, and fathering a child whom he loved but could never publicly acknowledge (an act of moral cowardice, but Tinker tried not to be too judgmental), who became a prostitute and who maybe even blew his

brains out. What a strange, lonely, embittering
life, with the frustrations being taken out on
certain unsuspecting malefactors who were unfortunate enough to cross the path of Detective
Harry Wilson, a man seething from his own personal injustices. No wonder Harry had been
such a good cop. Jesus almighty, Tinker
thought, what were ninth-inning heroics compared to any of this? How could you get excited
over a stolen base or a quarterback sneak with
things like this happening around you?

Tinker looked up at Charley, whose brooding
stillness exuded an almost palpable loyalty.

"You must be the gentleman," Tinker said,
"who worked on Quentin yesterday."

Charley's face remained impassive, but he
clasped his hands behind him, as though they
might incriminate him.

"Quentin was being abusive," Ettie said. "I
asked him to leave."

"I had to help the gentleman along," Charley
said, his soft resonant voice both explanatory
and unapologetic.

"What was Quentin doing here?" Tinker
asked Ettie.

"Warning me not to say anything, not to 'disgrace' Harry's good name."

"He knows the whole story?"

She nodded.

"I don't suppose it sat very well with him,"
Tinker said.

"Do you know Quentin?" she asked.

"I'm beginning to."

"Then you know it didn't sit very well with him."

"When was the last time you'd seen him?"

"Not for years. Before the war. Years before that. There was no reason to see him. We didn't care for each other," she said with icy delicacy.

"That man is troublesome," Charley said. "He is damned troublesome."

"What did Harry do about him?" Tinker asked.

"There wasn't much he could do," she said. "Harry was a most unusual man. He was able to love me and he was able to love his brother, although he had no illusions about Quentin. Harry admitted he didn't understand him, but he was always concerned about him, and protective. He recognized that Quentin was unstable and not always to be held to account. I had no quarrel with that, as long as the son of a bitch kept away. I was a little bit afraid of him, and I told Harry that."

"How often did you see Harry?"

"Oh, less and less as the years passed. Sometimes not for months. Then he'd call and come by and we'd have a quiet dinner together here, and then he'd leave. It was all very strange, and mellow."

"Listen," Tinker said, "do you really think Quentin is unbalanced?"

"Yes," she said.

"No," Charley said with an emphasis that

137

surprised them. "He's just bad. He's just mean. He gets around colored people, he wears that white skin like it's a tuxedo." He unclasped his hands from behind him and let them hang at his sides. He was staring sternly down at Tinker. "That son of a bitch better keep away and leave her alone," he said. "He talked rough to her—'Keep your mouth shut. Don't make the disgrace worse.' I told him to watch his mouth. So he said some things to me. Not very nice things. He think he could get away with that? In this house? I told him to get out, he wouldn't, so I helped him. First time I ever hit a white man."

Tinker smiled wryly. "Feel good?"

Charley's face was impassive.

sive. He was a husky man, rugged, his full head of hair still black. People who shook hands with him were surprised at the size of the hand, the strength in the fingers. Not many people remembered anymore that he had been a fine athlete at Ohio Wesleyan around the turn of the century, playing football, and catching on the baseball team, and had in fact been good enough to catch in the major leagues for a short time.

They called him other things besides the Old Man. Some writers delighted in labeling him "El Cheapo" because of his tight grip on a dollar. Well, in what other way should you hold your money? Baseball was a business, wasn't it? It may have been a business that packaged a child's game as entertainment and cultivated sentimentality and nostalgia, but if not run as a business it would soon cease to exist, taking with it the romance and the excitement that its fans cherished so highly. Every big-league club owner shut his fists when money was in hand, but there were more canards about Rickey's parsimony than there were about anyone else's. "He'd sell his own mother if the price was right." How many times had he read that profoundly witty line? And now it was being said he would even bring a black man up to the big leagues, just to sell a few extra tickets.

And they called him a windbag and a blowhard. In certain quarters some smart alecks referred to him as "The Mahatma." All of it wryly amused him. He was not part of an industry noted for its intellectuality, and he would not compromise his own intellect for it. He could weave bouquets of rhetoric, embellishing them with quotes from Shakespeare, Virgil, Homer, and most of all the Bible. Sometimes, to amuse himself at the expense of his detractors, he would gush forth until the air turned purple. But most of the time his rhetoric was purposeful. Men unused to grandiloquence paid attention when it came from the Old Man, because Rickey had a history of success. He was credited with having ideated the concept of the farm system when he was running the St. Louis Cardinals in the 1920s and 1930s, and from it had come all those talented players and ultimately nine pennants, including this last one in 1946, when a Rickey-built Cardinals team had edged out the Rickey-run Dodgers. Those who dealt with him knew to look out for the thorns in the bouquets, for he was known to be sharp and shrewd and devious (though for the last he would have preferred "subtle").

The Mahatma. They used that one to poke fun at him. That was their facetious or sarcastic way of mocking his intellect and its lavishly employed resources. But that particular bit of mockery was beginning to come closer to a laudable truth than they imagined. In the system of philosophical and religious thought known as theosophy the mahatma was the eminent sage who had renounced any further spiritual development in order to help those who were less advanced. Mahatma Rickey was not doing exactly that, but a variation on it. Those whom he intended to help had no spiritual problems, but in other ways—in equality and opportunity and certain basic freedoms—they surely were less advanced.

Behind him, hanging on an otherwise bare wall of the office, was a picture of a beardless Abraham Lincoln, snapped when Lincoln was in New York City to speak at Cooper Union on February 27, 1860. The Mathew Brady portrait showed the then little-known Illinois lawyer from the chest up. At the time a year from the presidency and five years from martyrdom and apotheosis, Lincoln had sunken cheeks, the bones prominent and edged, and in his eyes a clearly resolved gaze.

Rickey knew that some people found the presence of the Lincoln picture pretentious, ever since that October day a year ago when from this office had gone forth the announcement that the Brooklyn Dodgers were signing the first black man to play in organized baseball. Certain of the newspapermen had taken note of the picture, the cynics nudging each other. The photographers had made sure to angle their cameras to snap Rickey and Jackie Robinson with the picture in the background.

A black man was coming to play America's game, with the Dodgers farm club at Montreal, of the International League. Rickey knew it would hardly be a popular move, not among a certain segment of the press, nor with a lot of the men Robinson would be playing with and against, and certainly not with Rickey's fellow executives around the major leagues. Those venerated patriarchs, Washington's Clark Griffith and Philadelphia's Connie Mack, had blistered his ears with phone calls after the announcement had been made. They wanted to know what the hell he thought he was doing. "A nigger?" asked a flabbergasted Mr. Mack, the game's most saintly figure, at eighty-four years old still managing his Athletics. "A nigger, Branch? A nigger?" "Yes, Mr. Mack," Rickey said politely. "A Negro." He saw no point in trying to enlighten old Connie, to explain that the war had changed many things forever, and in so doing had released caldrons of pent-up, long-deferred hopes and dreams and aspirations. Too much for a benighted saint to be able to grasp. And anyway, some things were so transparently right that you either saw them or you didn't, and not seeing meant not wanting to.

He was dealing, Rickey knew, not with evil but with ingrained prejudices, held in some cases by honorable and decent people, their convictions conscience-proof and consequently nearly unalterable. A black man who demanded his rights would win little sympathy from these people. One who was perceived by them to have been denied those rights might be given a chance; but one who demanded was denying those people the sense of magnanimity they would feel in bestowing upon the black man what was rightfully his to begin with. Human nature, Rickey knew, could be maddeningly quirky, but at bottom always was a certain logic, if you had the patience to get through the labyrinth and reach it. Once you possessed understanding of that logic, you were securely armed for the conflict.

Rickey lifted a wooden match from the box now and struck it. He twirled the burning match in his fingers as he held it to the tip of the cigar, then began puffing rolling clouds of smoke into the office. He shook the match slowly to extinction, gazing into the smoke. He was now sixty-five years away from his birth on a farm in Pike County, Ohio, and it had been an active and industrious sixty-five years. Baseball had been only part of it; there had also been studying and learning and piety, and a law degree that he had barely used, and marriage and raising a family and becoming a grandparent. A full and busy life, oh yes; interesting, exciting, challenging, with opportunities to use his intellect and his imagination. And prosperous too. He could well afford to spend the rest of his days at leisure.

But now he felt as if his life were just beginning, that what lay ahead would dwarf all that had gone before, with turbulence of unforeseeable character. He knew it and his family knew it. They had, in fact, been opposed to his signing Robinson, their reasoning being that Rickey was too old to contend with the storm that was sure to come. He had earned his rest. "Let a younger man do it." Younger man? Who? Which one? Which one was even contemplating it? And anyway, it wasn't simply doing it—it was doing it right. You didn't just go ahead and *do* something like this. You had to plan it, in a moral sense have been planning it all your life. You had to believe in it to the marrow, because too many things could go wrong, and if even one of them went wrong it could undo everything, set the Cause back twenty years.

The Cause. That was how he thought of it, how he referred to it in conversation with his closest confidants. One thing Rickey was not doing was thinking of himself as an emancipator (Mr. Lincoln's picture was inspirational rather than fraternal). This business was much too complex and risky and even outright dangerous for him to have any grandiose notions about himself. This thing had to be planned shrewdly and executed carefully, and you needed a clear and practical mind for that, something you couldn't have if you were concerned with the verdicts of history. Not only did you have to be prepared to appeal to reason and decency, but you had to be ready to bluff and threaten, and if necessary make good on the threats, not relent, never relent, never take a step back. When allies were few and enemies many, you had to be prepared for the abruptly dangerous, the violently deranged. You were going to have to slip by the coldly neutral, the cynically indifferent. You were going to have to contend with hundreds of years of unquestioned belief and tradition that held that one race was superior to another. Yes, Rickey thought, he was going to have to get into that old, old darkness with his light. He was going to have to fight a war. With one soldier, whose only armor would be courage and pride and dignity—and athletic talent—no matter what the fire. "One incident, just one incident," he had lectured Robinson in this office, "can set us back twenty years."

Rickey was so obsessed with the Cause, in both its judiciously planned tactics and the revelations of its larger vision, that he sometimes found himself overlooking his soldier. It was Robinson, not Rickey, who would be out in the open alone, enduring the invective and the provocation. It was Robinson who was living with the threats, some of which came sinisterly whispered over the telephone or in anonymous crudely lettered mailings.

Good Lord, Rickey thought as he dug another match from the box on his desk, swiped it across the sandpapered side, and relit his cigar. What had he begun here? It was intended as a righteous challenge, an assault on injustice. He had anticipated the thunder of the old guard, the bigots, the obstructionists. He had plotted his strategy against the South's Jim Crow laws. He had warned Jackie there would be, in addition to verbal abuse, beanballs and spikings and deliberate heavy contact. But then Wesley Branch Rickey, who in his sixty-five years had thought he had heard it all, had sat behind his desk and listened to a stony-faced, grainy-voiced New York City detective say, "If an assassin wants to plug somebody there's not much you can do to stop it. He picks his time and place. That's in his favor. What's in your favor is they're usually deranged, nervous, and incompetent. And lousy shots. The ones you worry about most are the ones who have got a political motive. You see, they'll take the most flagrant risks because they're not worried about getting caught. They don't mind being martyrs. The others, the ones dealing out of personal hatred, aren't nearly as lethal. They end up saying to themselves, 'Why should I go to the chair because of that son of a bitch?' So they usually go out and get drunk instead, or knock the shit out of their wives. Most of these people are crackpots, just letting off some steam." *Most*? Rickey thought. How many did you need to make it a reality? "A bona fide potential assassin," the detective said, "doesn't make any threats or give any warnings. That wouldn't make any sense, would it?" "Then we have to be afraid of the unknown," Rickey said. The detective laughed. "That can make you crazy," he said.

They would investigate them all, Rickey was assured. Every call, every letter. They took them all seriously. But he really didn't think, the detective said, that there was all that much to worry about. And then the flatfoot wanted to know: did the Bums have a chance to win the pennant this year?

So far Jackie had performed admirably, both as a ballplayer and as a man. He had done everything Rickey had asked. The people of Montreal had welcomed him warmly, but there had been other problems: black cats thrown onto the field in Baltimore, death threats in Louisville, furnace blasts of racial insults from opposing dugouts. Through it all Jackie had responded as he had been commanded to, and as he knew was the only way, by turning the other cheek.

But that had been in the minor leagues. The major leagues were another story. Everything was scaled to greater dimensions. The focus was sharper, the pressure unrelenting. The opposing players were more self-assured, the fans more passionate, the press more penetrating. Among the perils was that of Robinson becoming a freak show, a side attraction to the game rather than part of the game. Rickey made a mental note to stress that point in a speech he was planning to give in a Harlem church this winter: if Robinson made it to the Dodgers, it was important that the black people try and restrain themselves when they came to the games, not become too emotionally partisan lest they make themselves offensive to whites and place even greater pressures on Robinson. But even this carefully calculated plea would, Rickey knew, be considered by some blacks offensive. This was discrimination of another sort: why shouldn't they be allowed to give vent to their feelings?

But what about Jackie? Again Rickey reminded himself that he sometimes lost sight of the man, that intelligent, highly committed young athlete, husband, son, brother. Sometimes it seemed to Rickey that the Cause was a chessboard and Robinson a piece to be shrewdly manipulated from square to square. Inside that baseball uniform was a man being asked to go where no black man had ever gone before, to face all the dangers, run all the risks. Alone. Jackie had complete faith in Rickey, and that made it all the heavier for the Old Man.

There was no question in Rickey's mind about Jackie's abilities on the field, but this scouting report had been like no other. It had included a study of Robinson's history, his brain and his heart and his emotions. In his time Rickey had signed all sorts—scoundrels, rascals, boozers, womanizers, nitwits—because the criterion had always been elemental: can he play? But this was different. Ability was only a part of the evaluation. And when reports came in that Jackie was known as a "militant" and a "troublemaker," a man who was adamant about speaking out for and demanding his rights, Rickey did not turn away. The Old Man had not wanted a foot-shuffler; he wanted a man who was committed, a man who had already taken risks and would understand the need for taking more. A man who understood that stoicism under fire could be the most potent of responses.

When Robinson had finally been brought to this office in August 1945, several weeks after the end of the war, the two had spoken for hours and Rickey was convinced he had the right man. After decades of waiting, the time and the man were both right, and the challenge was going to be made to baseball and to society. *Challenge?* the Old Man asked himself on reconsideration. *No,* he thought. *We are rendering baseball and society an opportunity.* Rickey was going to send his man through that odious barrier and shatter it once and forever, dismantling the hypocrisy and self-righteousness that had long stained America's game.

But now Rickey was afraid. The Cause was mighty and it was correct, but the chesspiece was a human being, not just a thing to be lifted between two fingers and placed here or there. Mine is the responsibility, Rickey thought, his the danger. While he never for a moment doubted the Cause, Rickey could question the risk. Was it worth it? A man's life?

He had discussed it with Robinson late last summer, on a trip over to Jersey City, where

Montreal was playing. By then there was no question in Rickey's mind that Jackie would be with the Dodgers in 1947. (The truth was, if Jackie had been white he would have been brought up late in the 1946 season and won the pennant for the Dodgers. But trying to break the barrier in a bitterly contested pennant race would have been an appalling mistake.)

Sitting alone with him in a hotel room in Jersey City, Rickey had asked Jackie, "Do the death threats bother you?"

"Yes," Jackie said. No feigned indifference, no bravado. Direct, as always.

"How much do they bother you?"

"I'll be out there tonight."

"Do you think about them?"

"Not during the game."

"But later?" Rickey asked.

"Sometimes."

"And how do you feel?"

"Angry," Jackie said.

When he saw the concern in Rickey's eyes, Jackie leaned forward and said, "Mr. Rickey, we started something and we're going to finish it."

"Amen," said the Old Man.

12

Tinker had gotten drawn into something he did not understand, and drawn still deeper by the fact that he knew something that nobody else did, not the police, not any other newspaperman, not even Tony Marino, that sharp, Aquinas-quoting dago who was supposed to be checking every fact right back to the Garden of Eden. Harry Wilson was Angel's father. Angel was Harry's daughter. Any way you care to say it. It made the pistol shot that killed Harry louder, and more explosive.

Tinker had always prided himself on being a knowing guy, a smart kid who knew his way around. Nobody had been able to con him, not since his preteen years. People liked him and trusted him, and he appreciated the value of that, and he knew too how to maintain that respect and esteem. Right now he had the admiration of the men he himself most admired, the top guns in his profession: Cannon, Runyon, Granny Rice, Red Smith. The kid from Capstone hung out in Lindy's and Shor's, sitting

152

with the ornaments of Broadway's nocturnal world. Tinker was on the inside.

He could go on writing sports until time anointed him the doyen. A good and enviable life. But nothing in sports had ever gripped him like this new, confounding, and elusive business. He wanted to understand it, and solve it. The white man not just living with the colored woman (and the two of them loving one another), but fathering a child with her. Tinker wouldn't condemn or condone it; it was too exotic for him to pass judgment on. Oh, he knew plenty of sports who went up to Harlem to get their jollies. But that was different; that carried a spirit of life much closer to what he understood.

What did Harry feel when he saw the baby for the first time? Fear, dismay, despair? What goes on inside you when you have a kid you love and can't tell anybody about? And Angel, having to deny she had a father. Christ, what did that do to a person's self-esteem? She could have cracked finally, after all those years of having to disavow and be disavowed. Tinker realized there were satellite worlds around him that he knew nothing about. He was shockingly uninformed.

He had to admit that he never thought about colored people, about how they felt or thought. Somewhere along the line the sharp kid had been conned, had accepted too many givens. He'd been there one night in Shor's when some

Broadway widemouth had called Joe Louis—jocularly, of course—"nigger" and that notorious poker face had never altered a muscle. But nobody ever called DiMaggio "wop." Tinker couldn't even imagine it.

He had come home from the war something of a cynic. He was now capable of the cold, self-isolating veneer of the survivor. But the deaths he had seen on those Pacific islands had been brutally impersonal, cases of bad luck or bad timing. You were plucked randomly and without logic. Altogether different from what had happened across the way on Christopher Street the other night. That death had not happened randomly. In retrospect it did not even seem sudden but rather of long and rancorous gestation.

Tinker could see by the expression on Scotty's face that this was going to be futile. The sports editor was sitting behind his desk with a motionlessness that implied an exertion of forbearance. He was back in his chair, hands on knees, head cocked slightly, eyes sliding from side to side as they followed Tinker's agitated pacing. Tinker's backdrop was the sports department behind the glass wall, where the desks were arranged so that no one sitting at any of them directly faced the sports editor.

"Scotty," Tinker said, arms flying out for a moment like a man trying to propel himself into the air, "you don't understand this. You don't understand *me*. I'm not the same guy who went off to war in 1942. Honest to God. Take my word. And it's not fair to me or to you or to the sports department or the whole goddamned paper to go on thinking so. Look how I fucked up during the World Series. Don't you see what was happening? The *World Series*, for Christ's sake. What does that tell you about a sportswriter when he blows that kind of assignment?"

"That he shouldn't be covering sports," Scott said quietly.

Tinker paused and, aiming his forefinger at his watchful boss for a moment, said, "Correct. Writing sports can be great—it *is* great—if that's what you want to do with your life. But, finally, it's limiting, confining. It's all diagrammed, dictated by the rules and the clock. It goes back and forth over the same rails like the Toonerville Trolley. No depths, no surprises."

Tinker picked up the barely perceptible elevation of Scott's eyebrows at that last.

"I don't mean no surprises the way it sounds," Tinker said. "I think you know what I mean. No surprises in the sense that we know somebody's going to win, somebody's going to lose. Nine innings. Four periods. Ten rounds. The drama is artificial because it's programmed to happen. We make it happen. It occurs because we're there. But in reality it's banal, because it's going to happen again tomorrow, or next week. It's *scheduled* to happen."

"You've got a problem, Joe," Scott said, not unkindly.

"It's fun and it's often exciting, but that's all it is."

"Not in the hands of the good writers. You know the literature. Sports can give us some very meaningful insights into people. Sports as myth and metaphor. Sports as a window upon the human spirit. It's got a lot to offer, Joe. It can be a hell of a lot deeper than you think."

"I know that, Scotty," Tinker said, sitting down. "Believe me, I appreciate your patience."

"Joe, I know you went through a hell of a lot in the war. That kind of experience tends to have a diminishing effect on so many other things and can leave a man unsettled for a long time. Maybe you just haven't adjusted yet."

"It's been more than a year."

"Well . . ."

"Maybe I don't want to adjust."

"Look, Joe. Writing sports is what you know, what you do best. All your bullshit notwithstanding, I wish I had a few more like you. Stay at it and in ten years you'll be at the top of your profession."

"If I'm so good," Tinker said, "then why am I taking so much time on that Wilson story?"

"Yeah," Scott said. "Where the hell is it anyway?"

"I feel like I'm working on just a slice of it. A dull, dry, meaningless slice. Jesus, Scotty, the guy was murdered. That's what I want to dig into. This was no gunshot in the night; this goes back a long time. I've dug up a lot of stuff—without even trying," Tinker felt constrained to add.

"That's not your beat. You're not a police reporter."

"A guy gets into a story, he should be allowed to run with it."

"But you're not into that story," Scott said sternly, coming forward and flattening his hands on the desk. "You're into one aspect of it, one *narrow* aspect, where you happen to have expertise."

"I know," Tinker said sullenly.

"Look, Tinker-boy, let me tell you something. The way you talk about sports, you're demeaning something that *I've* worked in all my life, with pride. Sports are very goddamned important in this country. Maybe more than you think. Now there's nothing wrong in wanting to go out and knock off a few Pulitzers for solving murders and exposing municipal corruption, et cetera. But I don't want to hear you doing it by stepping on the neck of the sports department. I won't stand for that. Right now you're drawing your pay as a sportswriter, working for me and for this newspaper, and as long as you're doing that you're going to write sports and you're going to do it as well as you can and meet your deadlines."

"Or else," Tinker said dryly, as if completing Scott's sentence.

"You bet your ass 'or else.' Be ambitious, Joe, but not at the expense of anything or anybody else. And I'll tell you some more. Maybe you haven't given this all the thought it deserves, but you're covering the Dodgers and you ought to count yourself lucky, because pretty soon that team is going to break one of the biggest stories in the history of sports."

"You mean Robinson."

"It's a story that transcends sports, Joe."

"Scotty, I know my baseball history and I know what's going on in the world. What's happening with Robinson is interesting, and in its way important. But what it comes down to, finally, is baseball: can he cut it or not?"

"With that attitude, maybe I ought to reassign you and send somebody else." Then Scott allowed the faintest of smiles. "You're really hooked on this Wilson murder, aren't you?"

"It's my story, Scotty."

"It's Tony Marino's story."

"Tony's damned good; but for this one, I'm better."

"Joe," Scott said quietly, his tone paternal, "stick with your beat for a while. Go about your job. Let some time pass. Then we'll sit down again and have a whither goest Joe Tinker discussion."

"You're the boss," Tinker said.

"Exactly," Scott said. "In late February you're going to pack your bags and head south with the Dodgers. It's going to be a fascinating spring training, believe me. And if you fuck up one more time, I'm going to run your ass right off this newspaper."

"You're the boss all right," Tinker said, slapping his knees and getting up. "Only a boss could convey that message with a sweet smile."

13

Crossing the Atlantic on the troopship home after the war, Elmer was offered $250 for the pistol by another GI and turned it down. It wasn't just that the Walther 9mm 38 automatic was a first-class weapon and highly prized souvenir, but it so happened that this particular piece had a morbidly sentimental attraction for Elmer.

He had taken the gun from an SS major in Belgium at the end of December 1944. The major and about a dozen of his men had surrendered after being flushed from some shattered buildings in a small crossroads town. It was about two weeks after word had got around that soldiers of the 1st SS Panzer Division had machine-gunned eighty-six American prisoners in a field at Malmédy. With that news came a tacit agreement among the GI's in the area that no SS taken prisoner would survive.

The Germans, with their smoke-blackened, white-eyed faces, came walking out of the buildings with arms raised. The major's pistol was still in a holster strapped around his overcoat and Elmer got there first, opening the holster and lifting out the Walther automatic. He grinned foolishly at the major, whose coldly aristocratic eyes regarded him with sullen contempt. Elmer glanced at the death's-head badge on the major's high-crowned garrison cap, winked conspiratorially at him, slipped the pistol into his own overcoat pocket, and stepped back.

The SS troopers were pushed and prodded around to the side of a building and forced to stand two and three deep against the wall. The Germans knew what was up. One of them, in sharply accented English, began saying that they were merely a tank maintenance crew. The major, a realist, passed him a disdainful glance, then turned back to his captors, who were raising rifles and Thompson .45 submachine guns.

"Malmédy," an American lieutenant said, and the racket was sudden and intense. The SS troopers were hurled back by the close, concentrated fire and then pitched into the snow, where their bodies were sprayed by Thompsons that waved back and forth, causing some of the bodies to whirl spastically.

The lieutenant walked over to Elmer.

"What did you take from that officer?" the lieutenant asked.

"A pistol."

"Give it to me."

"Ask me again and I'll give it to you," Elmer

161

said, walking away. He glanced back over his shoulder. "When you're not looking."

The Walther 9mm automatic, known as a P-38, was by general consensus considered the most reliable and technically perfect weapon of its kind during the war, superior to the world-famous Luger which it had replaced. It used a double-action trigger lock so that it could be carried with the hammer lowered onto a loaded chamber and fired merely by pulling the trigger. It fired eight rounds from a handle clip and had a reputation for extreme accuracy up to 75 yards, discharging a bullet at a velocity of around 1,150 feet per second, about a third faster than the U.S. Army's Colt or Smith & Wesson, while the only thing close to it in the British arsenal was the Browning GP35, which had an FPS velocity of 1,100. The P-38's bullets were said to possess an exceptionally high striking energy.

Elmer kept the pistol wrapped in tissue paper in a shoe box on a closet shelf. Several times he had taken it out and sat in his armchair hefting and aiming it. Its grip and balance gave it a comfortable feeling in his hand. To Elmer this admirable weapon was the war. Though the circumstances of its possession barely brushed across his memory, the P-38 was capable of evoking scenes of combat with all their gruesome horrors and gluttonous consuming. Elmer was not one to brood on the bitterness or the ironies of war. He had gone in unwillingly, seen it through, and emerged with sensibilities unscathed. If war was a brutal preceptor to all who passed through it, the experience had slipped right by Elmer Cregar. The only real thing the war had left behind for him was this pistol. There was no compelling reason for its mystique—Elmer never bothered his imagination with such pursuits. The gun was neither a symbol of pure evil nor an icon representing the triumph of good over that evil. It was simply something that was light yet powerful in his hand.

The idea of using the pistol was almost as appealing to Elmer as the thought of Quentin's five thousand dollars and the saloon Elmer would be able to buy into. Quentin, that prick, had mocked the idea of hanging framed pictures on the walls, but Elmer could already see them. They gave a place class. Mickey Walker's had them, and so did Moore's and Dempsey's and all the other places the sporting crowd stopped at. He'd go up to Nat Fleischer's ratty *Ring* magazine offices in the Garden and get the pictures and then have some fun going around getting the boys to autograph them to Elmer Cregar. Louis and Dempsey, of course (but not Tunney; Elmer didn't much care for that snooty bastard). He'd want Walker, Benny Leonard, Sid Terris, Barney Ross, Tommy Loughran, Tony Canzoneri. And naturally he would have to have Conn and Zale and Sugar Ray and Willie Pep and Ike Williams and the Rock. There were plenty of them and they all either lived in New York or came through sooner or later. *To Elmer, From His Buddy. Best Wishes To Elmer From His Old Friend.* He'd frame each one and decorate the walls with them. Let everybody know whose place this was, who Elmer Cregar was. And any bartender who tried to clip at the cash register would be chewing teeth for a week.

Elmer's daydreams about his saloon-to-be were so pleasurably real and diverting that he began getting anxious about Quentin. Several weeks had passed since their conversation and he had heard nothing further. The idea that Quentin might have changed his mind began to rankle Elmer, who had made the commitment, had already—in the deeper reaches of his mind anyway—taken the black ballplayer, and now was ready to start enjoying what he had earned.

When he picked up a ringing telephone one evening and heard Quentin's voice, Elmer shouted with both anger and relieved anxiety, "Where the hella you been?" He immediately became self-conscious. He had given himself away and you never wanted to do that with somebody like Quentin. You never wanted that son of a bitch to know too much about you or how you were thinking.

Quentin's message was succinct: he would meet with Elmer the day after Christmas in a lunch wagon near the Hunters Point subway station in Long Island City. At that time, Quentin said, Elmer would receive the first half of the payment.

Elmer felt exhilarated after the conversation, as though it had cleared away all doubts and obstacles. He even sat down with a pencil and paper and began printing in block letters possible names for his saloon. THE ROPED SQUARE. THE KNOCKOUT. THE WINNING CORNER. He began considering locations. He knew a bar in Forest Hills that he might be able to buy into. It was on Queens Boulevard, not far from the tennis stadium. Elmer had heard that all of those empty lots on Queens Boulevard were soon going to have high-rise apartment buildings raised on them. The sooner he got in there the better it would be for him.

On a cold gray morning two days before Christmas, Elmer took the shoe box from the closet, put it into a canvas overnight bag, and left his apartment. He borrowed a black DeSoto coupe from a friend and began driving out to Long Island. He knew the kind of surroundings he was going to need right now but he wasn't quite sure just where he was going to find them. So he kept driving, relaxed, in no particular hurry, passing the South Shore towns lined up on or just off Route 27: Freeport, Wantagh, Babylon, and then even farther out past Patchogue, Moriches, Hampton Bays.

The day remained gray, cold, with an occasional Atlantic mist forming like perspiration on the windshield. The land around was flat, empty, populated mostly by potato farmers. A New Yorker all his life, Elmer had never been this far out on the island, nor did he know anyone who had, although he could remember some guys talking once about fishing out at Montauk.

When he saw a sign that said Amagansett he got off of the blacktopped highway and turned in the direction of the beach. He bumped along a dirt road, passing fields of high dun-colored grass that nodded to and fro as the sea breezes came and went. There was nothing out here except a few boarded-up fishermen's shacks.

He could see the ocean up ahead now, flat and tremendous, a wintry gray surface expanding monotonously toward a horizon that was engulfed in gloomy overcast, with only an occasional unfurling whitecap disturbing the vast symmetry. The dirt road gave out where the dunes began, and Elmer braked the car to a halt. When he got out he heard the wind slithering through the high grass and the slow, languorous discharge of waves on the beach. After looking around for several moments to make sure of his solitude, he reached back into the car and removed the P-38 from the shoe box with several cardboards that had come back with his clean shirts from the dry cleaners and a sealed white envelope blank on both sides.

Slipping the pistol into his coat pocket and

holding the other articles in his hand, Elmer crossed the dunes toward the beach, the cold, wind-sculpted sands yielding under his two-toned brown and white shoes. The steady sea wind with its keen December edge made him turn up his overcoat collar and pass a glance of morose hostility out at the great gray ocean as though contemplating retaliation against it.

He strode along the beach, just beyond the water's edge, each stride parting the overcoat around his knees. When he saw the lifeguard's elevated observation chair looming ahead he smirked. Moving toward the wide chair perched on its structure of nailed-together planks, he removed the white envelope from his pocket and tore off part of one corner. Tilting the envelope over his hand, he spilled out several thumbtacks.

Standing at the base of the structure, he used two tacks to hang one of his shirt cardboards to a leg of the chair, and then tacked a second to another leg.

He then measured off what he approximated to be around one hundred feet in a straight line from the chair. He lifted the P-38 from his pocket and sighted one of the cardboard targets, clutching the weapon with both hands. The light was less than perfect, but good enough. Bracing himself against the recoil, he fired twice. Then he went near the water's edge and took a diagonal position as he drew a bead on the second cardboard. He fired twice, quickly, seeing the chair shudder each time.

He walked back to see the results. The first two shots had missed, the second two had torn into the cardboard and shattered most of the wood behind it. He tacked up a fresh cardboard and again paced off a hundred feet.

After emptying his clip and refilling it with shells he had bought in a sporting goods store on Madison Avenue, Elmer banged away again. On depleting his second clip, he could count only five hits out of sixteen shots. This brought him to the conclusion that while the P-38 was supposedly accurate at seventy-five yards, his own eye was not totally reliable at a hundred feet. Well, he thought, that meant he'd have to take the guy at under a hundred feet; either that or use a rifle, with which he had been very accurate. But he didn't like the idea of that. A man with a pistol could go anywhere; a man with a rifle was restricted. But there was no reason why he couldn't get within fifty or a hundred feet of Robinson. What the hell, the guy wouldn't be walking around with armed guards. According to Quentin, the guy would probably be staying in a nigger hotel in a nigger neighborhood, and further according to Quentin, a shooting on the streets wouldn't draw immediate attention because of the niggers' tendency to look the other way and keep their mouths shut. But that was Quentin talking.

Elmer would figure it out and do it his own way.

Before he left the beach, Elmer inserted another clip and from fifty feet fired at the lifeguard's chair until its support struts disintegrated and it fell into the sand.

14

Tinker hadn't been looking forward to Christmas and when the day came it bore out his worst expectations. The afternoon before, he had taken Sally up to the Greyhound terminal on West Fifty-first Street, from which she was departing for a five-day holiday visit with her parents in New Hampshire.

After waving the bus on its way, he walked east to Fifth and then began heading back to the Village, walking. The avenue was crowded with last-minute shoppers carrying armfuls of packages. Tinker, his overcoat collar turned up, a cigarette worked into the corner of his mouth, moved through the crowds, listening to the sidewalk Santas tolling off the minutes to Christmas with jingling handbells. The crowds thinned once he got below Forty-second and passed the library. When he reached Twenty-fifth Street his feet began feeling cold and he flagged a cab and completed the journey home in style.

Once upon a time Tinker had been sentimental about Christmas Eve. He supposed everyone had at one time or another, thanks to the convivial times and the sweet smells and tastes and warm laughter of old Christmases. Today's cynicism, he guessed, might merely be a defense against the mellow ache of those irretrievable good times, when the world was warm and snug and your parents were young and strong and would ward off whatever might threaten. Tinker's parents were both dead; Tinker had had to ward off World War II all by himself.

He sat at the window on Christmas Eve 1946 sipping from a pint bottle of bourbon he held in his long, thin fingers. The radio was not on. If he was consciously trying to feel unsentimental, then he didn't want to listen to the carols.

He was annoyed because he could not move his moodily staring eyes from the dark unoccupied apartment across the street. Lighted wreaths and gaudy bulbs hung in most of the windows of the tenement, but these few still bespoke their sullen gloom.

Tinker turned around for a moment and surveyed his own dark bedroom. This building was what—fifty, sixty years old? Who knew what might have taken place right in this room. No doubt plenty of drinking and screwing and laughing and crying and loving and hating, as well as mourning and celebrating and hoping and despairing. But all those strangers in the light and the dark of their lives had left behind not a sound, not a trace. Human transience was probably the most puzzling and disheartening of all realities; it was the mockery of all effort and all passion. Five years from now who would give a rat's ass that ace sportswriter Joe Tinker had lived here with his beautiful, genteel Sally, who sometimes read Andrew Marvell and Robert Herrick aloud to him in bed before they went at it in ways that would have made a satyr wince? (Was it perhaps a primal sense of that very transience which made it all so intense and frantic, a sense of clock, calendar, and grave?) By then Rush and Angel would have had their asses fried in the electric chair and whoever was living in that apartment would—if they knew what had happened there—make morbid jokes about the whole episode. Tragedy without immediacy was not tragedy.

At midnight he opened the present Sally had left for him. He could tell from the shape and heft of the small package that it was a book. It was Palgrave's *Golden Treasury*. She had often told Tinker that his sensibilities needed broadening as well as some other, undefined modifications. Well, he disagreed. He felt his sensibilities were in good order. Palgrave remained unopened.

At one A.M. he ate a ham sandwich, washed it down with a cup of coffee, and went to sleep.

Christmas Eve, 1946.

On Christmas morning Tinker walked through a lightly falling snow until he found a candy store that was open. The proprietor, a small impassive old man, was sitting on a wire-backed chair behind the counter.

"I want to buy a baseball," Tinker said. "You got one?"

"I got a baseball."

The best the old man had was a ball with McGregor-Goldsmith stamped on it. Tinker bought it, then sat at the marble-topped soda fountain and with his pen began writing names on the ball, laboring to make each signature appear the work of a different hand. While the old man sat and sourly watched him, Tinker inked onto the ball's smooth white surface the names of Dodgers Dixie Walker, Pete Reiser, Cookie Lavagetto, Eddie Stanky, Hugh Casey, Carl Furillo, and Pee Wee Reese. When he was finished he replaced the ball in its red and black box and put it in his overcoat pocket. Then he bought a box of chocolate-covered cherries.

"Merry Christmas," he said as he prepared to leave.

"Why not?" the old man said.

Tinker walked several blocks through the snow to the Women's House of Detention on Greenwich Avenue. Although it wasn't even fifteen years old, the jail, built on the site of the old Jefferson Market Prison, was beginning to look old and sorrowful. Tinker had once heard that the external appearances of dwelling places eventually came to reflect the lives and characters of their inhabitants. Well, the fact of Christmas morning certainly didn't help.

When he walked inside he got as far as a small, cheap desk manned by a sergeant whose strong Semitic features wore a distinctly inhospitable expression. You found a lot of Jewish cops working on Christmas, having swapped time with their gentile partners, though this one didn't look any more happy about it than one of them would have.

"Merry Christmas, Sarge," Tinker said, standing before the desk, the snow melting from his shoes onto the marble floor.

"What do you want?" the sergeant asked, looking up from his *Daily News*. It was last night's pink edition, probably left behind by the preceding shift.

Tinker was now oh-for-two with his Merry Christmases.

"I'd like to see Angel," he said.

"You a relative?" the cop asked. Tinker couldn't tell if the guy was trying to be smart or was just plain stupid. A sense of humor wasn't required for civil service jobs, but New York cops could be pretty droll at times.

"I'm a newspaperman."

"What paper?"

Tinker pointed. "You're reading it."

"What's your name?" the cop asked.

"Joe Tinker."

"You're a sportswriter."

"That's right."

"You did a nice story on Harry. What do you want to see her for?"

"A follow-up."

"She's not too sociable."

"I brought a present," Tinker said, showing the box of cherries.

"Laced with arsenic maybe?"

Tinker laughed. "I don't think so."

"You'd save the state a lot of money."

"The state's got plenty."

"Well, since your cherries are clean, why don't you just eat them yourself?" The sergeant's eyes had a flat, obstructive, bureaucratic expression.

"You a baseball fan, Sarge?" Tinker asked. Getting no response—these guys often clammed up when the conversation took an unexpected curve—Tinker took the box from his pocket, removed the ball, and set it down on the desk. The sergeant regarded it suspiciously, as though it were something put down by an anarchist. Then he picked it up and revolved it with his fingers as he read the signatures.

"These for real?" he asked.

"The boys signed it for me at the end of the season."

"That's not a big-league ball."

"They use those in batting practice," Tinker said.

The sergeant nodded knowingly at the names. He looked up at Tinker.

"What's the story with Robinson?" he asked. "They bringing him up?"

"That's a secret, Sarge. I can't tell."

"You mean you don't know." The sergeant opened a desk drawer and carefully put the ball inside, then slid it shut again. "Go on up to the third floor," he said. "I don't know if she'll see you."

Tinker took the elevator to the third floor. There was another sergeant sitting at another desk here, this time with a police matron in a brass-buttoned blue tunic and blue skirt and black, stubby-heeled shoes. The matron was just emerging from a dimly lit corridor defined by two long rows of steel bars. She stepped through another wall of bars, this one dividing the open area from the confined, and slid shut the barred door with a rattling metallic clash.

The desk the sergeant was sitting at was actually a card table covered with a padded material and a green blotter framed into four brown leather triangles. His feet were drawn back and crossed at the ankles underneath his folding chair.

"Merry Christmas," Tinker said as he walked from the elevator, the box of cherries in hand. He made a quick appraisal of the cheerless institutional surroundings, the bare gray walls, the neon tubing burning in the gray ceiling. A small table against a far wall held two telephones and a small stack of manila envelopes, and next to it stood a row of four folding chairs. There wasn't much else to see.

"Merry Christmas," the sergeant said, the response obligatory more than anything else, as if he were reading it from a piece of paper. The matron, a tall, angular woman with her hair drawn severely back into a bun, stood stock still, staring at Tinker with churlish curiosity. The sergeant was broad through the chest and shoulders, with a large close-cropped head whose weight seemed to have squashed his neck into his shoulders. His pink face looked like a ham studded with small, mean features.

"I'd like to see Angel," Tinker said. "I'm Joe Tinker of the *News*. They sent me down to run an interview."

The sergeant swiveled his bruiser's head and looked up at the matron, who was standing just off to his right. The matron looked at the sergeant. Tinker had seen more animation in the faces on postage stamps.

"I know she's not talking much," Tinker said. "The sergeant downstairs told me," he added, letting them know he had already been checked out. "Believe me, I'd rather be home with the wife and kids on Christmas Day, but my editor said to come down and give it a go."

"She won't talk to you," the matron said.

"Maybe these will soften her up," Tinker said, raising the box of cherries.

"Leave them here," the sergeant said. "We'll see she gets them."

Tinker put the box on the desk. Then he was following the matron along the corridor, walking between the two rows of cells. He was aware of women sitting silently behind the bars on either side of him, watching him pass—they had to be watching him—but some nagging sense of honor or discretion kept his eyes straight ahead, fixed on the ironing-board back of the matron, who was taking crisply measured strides, her ring of heavy keys rattling in her hand. Some of the small, barred cell windows faced out on Greenwich Avenue, and Tinker heard an automobile horn. It sounded remote, incongruous.

The matron stopped in front of the last cell on the right side of the corridor. She waited for Tinker, then began retracing her steps, shrugging at him as she passed.

He watched the matron for several moments, then turned and looked into the cell. Angel was sitting on the far end of an uncomfortable-looking cot that hung from the concrete wall by two taut diagonal chains. The light coming from the wire-caged fifty-watt bulb in the corridor ceiling did little more than gray the shadows inside. She was looking at him, or more precisely was looking toward where he was standing. He knew immediately that she wasn't going to talk to him, not even to say "No" or "Go away." He felt like an alien, unwanted and intrusive.

"May I talk to you?" he asked quietly, raising one hand and closing his fingers around a bar.

"My name is Joe Tinker. I'm a writer. Will you answer some questions?"

She continued to sit and look at him. Her hands were pressed flat on the cot, causing a slight rise in her shoulders. Her feet were crossed at the ankles and drawn back under the cot. She was wearing prison garb, a drab smock with short, baggy sleeves.

"I wish you would talk to me, Angel," he said. "I don't know that I can help you. But maybe you can help me. Not just because I want to write this story, but because I'm trying to understand ... certain things."

It was too dark in there for him to see what expression—if any—was in her face. He could feel the terrific gulf that lay between them, the utter lack of any connecting point. He had never in his life felt so distanced from another human being. With sadness he thought, *I could stand here for a thousand years and it would stay exactly the same.*

A few minutes later the matron was unlocking the barred door and letting him through. The sergeant had stepped away.

"Nothing, right?" the matron asked as she crashed the door shut behind him.

"What is it with her, do you think?" Tinker asked.

"She's scared."

"It seems more than that."

"I wouldn't know. She doesn't seem like a bad kid. I think she's just scared."

"Does she say anything at all?" Tinker asked.

"She says 'Thank you.'"

"It's like she doesn't know where she is or what's happened."

"I think she knows."

"And so goddamned alone."

"That's what happens when you're accused of murder," the matron said with a sad smile. "There's no loneliness like it."

When he was outside again he stood on the top step of the stone flight that led from the entrance to the sidewalk. The snow had stopped. The cold air felt refreshing; he supposed everyone who walked out of this place immediately remarked on the contrast.

He did not recognize the package-laden black woman coming up the steps until he had stepped back to open the door for her.

"Miss Pearson," he said.

Ettie Pearson stopped. She was wearing a fur coat, brown kid gloves. A white knitted shawl lay halfway back on her hair.

"Mr. Tinker," she said matter-of-factly, not surprised.

"I was up to see Angel," he said.

"Why?"

"To talk to her."

"And did you?"

"Yes, but she didn't answer."

Ettie's lips formed a knowing, sympathetic smile.

"Does she talk to you?" he asked.

"I'm her mother."

Tinker grinned sheepishly.

He followed her into the building. She placed her packages on a bench near the door, then slid the shawl from her hair, folded it, and slipped it into her purse. The officer at the desk stared at them across the stark, empty lobby.

"What are you doing here on Christmas Day?" she asked.

"That shooting has been on my mind."

She raised one eyebrow slightly.

"A girl shooting her own father," he said. "Why?"

"You have to look to history, Mr. Tinker," she said, maintaining a poise that made him uncomfortable. "It explains everyone."

"Everyone?"

"Oh yes," she said emphatically, not wanting to be misunderstood.

"Angel too?"

"Especially her. I told you something about her. What she had gone through, what she had seen."

"But Harry went there to try and help her, to get her into a better life."

"That's right. But then what happened? You have to be able to see what happened. The way she saw it."

Tinker began trying to work his way through it, re-create it.

"Rush was there," he said, "and that's what set it off. It would, wouldn't it? Harry became

181

angry. Rush wouldn't know Harry is her father, possibly wouldn't even know he was a cop. So Harry starts using some muscle, Rush hits back, and Harry really goes at it."

"He was a brutally strong man," Ettie said, as if trying to fill in the picture.

"Angel tries to break it up, but she can't. She's screaming at them, but they won't stop."

"Harry wouldn't stop," Ettie said dryly.

"So Angel picks up the gun," Tinker said, in the midst of it now, seeing it happen, "maybe just to scare them into stopping."

"Not *them*: Harry. You have to understand that."

"But that doesn't do it either. She fires the thing, maybe just to startle them, or maybe even at Rush; only she hits Harry. It was an accident. What the hell, the two men were rolling around on the floor."

Ettie moved her head slowly from side to side. "No," she said.

"Then what?" Tinker asked.

"What does the girl see?"

"She sees . . ." Tinker turned away from Ettie's soft, inquiring eyes. He was there now, he had reached it, and he was appalled by the simplicity of it, the bitterness, the awful sadness. "She sees," he said, turning back to her, "a white man beating the blood out of a colored man."

"That's what she sees. And for a split second that's all she can see."

"And it's just one time too many, isn't it? So she takes the gun . . ."

"History, Mr. Tinker," Ettie said, reaching for her packages. "There's just too much of it."

And Harry never knew why. Tinker thought about that later, when he was back in the apartment, sitting alone, listening to that curious silence that is Christmas night in a big city. Harry never even knew why. Tinker wondered if at the last moment Harry had looked up and had seen that gun pointed at him, and if so, what he had thought. Jesus, what could he have possibly thought? That would have been the only mercy, Tinker told himself, Harry never knowing what hit him.

15

Elmer was the only customer in the lunch wagon. He had come in twenty minutes earlier than the appointed time and taken a booth that had a clear view of the door. The bus-shaped, aluminum-roofed eatery was a half block from the subway station, set on an embankment overlooking a vast freight yard that seemed to be the final resting place not just for hoppers and boxcars but for outmoded Long Island Railroad coaches too.

Elmer was staring out the window, an untouched cup of coffee on the table in front of him. The streets were empty; this was an industrial area and most of the surrounding factories had closed down between Christmas and New Year's. From here it was a five-minute subway ride under the East River to Grand Central Station.

Elmer was wearing a pea jacket he had bought at a war surplus store on Forty-second Street and its thick navy-blue wool was warm in this place, but he did not remove it. The counterman was sitting on a wooden stool at the cash register, staring out at the bright cold day with an expression on his face that suggested that what he was seeing was inside his head rather than out on the quiet streets.

Quentin arrived by cab, a fact that made Elmer smirk. He watched disdainfully as the rear door opened and one dark-trousered leg appeared, looking as though it were taking an overly large stride. Quentin was wearing a belted tan trenchcoat, the snugly cinched belt accenting his thinness. A red silk scarf was around his neck. His hair was slicked down. He waited for the cab to pull away, watched it for a moment, then looked at the diner, groomed himself with his hands, and headed for the door. Playing his role, Elmer thought. The actor. Whatever personality he had always submerged in whatever was the role of the moment. Sly, calculating bastard, Elmer thought, watching Quentin approach. Look at him pull back on the door, each gesture crisp and precise. That's it, Quentin, a cold little glance for the counterman and then the quick stride like a brand-new second lieutenant's across the tile floor, leather heels rapping. One shot in the breadbasket, Elmer thought. Just to douse the footlights and draw the curtain.

Quentin slid into the booth.

"You're going to Cuba," he said.

"Cuba?"

"Rickey is sending the ball club there for

spring training instead of Florida. To reduce the pressures on Robinson. It's probably a favor to you. If they put that nigger on the field with whites in the South some cracker is likely to pick him off and do you out of some money."

"Havana?" Elmer asked.

"Yes."

Not so bad after all, Elmer thought. A lot of the sharpies he knew, the boys who packed their heat in shoulder holsters, liked to skip down there. The place really moved, so he was told. Casinos, cathouses. Everything wide open, owned and run by the same frozen-faced bastards who were at ringside for the big ones. He knew some Mick lightweight from Bensonhurst who'd gone down there for a fight last year, won the fight but then lost his whole purse at the tables and then got the clap at one of the houses and came home begging his manager to get him booked down there again. Through Elmer's mind went appealing visions of smoky, dice-rattling evenings and perspiration-soaked bed-sheets under languidly turning ceiling fans.

"It's got to be done there," Quentin said. "Size it up and then do it. As soon as you can. That's very important. As soon as you can."

"Why?"

"Psychology. He gets there, he gets picked off. The more sudden the shock, the more stunning the effect. After that, none of them will have the guts to try it."

"Not while he's out on the field, Quentin," Elmer said.

"I don't expect that. It would be perfect if you could, but much too risky."

"I'll figure it out."

"He'll have certain habits, a routine. Once you pick it up you'll have plenty of opportunities."

"I'll figure it out, Quentin," Elmer said reassuringly. "You just keep your eye on the newspapers; you'll see it."

"This will come over the radio, Elmer. This is going to be big. They're going to interrupt programs for this one."

The peculiar light in Quentin's eyes made Elmer uneasy, for even though Quentin's gaze was directly on him, Elmer felt as though it were going beyond him, was focused on some insanely satisfying vision. The ex-boxer fancied himself an authority on eyes—in the ring he had always been able to read them, knew when he was at it with a man who was unsure or afraid or cocky or—that most unsettling communication of all—an unceasing and unshakable self-confidence, the kind of impervious concentration they said was always in Louis's eyes. But what Elmer was seeing now in the eyes of Quentin Wilson was something he knew he did not understand; and then its disturbing quality slowly vanished as though the vision had dissolved. Quentin smiled faintly, self-consciously.

"You got an envelope for me?" Elmer asked.

Quentin drew the packet from inside his coat and pushed it across the table. Elmer glanced for a moment at the moodily self-involved counterman, then picked it up and stuffed it into his pocket.

"There's three thousand in there," Quentin said. "Half your fee plus expenses."

"Now look, Quentin," Elmer said, "I know you want this done as fast as possible, but don't go looking for miracles. They may have security on the guy. It could be trickier than you think. Remember, this ain't going to be any kamikaze mission. I plan to get out of there with my skin on. So I may need some time to dope it out. I'm going to have to track the guy without looking suspicious, so when I do pull the plug on him nobody will say, 'Yeah, there was some guy with a busted nose spooking around.'"

"I have every confidence in you," Quentin said. "Remember, I saw you in action under the worst possible conditions. You were always the guy I wanted to be around when things got hot. I always said to myself, 'Stay near Elmer. If anybody's going to get through this, it's going to be Elmer.'"

More Quentin bullshit, Elmer thought. Or maybe not. Either way, he liked the sound of it.

16

Jackie had to keep reminding himself that he trusted Mr. Rickey. He had never put such faith in a white man before. Sometimes, lying in bed late at night, unable to sleep, listening to the warm Caribbean stillness, he found himself smiling wryly at the darkness. He had put his trust, his faith, maybe his very life, into the hands of a white man. Of course Mr. Rickey was no ordinary white man. Was no ordinary man, period.

In agreeing to go along with Mr. Rickey's crusade Jackie had accepted all the compromises that would have to be made. The hardest, so far, was the promise not to fight back. Jackie had abided by it and it had become, oddly enough, easier as the season went on. He wasn't sure whether his adversaries were becoming less abusive or he was becoming less attentive. Maybe always having been the sensitive, uncompromising militant had been a good thing;

it had always provoked extra helpings of abuse, mindless and subtle both, and it had served to make his resolve ever more unyielding and intense. He had heard it all before—in stainless white Pasadena where he had grown up, and then all over again in the segregated precincts of the United States Army—and he had always made it a point to pay attention. He allowed the words and the gestures and the snickers to burn themselves into him, and he would respond with words of his own, or a cold steady glare that could make a man turn aside.

The year at Montreal had gone well, better than anyone expected. His performance on the field had been dynamic. Ordinarily, there would have been no question about his joining the Dodgers for spring training. But Jackie Robinson was different. He understood that. In January, the Associated Press had conducted a poll among the country's sports editors and found that a large majority of them said that the most compelling question of the year was whether the Dodgers were going to bring Robinson to the big leagues, and if so, would he be able to make the grade.

Jackie had no doubts about any of it, though Mr. Rickey had so far confided nothing. Jackie was confident he could hit big-league pitching. It wasn't simply that he had torn up the International League in 1946. After all, a lot of men had had spectacular minor-league seasons and then failed abysmally in the bigs. He didn't buy that crap about being "a man of destiny" either. Some writers were implying that, as though his base hits were preordained. Jackie had too much respect for big-league curves and fastballs to believe that. It was simply that he had faith in himself as an athlete, with an athlete's primal self-confidence in his strength, his muscles, his reflexes, his judgment. If it all was wound tighter and galvanized more by the brainless taunts of fools, so much the better.

And yet as he lay in the darkness of his room in a fleabag hotel he could feel the flames of resentment still burning. All right, he understood why he wasn't training with the Dodgers; but why the hell was he quartered in this place while the rest of the Montreal club were in the more palatable Havana Military Academy? This was Mr. Rickey exercising the utmost caution, unwilling to risk any incidents. And Jackie—segregated—had to go on trusting Mr. Rickey, like it or not, and he did not entirely like it, because that was the other thing he had been asked to put in abeyance along with his combative nature—his independence. The taunts and the insults he had long ago learned how to absorb, and his pride and dignity had never been penetrated because he always had his independence. He had never indicated it to Mr. Rickey, but this loss of independence rankled him more than anything else. He understood the gamble Mr. Rickey was taking, the terrific pressure that was unrelentingly on him; nevertheless, there were times when the idea of being a chessboard piece, a pin on a field marshal's war map, made Jackie resentful.

Jackie felt that Mr. Rickey was being overly cautious. Jackie had got on well with his Montreal teammates the year before; even his Mississippi-born manager, Clay Hopper, who had initially found the idea of having a black man on his team repugnant, had gone to Rickey at the end of the season and extolled Jackie as "a great player" and "a gentleman."

Jackie hadn't argued with Rickey about being segregated in this hotel, nor had he even raised the issue. There was no need to—Mr. Rickey was with him, thought for thought.

"Even though we're in Cuba and the races are compatibly mixed here," Rickey said, "the situation is still delicate. Believe me, no step is being taken without the most careful planning and consideration."

If you wanted segregation, we didn't have to come here. We could have stayed in Florida. That was what Jackie wanted to say, but didn't. Nor did he say that it was all right, because it wasn't, or that he understood, because he didn't entirely. He merely stared at Rickey and let the Old Man read his thoughts: I trust you.

I don't want you to avoid them or be anything less than honest with them, Rickey told him, but the less you speak to the press the better. Working out with Montreal as you are, you'll be seeing fewer of them. Overall, it's best you remain as inconspicuous as possible. Take your meals in the hotel and then go back up to your room and relax. These are all suggestions, of course, Rickey hastened to add. But I know I can rely upon your good judgment.

Two other blacks were also working out with the Montreal club and also staying in the hotel—Roy Campanella and Don Newcombe. If anyone still had doubts about Rickey's commitment to the Cause all they had to do was take a look at these two on a ball field. Campanella had years of experience in the Negro leagues and was probably the equal of any catcher in the big leagues, while young Newcombe was a big right-hander with a blazing fastball. The two had played together in 1946 at Nashua, New Hampshire, in the New England League and had done well. Campanella was an amiable man, apparently without Robinson's smoldering inner tensions. While what he considered Campanella's philosophy of expedience sometimes nettled him, Jackie conceded that Roy's conciliatory disposition was probably a positive influence on the twenty-year-old Newcombe, who could be impulsive and unpredictable.

Despite the presence of Campanella and Newcombe, the focus remained on Jackie. On the field his every move was cheered lustily by the Cubans, especially the dark-skinned. In the evenings small boys would come shyly into the hotel lobby, where the frayed rugs were not always successful in covering the missing tiles, and ask to see "Señor Jackie," and if Jackie was available—he sometimes sat in one of the crackly straw-filled easy chairs after dinner— the boys approached him with raptly staring eyes, hesitant but determined. The visits were not the usual small-boy homages to star ball-players; there was no small talk, no request for an autograph: they simply wanted to get up close and look at him. Sometimes they squirmed and shrugged their shoulders and mumbled a few words, and Campanella, who had for years played winter ball in Latin America, interpreted. *"Gracias,"* Jackie would say to the shy offerings of praise and good luck. And then the boys would retreat, staring solemnly over their shoulders at the thick-bodied, muscular man in the chair.

The hotel was a depressing place. It was situated on a side street in a run-down residential district of scattered, flat-roofed houses, many of them little more than shanties. In bed at night, Jackie could hear the elevator's clanky machinery and weary humming whenever the contraption had been signaled for. Hotels were supposed to face out on lights and traffic and a vital urban resonance, have revolving doors and thriving lobbies. You entered this place by walking in from a dark and dead-ass street and pushing aside a front door and walking across a funereal lobby that looked seedy and smelled musty. The employees were pleasant but they spoke no English and when Campanella and his smattering of Spanish weren't around, Jackie felt helpless.

The dining room where they took their meals almost every evening was seldom more than a quarter full. The other guests, the brooding Jackie noted, were dark-skinned Hispanics in dark suits with shiny trousers and frayed white shirts. An empty bandstand, with skeletal music stands, emphasized the cheerless atmosphere. It contrasted sharply with the glittery Hotel Nacional in Havana where the Dodgers were staying, and the Havana Military Academy, a school for the sons of wealthy Cubans, where Jackie's Montreal teammates were billeted.

Occasionally they cabbed into Havana for a decent meal, but mostly they stayed in the hotel, taking their meals in the dining room with its ghostly bandstand and then sitting in the lobby, receiving nods and smiles from the desk clerk whenever they happened to catch his eye. At times Jackie would be irritably adamant about not leaving the hotel; when the other two suggested a ride into the city for a meal, he would say acidly, "No. We're supposed to stay here. We're not supposed to be seen in public. You don't want us to disgrace the Brooklyn Dodgers, do you?"

When Campanella and Newcombe went off by themselves, the restive Jackie would leave the hotel and walk around the surrounding area, hands in pockets, face fixed in a scowl. He never tried to suppress the anger within; it was an old and trusty gauge and weapon and he let it seethe, let it irritate and disquiet him. That unrelenting anger was one of the reasons Mr. Rickey had chosen him; Jackie would not permit one drop of it to be stifled or rationalized.

Campanella and Newcombe were gone tonight and Jackie felt particularly restless and increasingly irascible. Dinner in the ever grimmer dining room helped neither his disposition nor his digestion and he left in the middle, strode across the lobby, threw open the front door, and went into the night.

What voices he heard as he paced through the warm tropical darkness were Spanish, what music he heard coming from radios behind the lighted windows of the small houses was Spanish. It alienated him further, heightened his sense of apartness. Now and then a stray dog loped toward him, paused, then swung its shoulders and padded on four floating legs back into the night. He passed the only sign of life in the area, an open-till-midnight bodega where several youths were sitting out front on their haunches drinking from bottles of soda pop.

He walked for several miles, out to where the sugarcane began to appear. In the morning they rode past these fields on the fifteen-mile trip to the Montreal training site and saw the cutters, white shirts dark with perspiration, hacking away at the stout jointed stalks.

He stared moodily at the fields for several moments, listening to the rippling sounds of crickets, then began the long walk back. Out here, the streets were dead; not a single automobile had passed, nor had he seen a single person. The scattered houses seemed sealed into the night.

He was about a half mile from the hotel, walking on a dirt sidewalk, when he heard someone behind him, footsteps scuffing softly across the dirt. He raised his head slightly and listened attentively, trying to gauge the distance between himself and the maker of those sounds. He continued on, listening to the footsteps that seemed in steady beat with his own. He became more conscious of the darkness—there were no streetlights, no light of any kind—and of the deadening silence that was entered only by those companion footsteps. A three-quarter moon was buried in a heavy, quilt-like cloud bank. He lifted his hands from his pockets but did not turn, other than to shift his head slightly aside to enable himself to more clearly register the pace of those steps.

Why am I so suspicious? he asked himself as he continued moving forward, and not through words but through emotions came the response: because he was not a placid man, because his days were rubbed with unrelieved tension. Had somebody spotted him and decided to try and take him? See the nigger boy walking alone and decide to clean his pockets? A surge of anger almost made him wish it were so. He was in the mood. Purposefully he began slowing. Those taunting little footsteps were infuriating him. He'd tear the son of a bitch apart. But then again, maybe it was just some unoffending Cubano who happened to be walking this way.

You think you're being followed, a worldwise, world-weary old teammate on the Kansas City Monarchs had said to him once, you cross over the street and when you're lookin' to check the traffic you take a peek. Or, you want to be bold, you turn around and start walking back, real fast and mean-like. Whoever looks like he just shit his pants, he's the one doggin' you.

He was now consciously resisting the urge to spin around and start heading directly at whoever was there and make him pay for all the anger and the resentment, today's and yesterday's and all the rest of it. How much easier it would be to turn the other cheek tomorrow if he could spin somebody's head around tonight.

But he kept going, listening intently, his own accelerated footsteps being matched by the other's. When the moon suddenly broke free of the clouds and delivered a pale silvery pool of light, he abruptly crossed the street, allowing himself a wry smile as he turned to check the "traffic" and saw the man about a hundred feet behind. It seemed to be a white man, but in the frail light Jackie could not be sure. But of one thing he was sure: crossing the street had brought the man to a halt. When he reached the opposite side, Jackie stopped, turned slowly, and faced him, feeling within himself a severe calm, something taut and dangerously poised.

The man remained motionless in his own pocket of soft light, which was already beginning to diminish as the clouds began re-covering the moon. He was standing diagonally across the empty street from Jackie, staring back.

He knows who I am, Jackie thought, his eyes narrowing at the corners. It was no innocuously strolling Cuban. The light was gone now and Jackie could no longer be sure if anyone was there or not. He turned and began walking again. He cut across a garbage-strewn empty lot and into an intersecting street, heading back to the hotel, as far as he could determine unfollowed and unobserved. At the hotel's door he paused and looked back once more into the deep and unrevealing night.

Who had it been, he asked himself, and what had he wanted?

17

Tinker was surprised to learn that Larrimore Henry, the eminent and sometimes standoffish sportswriter, was a bigot. Tinker didn't know why he should have been surprised; just because a man could spin metaphors like arabesque motifs through his column and quote aptly from poets as diverse as Pope and Whitman was no reason to suppose he was free of prejudice. That an enlightened mind was necessarily an unsullied one was, Tinker supposed, one of his own prejudices.

Larrimore Henry certainly wasn't one of the boys who came out to watch Robinson and yell "porter" and "shoeshine," as though the black man had been provided for their personal entertainment. Larrimore even filed copy back to New York saying that things "crude and vile" were being shouted openly and clearly at Montreal's "colored boy" without regard for anyone's sensibilities. Robinson, he wrote, reacted with "admirable detachment, as if he heard nothing."

"It's going to be a problem," Larrimore told Tinker.

"What's going to be a problem?" Tinker asked.

"This Robinson business."

They were sitting in the shade of the visitors' dugout at El Gran Stadium, watching the Dodgers working out in the hot sun. For the intent, appreciative observer, there was a lovely rhythm being enacted out on the field. As soon as the ball struck by the batter in the cage had been gloved, a coach standing in foul ground next to first base lofted a long, high fungo shot to a group of outfielders gathered in left center who took turns catching it and firing one-hop pegs to the player "catching" for the coach. As soon as the peg struck the grass, the pitcher swung forward on the mound and wound up to deliver another batting-practice meatball to the man in the cage. Deep in the outfield, another coach was running a brigade of pitchers back and forth, from the left-field corner to the right-field corner.

Tinker's eyes rose with every fly ball, watching the tiny white pellet soar into the bright cloudless sky, reach its apogee, and then drop with a seeming gentleness that belied its velocity. He listened with a comforting sense of familiarity to the infield banter, which was punctuated by the alternating cracks of the bat coming from the cage and from the coach behind first base.

In the first-base dugout Leo Durocher was sitting and talking to newspapermen and assorted visitors, but whenever Tinker glanced over there he noted that the skipper's eyes were always fixed on the field, taking in every movement and nuance.

Rickey had said that Leo would make the final decision about Robinson. "If Leo thinks Robinson can help the Dodgers," the Old Man said, "then Jackie will join the team." Tinker and the other writers weren't buying it; they believed the decision had already been made and that Robinson would be on the roster by opening day. But at what position? Jackie had been a second baseman at Montreal, and the Dodgers had a good man at that spot in Eddie Stanky. Shortstop? Reese was the shortstop and nobody was moving Pee Wee aside. And anyway, Jackie didn't have the arm for short. Word was that Jackie was working out a lot at first base with the Montreal club, and people were wondering what Rickey was up to now. It was true the Dodgers were weak at first base, but it hardly seemed likely they would break baseball's first black player in at a strange position, considering all the other pressures that would be on him. Some cynics among the press corps suggested that Rickey was deliberately setting Jackie up to fail, enabling the Old Man to then claim that he had tried to break the color barrier but that the man just hadn't worked out, thus getting credit for the effort, pacifying the integrationists, and in effect finessing the issue. Tinker didn't believe this theory, nor did Larrimore Henry.

"Robinson is going to be on this team," Larrimore said, "and the problem is going to be how do we cover him, cover the story. Suddenly we have a blend of sociology and baseball. Instead of spending pleasant afternoons in the sunshine watching the skills of big-league baseball players, we're going to have to concern ourselves with the subtle, and sometimes not-so-subtle, manifestations of racial prejudice, with what passes for social progress, and a lot of other things that will be burdensome, tiresome, and unnecessary."

"You think there's going to be trouble?" Tinker asked.

"I think the potential is there for it, some of it quite ugly. I'm all for social progress, but for God's sake this is baseball. I'd rather see darkies running the Bank of America or Jews in the State Department." Larrimore laughed at his own analogies.

Despite the heat Larrimore was wearing a three-piece white linen suit, replete with a polka-dot bow tie and a Phi Beta Kappa key on a chain looped across the slight paunch under his vest. He spoke with the studied, cultured enunciation that had been refined at Yale three decades before. Larrimore was something of a snob, but Tinker had always forgiven him that; it seemed to Tinker that a man who had worked for the OSS in London during the war, dined occasionally with Walter Lippmann, and attended the opera, in addition to being a first-rate sportswriter, had earned a peculiar status.

"The man is a hell of a ballplayer, Larrimore," Tinker said.

"Nobody has said he wasn't. Frankly, if Robinson was different he would probably be the most interesting player in the Brooklyn organization."

"By different you mean white."

"Yes, Joe," Larrimore said agreeably. "That's exactly what I mean." The way the man's mouth was shaped you always saw his bottom teeth when he spoke. It added a trenchant quality to even his blandest comments. "This is the last goddamned thing we need—a darkie coming into the major leagues. Why are we in Cuba instead of over in Clearwater where the cuisine is better and the people speak your language? Because of Robinson. Why are half the Dodgers skulking about wondering when the other shoe is going to drop? Because of Robinson. Why are otherwise normal and placid people going to come out to the ballpark and scream the vilest epithets? How in the hell are we supposed to cover this story?"

"It's a story," Tinker said. "You write down what happens and you send it out, just like any other story. Jesus, why am I telling this to *you*?"

"This is a different kind of story, Joe. Usually we're objective. Oh, we have our favorites. I love it when Dixie bangs out three hits, that sort of thing. Covering sports is enjoyable. But this is different. This is creating a disturbing sort of tension. Spring training used to be a grand time. That last one we had down here in 1942, before everybody went off to war, that was a ripper. The drinking, the brawling, the whoring. There was a good, healthy, noisy emphasis here then, even though the world was on the brink of going to hell. But now this. I don't like it. Frankly, I resent it. And I'll tell you another thing: it's tearing up a first-rate ball club, one that should be a contending team this year. Talk to some of the boys, they're sullen as hell. Some of them say they won't play on the same team with Robinson. Walker, Higbe, Casey. To name a few."

"I don't know, Larrimore. Sometimes I don't think it's fair."

"What?"

"Being against a man because of his color."

"Would you like to see Robinson in the big leagues?"

"I haven't asked myself that question," Tinker said. "It's outside my province."

"But don't you see that it isn't? You're a sportswriter, Joe, and we're talking about the major leagues. The National League has existed very nicely for more than seventy years without them. Why all of a sudden do we need them now? We cover the team, Joe. We practically live with these men for half a year. Why is Rickey doing this?"

"Egalitarian reasons," Tinker said.

"Nonsense. Don't you ever believe any of that idealistic crap, not about Rickey, not about anybody. It's materialistic, that's what it is. Pure and simple. Nothing wrong in that, except in this case it becomes irresponsible avarice. There's no question a colored boy will draw some fans—but will they be the most desirable ones? And have you figured into the equation how many will be driven away? Does it balance out? Is it worth it?"

"I don't know."

"Big-league baseball had record-shattering attendance figures last season," Larrimore went on. The dugout roof was cutting the sun in a straight line just at the tips of his neatly buffed white shoes. "The Dodgers set a single-season National League attendance record last year. How many more tickets does Rickey want to sell? How many more people does he think he can stuff into that ballpark of his? I would like to write a column in which I say exactly how I feel about this."

"You think they'd run it?"

"Sure they'd run it. What's wrong with honest journalism? I'd be saying what most people are thinking."

"So why don't you?"

Larrimore made a weary gesture with his hand.

"Who needs the furor?" he said. "But it would be preferable to the hypocrisy we're filing now."

"What's this 'we'?" Tinker asked with a smile.

"Look, they have their own league. Let them stay in it. I think everyone should stay in their own place."

"Who decides what that is?"

"It's been decided," Larrimore said firmly. "Don't you think it's been decided?"

"I don't know, Larrimore. I'm just a sportswriter."

"Not anymore, Joseph. You're a sociologist too, now."

"Probably," Tinker said. "When I was over at the Montreal camp the other day I heard a lot of crap coming at Robinson from the stands, from whites. But I also heard the dark-skinned Cubans cheering every move he made."

"Maybe down here in Cuba. But you'd be surprised how many colored people back home are nervous about this thing. Some of them have told me they'd rather not see Robinson make it."

"They're kidding you."

"No they're not. They're content with things as things are. They'd rather not have attention drawn to themselves. Believe me, colored people prefer staying out of the limelight."

"I think they're bullshittin' you," Tinker said.

"What do you know about them, Joe?"

Tinker thought back to his Christmas Day conversation with Ettie Pearson. *One time too many. It had been one time too many.* Those disturbing words, and their implications, had remained with him, ominous and sobering.

"I'll tell you what I know," Tinker said. "This business goes a hell of a lot deeper with a hell of a lot more people than you think."

"Well, I don't see why baseball has to be dragged into it."

"Why not?" Tinker asked. "Is it so innocent?"

18

Tinker had interviewed plenty of athletes, including such Valhalla niches as Ruth, Louis, DiMaggio, Dempsey. But he had to admit that he had never met anyone like this Robinson. No one had ever exuded such tension. You could feel it as you neared him, as he sat in what seemed profound self-awareness alone in the shade of the ramshackle dugout, legs crossed, arms extended along the top of the bench, a towel around his neck, head slightly cocked, watching Tinker walk across the infield grass toward him.

Tinker could feel himself being measured, contemplated, and not merely because he was the only person on the field, but because this was the way Robinson was, had conditioned himself to be. Some people—depending on the content of their own minds—might have read hostility in the man sitting alone and utterly motionless in that dugout. But to Tinker, as aware of Robinson as Robinson was of him, the black man in the Montreal Royals uniform looked self-possessed, wary, perhaps a touch skeptical. Tinker had never been stared at like that by a black man, and he was conscious of the thought, acutely aware that he was thinking it—and on that he had the further, discomfiting thought that Robinson knew exactly what he was thinking.

"I appreciate your hanging around for me," Tinker said as he stepped down into the dugout.

"I don't mind," Robinson said. "There'll be more room in the shower when I do get in there."

"I hope they leave you some hot water."

Robinson smiled politely. The voice was pitched a bit high for the broad, powerful body, which looked almost too bulky for the agility and suddenness with which it could move.

"Joe Tinker, *Daily News*," Tinker said rather formally, as if stating it for the record. He sat down next to Robinson. The dugout bench was put together with slats, like the benches in Central Park, except the park benches didn't give like this one when you sat down on them.

Robinson brought his arms down and offered his hand. As they shook hands Robinson watched Tinker with mild amusement, as if gauging the newspaperman's reaction to grasping the strong black hand. Tinker felt self-conscious, as though the brief handshake—normally reflexive and peremptory—was a cogent exchange of thoughts, except that Tinker didn't know what he was supposed to be thinking, and if nothing, then was he supposed to be conscious of that too?

Tinker had of course interviewed rookies before; they were always fidgety and somewhat insecure, their thoughts always transparently at the surface; not thoughts, really, but just the one thought: *Am I going to make the team, the big leagues?* But this rookie, with his unprecedented burden, was different. He seemed confident; or was that the tension, binding him?

"Hot as hell," Tinker said. He was staring out at the field, aware that his profile lay under Robinson's measuring gaze.

"How are things over at the big camp?"

"Oh, they're huffing and puffing. Everybody's filing stories on Snider. That's all Rickey's talking about. 'Another Ted Williams. Legs like steel springs.' "

"Duke can play ball."

"Maybe," Tinker said. "But notwithstanding that, I think Rickey's giving him all this buildup to divert attention away from you. To take away some of the pressure. By rights you should be training with the Dodgers, don't you think? I mean, a man who tears apart the International League the way you did, normally he'd be in training with the big club."

"Normally," Robinson said succinctly.

"Don't you think you should be over there?"

"That's Mr. Rickey's decision."

"Do you think they're being fair with you?"

Robinson folded his arms, settling back more comfortably on the bench.

"In what regard?" he asked.

"Working you at first base. You're a second baseman. With everything you've got on your mind, having to learn a new position seems a bit of an extra load."

"Whatever Mr. Rickey asks me to do, I'll do."

Tinker had been jotting notes with a stub of yellow pencil onto a small spiral pad. He closed the pad and placed it and the pencil in his shirt pocket.

"Off the record, Jack," he said, "do you think you're being set up?"

Normally, when he put away his pad and pencil and asked someone to comment off the record, Tinker would notice some telltale change of expression or slight shifting about, some indication that thoughts or facts were indeed being concealed or circumscribed. He exacted no such nuance from Robinson, who remained still, his expression steadily unchanged.

"For what?" he asked.

"To fail. So Rickey can tell the world he tried to integrate but that the man just couldn't cut it."

"That's very cynical, Mr. Tinker."

"It could be true."

"Then you're missing something."

"I am?"

"How well do you know Mr. Rickey?" Robinson asked.

"He's a tough man to read."

"How well do you know me?"

"Not at all," Tinker said.

"How well do you understand this whole situation?"

"I think I understand the significance."

"Good. Then you know I'm not just another guy. I would like to be. Maybe someday I will."

"You're not shy, are you?" Tinker said.

"What do you mean by that?"

"I've researched you a bit. You had trouble in college, had some problems in the army."

"The problems were there when I arrived."

"They're going to continue to be there, wherever you go."

Robinson smiled wryly. "That's one of the reasons I'm going—wherever it is I'm going."

"You were court-martialed down in Texas, at Fort Hood."

"For exercising my rights. Public transportation on army bases had been desegregated."

"So you sat in front of the bus."

"I was entitled to sit anywhere I wanted."

"But you knew it would cause trouble."

"It was the driver who caused the trouble, not me."

"And you were court-martialed for it."

"The judges accepted that I was acting within my rights," Robinson said. "There was no conviction."

"You got an honorable discharge instead. They got rid of you."

Tinker had been looking out at the field. When he turned his head he found Robinson's eyes on him, intent, inquiring.

"It looks like I may be making life difficult for some of you guys," Robinson said.

"How so?"

"Some of the writers don't like Negroes," Robinson said with a directness that startled Tinker and for a moment made him feel defensive. "And most especially Negroes who want to come in through the front door."

"What are you going to do about it?"

"Ignore it. Go about my business."

"What about your teammates? On the Dodgers I mean. You can't ignore them."

"They're not my teammates yet."

"There are a lot of Southern boys on the club."

"At least I'll *know* what *they're* thinking," Robinson said.

"I hear you've received some poison-pen letters."

"Where'd you hear that?"

"Is it true?" Tinker asked.

Robinson shrugged. "I get a lot of mail," he said.

"The letters I'm referring to contained either warnings or threats."

"I've gotten a few of those," Robinson said. "I turned them over to the ball club."

"What was the general content of the letters?"

" 'Get out of baseball, or else.' Nothing subtle."

"Or else what?" Tinker asked.

"One guy said he'd shoot me down right in the batter's box. Another one said he'd blow my head over the center-field fence."

"Jesus," Tinker said, "and we sit up in the press box holding our breaths when we think a beanball is coming."

"Listen," Robinson said, "the less said about this the better. That's the way Mr. Rickey feels and that's the way the police feel."

"What about you? How do *you* feel?"

"How the fuck would *you* feel if you got death threats in the mail?"

"Scared shit," Tinker said.

"Well, so am I."

Tinker sat silently for several moments, staring out across the empty field and beyond the gray weathered boards of the outfield fence and far out to the inert blue Caribbean sky. He had a terrific sense of Robinson sitting next to him, contemplating him. Tinker felt a vague irritability that he tried to account for. *Is it because I've never met a Negro like this one, or that I've never met a man like this one?* Tinker felt as though he were sitting through a severe tutorial, that his soft, unseasoned confusions were being mocked.

"Aren't you going to ask me if it's worth it?" Robinson said.

Tinker, leaning forward, turned his head and looked across his shoulder at Robinson.

"It seems to me," he said, "that you would have all that worked out by now."

"Listen," Robinson said, pointing at Tinker's shirt pocket, "why don't you take out that notebook and get on with your interview?"

19

Five days and still nothing. Quentin knew the waiting was going to be difficult. The sense of anticipation with which he awaited each moment was beginning to border on the excruciating.

He kept the radio on all day, listening to news, weather, music, those afternoon serials, the evening shows, and then the news again. That was how he, and everyone else, was going to hear about it—not in the newspapers but over the radio, because this was going to be breath-stopping news, a bulletin. And to Quentin it would of course be more than merely news; it would be a pronouncement, a warning, and "they" would hear it clearly and take heed.

The snow made it worse, as though sealing his sense of solitude and isolation. It struck early on the morning of the fourth day and by midafternoon was falling in an immense crowd of thick white flakes, soon swept about by a blasphemous wind that seemed to be on the attack, as though trying to tear itself free of some final restraint.

He stalked about the house, upstairs and down, always with an ear cocked to the running radio, waiting for the gunshot, damning the songs and the serials, as if they were standing in the way, blocking what he wanted to hear. The night of the storm he sat awake until three in the morning, listening to the radio and to the whiplashed furies outside and to the solemn creaking of the roof overhead.

On the morning of the fifth day the world outside was silent, exhausted. The piled snow glistened in the cold winter sunlight. It was dead out there and would remain dead for days, until the plows finished clearing the main thoroughfares and could begin working their way through the side streets.

He sat in the house all day drinking coffee and eating sandwiches made with bread so stale he had to toast it to make it edible. He could hear his neighbors digging out, long-handled scoop shovels scraping against the concrete, voices jocular and philosophical—men in discussion upon the aftermath of nature's fury.

In the afternoon Quentin put on his boots, overcoat, muffler, and ear-lapped plaid cap and kicked through the knee-high snow that covered his sidewalk, and headed down to Grant Avenue to buy some newspapers. The neighbors paused in their shoveling to greet him, lifting gloved hands as faint vapors accompanied their hellos. He ignored them, striding with his head down, face pinched in concentration. They shrugged and went on thrusting at the snow. They knew him well enough, knew he was strange, and more so since Harry's death.

He returned home with copies of the *Daily Mirror* and *Daily News*. He sat down next to the hissing radiator, put the papers face down in his lap and turned the back pages to the sports section. The *Mirror* had a bland story about the Dodgers' pitching staff. The *News*, however, had an interview with Robinson, accompanied by a picture. He stared sullenly at the black face under its Montreal Royals cap. That face always looked belligerent, defiant. Gazing on it, Quentin felt a wrathful stirring, but then he felt nudged by a sense of impending triumph, of gloating, and his lips curled in a malicious smile.

The story, under the byline of Joe Tinker, told of sitting with Robinson in the Montreal dugout after the Royals workout. It dwelled on the fact that Robinson was coming to camp every day with a first baseman's mitt and was working out at the bag under the supervision of George Sisler, the old 1920s first baseman who was considered one of the slickest gloves ever at the position. Did it mean a change of position was in the works for Robinson? Jackie didn't know. By whose orders was this being done? Mr. Rickey's. Did Jackie feel comfortable around the bag? No, not yet. But he said he was not worried. If asked to play first base he would learn to do it competently. Was he expecting a promotion to the

Brooklyn roster? He didn't know. He was simply doing what he was told and not asking any questions. He was just one man, part of a large organization whose collective goal it was to bring a pennant to Brooklyn in 1947.

The rest of the interview concerned the intricacies of playing first base: learning how to shift your feet, how to handle cutoffs and relays, how to lead a pitcher who was running over to cover the bag.

Again Quentin felt his wrath stirring. Who were they kidding? This was all part of Rickey's grand design to bring the nigger to the major leagues. Didn't they all know what he, Quentin, knew—that the Dodgers were fixed at short and second but not at first? Rickey was so intent on moving his nigger to the Brooklyn roster that he was willing to play the son of a bitch out of position. It was very clear to Quentin. Rickey had made up his mind. The calculating old windbag was going to bring a nigger into the major leagues—with the Dodgers, no less—and nobody was doing anything about it.

But that wasn't quite true.

Quentin let the newspapers fall to the floor. Where was Elmer? What was he doing down there? The shrewd combat infantryman, survivor of Omaha Beach and the Normandy hedgerows, the Ardennes and the Rhine crossing; the tough, bruising middleweight; a man with the morals of a snake. What was he doing? Stalking his prey? Being careful? True, this was no snap-of-the-finger job. The venture was definitely not without risk. But Elmer was a man who thrived on risk, wasn't he? Or was he? He was, after all, a survivor, and how could a survivor survive unless he avoided taking chances? Elmer had always been cagey, could always smirk after the smoke had cleared and the dog tags were being collected. But maybe that was all to the good now. He would pick his spot, do it clean, and get away with that smirk still in place. After all, he wanted the rest of the money, didn't he?

But in reality, Quentin asked himself now, sitting there in his frustrating solitude, how much did he really trust his old buddy (not that Elmer had ever been anybody's buddy)? He had trusted him in combat, but the truth was buddy Elmer had always been looking out for himself and had done a damned good job of it. That was why Quentin had stayed close to him, because Elmer had the cynicism and the stamina and the luck to survive, and Quentin had scented it. But that was over with now and Quentin was detecting a different scent.

He's going to try and stiff me, he thought.

20

Elmer met the woman on the morning of his third day in Havana. She was sitting at a white oval-topped table in the hotel coffee shop, looking as though she had been placed by a directorial hand, just near enough to the floor-to-ceiling glass wall to be touched by sunlight that softened her staring profiled face and lent it an aura of melancholy. Beyond her look of sculpted loneliness there was nothing remarkable about her. She was in her middle thirties, with shoulder-length brown hair, a roundish face, and though visible only from the waist up gave an impression of incipient dowdiness, like a small-town secretary who has remained at a humdrum job just long enough to have foreclosed any other opportunities.

In a casino lounge the night before he had met a couple of strong-arm boys whom he hadn't seen since before the war, recognizing them and wondering if they would remember him, not greeting them because you could never be sure if they wanted to be approached, called by name. So he was gratified when they noticed him and walked over to say hello, remembering him as that good tough middleweight who would stand toe to toe with anybody, recalling some of his better nights in the smaller New York arenas. They didn't ask him what he'd done during the war and Elmer didn't ask them, though he was pretty goddamned sure he'd had it tougher. But here they were now, slick as ice, alert as rattlers, working high up in one casino or another, sharks in tight-fitting double-breasted jackets with fresh carnations in their lapels, offering firm handshakes and deathmask eye-for-eye stares. For Elmer they were reminders of better days, when dreams were realistic and the future seemed a paved road.

Later in the evening they were joined by several sly-faced men whom Elmer didn't know but who impressed him because his companions deferred to them. They were subsequently joined by a couple of stars of New York's nocturnal life whose names Elmer recognized, who were generally characterized in the columns as "sportsmen," a convenient catchall that allowed them to be anything they wanted. They were accompanied by flashy ruby-lipped women of little subtlety. After having been introduced as "Elmer Cregar, the middleweight," he was relegated to the group's periphery, sipping whiskey, eyes broodingly riveted on whoever was speaking, smiling when the others laughed, saying little, glad to be there among them, but resentful of his sideline status.

And then even this group of self-confident and well-connected men fell silent when the large, bulky man entered the lounge, followed by an entourage of a half dozen men and women who were obviously trailing in his wake. Elmer didn't recognize him and realized that he was probably the only one in the place who didn't, for the tourists at the tables ceased their conversation when they spotted him and some Cubans at the bar called out familiarly and affectionately to him, "Papa! Papa!" Obviously accustomed to the attention and aware of the impact of his presence, the big man greeted the hailers with a comradely wave of the hand and a broad, tight grin.

When the big man passed close to Elmer's group, one of the New Yorkers greeted him, then with pride turned to introduce him.

"Ernest Hemingway, meet—" and so it went through the group, hands extended, greetings exchanged, an admiring word for this or that book.

Introduced finally—"This is Elmer Cregar, the middleweight"—Elmer reached his hand between a pair of sportsmen and had it engulfed by the large hand of the famous writer, whose name he recognized.

"Middleweight, eh?" said Hemingway, peering interestedly at Elmer for a moment before turning and moving on, a god of the immediate dominion.

As he lay in the cool impersonality of his hotel bed that night, Elmer thought about the strong-arm boys and the gamblers and the sportsmen and the famous writer, all of whom had shaken the hand of Elmer Cregar, the middleweight. *Ex-middleweight*, he thought, not morosely or wistfully but rather with a curious detachment, as if regarding himself from a fresh angle. He had appreciated the accord, even as he now thoughtfully acknowledged it was no longer enough, that its currency had been spent.

The woman's name was Irene Flagler, and when Elmer sat down uninvited at the white oval-topped table where she was sitting, she moved her eyes to him with a look of petulant annoyance.

"I'm Elmer Cregar," he said, listening to *middleweight* reverberate like a dying echo through his mind. "Excuse me, but this seemed the only place to sit."

When she looked around and saw every other table unoccupied, she turned back to him with a raised eyebrow and the curl of a knowing smile.

"Let's warm that up," he said, indicating her half cup of cold coffee, then raised his hand into the air and snapped his fingers. It occurred to him that he had never done that before—call for service with a snap of the fingers.

She liked his manner and his tough face with its hard smile and punched-around nose. His air of command titillated her and she could not help comparing it with the earnest plodding of her late husband, a man who always frowned and bunched his eyebrows before speaking, even if it was to say good morning. Even as he had lain dying from his third heart attack in three years, he had been full of apologies for the inconvenience he was causing her, though there had been no apologies for the sexual winter his chancy heart had imposed on their childless marriage during those final three years, probably because he hadn't seemed to mind and assumed she felt the same. She didn't tell Elmer this, of course, only that she was widowed a year now and that an appropriate period of mourning had passed and that she was in Havana on a vacation she described as "well-deserved." It was, she said, the first time she had ever been out of the United States and was frankly intimidated by the strange language and in the five days she had been there had done little more than write postcards to her friends back in Middletown, Connecticut and take half-hour walks, always in a straight line so she would be able to find her way back to the hotel.

With a patronizing smile, Elmer reminded her that she was in one of the most exciting cities in the world and would feel sorry later if she didn't "see it all dressed up." And who was he and what was he doing in Havana?

"Just traveling," he said. "I'm a sportsman."

So on his third night in Havana Elmer slept with Irene Flagler, who never in her life had known such sexual raptures. By the time the night had begun to expire into dawn, she had experienced fantasy into reality so many fervent times she was in a state near levitation. It wasn't just the full and steamy presence of a man inside her again, nor was it just that this man's tireless piston fury severed her lashings as she had never thought possible, nor was it just that her arms had never engaged back and shoulder muscles like that, muscles that made her aware of the primordial fullness of the total man. It was all of that and more: the balmy tropical air, the Caribbean breezes that so sensually curled the white curtains, the street sounds of a strange city, alien before, but now exotic. It was pure cinema and she was aware of her central role, allowing herself to drift through it with barely suspended disbelief.

On his fourth day in Havana a coolly confident Elmer showed her the city, and she was still so immersed in the wondrous unreality of what was happening that she was inattentive to the fact that he knew little about where they went and what they saw. He took her to the wharf, where they sat on the deck of an outdoor café and stared at tied-up fishing boats and the stolid sea-worn faces of the fishermen, and later to a fronton, where they watched a jai alai game that was incomprehensible to them both, and later to a restaurant that he claimed served the best steaks in Havana ("Flown in fresh every day from Florida," he said).

He had heard the name of a bar mentioned and so after dinner he told the cabdriver to take them to the Floridita.

"Everybody goes there for a nightcap," he said.

The Floridita was indeed full and lively when they walked in, Irene's arm locked into his. When he surveyed the place with its crowds and hubbub of convivial chatter, Elmer congratulated himself on his choice. As they headed along the bar toward a table Irene suddenly had a sharp intake of breath.

"That's Ernest Hemingway," she whispered, indicating a knot of people at the corner of the bar.

They walked slowly, Elmer's gaze riveted on the face of the big-shouldered writer, who was sitting on a stool entertaining his coterie, one elbow on the bar, frozen daiquiri in hand, broad smile on his tanned adventurer's face.

Walking with great deliberation, Elmer passed as close as he could to the famous writer. Front teeth softly in underlip, his eyes were fixed on Hemingway's face, trying to will a glance of recognition. As Elmer and Irene were nearly abreast of him, Hemingway's eyes suddenly shifted, picked up Elmer's painfully hopeful, almost pleading face and Irene's wide-staring adulation, took a quick reading and though not always noted for grace under social pressure, reached out and heartily shook hands with Elmer, saying, "Elmer. Good to see you again."

On his fourth night in Havana, Elmer lay in bed with Irene discussing the best way to invest the money her deceased husband had left her. Elmer didn't know exactly how much it amounted to, which was just about the only thing she hadn't told him thus far, but that it was a sizable sum there seemed to be no doubt. She had mentioned the possibility of buying into an inn in Vermont or backing a beauty parlor in Middletown. When Elmer suggested opening a restaurant in Hartford, she found the idea appealing, especially when it seemed that he would be willing to manage it for her, something he vaguely indicated he had experience at doing.

"We could make it the most exciting place in Hartford," Elmer said. "That city's got a lot of class; it would welcome this kind of place with open arms," he said, speaking of a city he had visited once in his life, in 1941, when he had been knocked cold in the sixth round of an eight-round semifinal. "You make it a hangout for the sporting crowd," he told her, "and all the celebrities will come there."

"Like Ernest Hemingway," she said, still aglow from the radiant moment when the writer had reached out to greet Elmer.

"Sure," Elmer said. "You can be sure Ernie'd drop in whenever he was in town."

On the fifth night, after another session of wildly gratifying lovemaking, Irene lay in bed, her shoulders resting on a pair of propped-up pillows, covers drawn up over her plump breasts, drink in hand, discussing the restaurant (already named "The Champ's Corner") that was so vividly in mind now that they were considering the decor, the number of tables and booths that would be on the other side of the half wall that would divide the dining area from the bar. Elmer, clad only in white trousers, chest bare, was sitting in a chair, feet crossed at the edge of the bed. He kept reminding her that it was important to have autographed pictures of prizefighters on the wall, to give the place "style."

Before they went to sleep he told her the idea was surefire, that it couldn't miss, even if it turned out that he was unable to come to Connecticut and help her with it. She made no response to that, didn't allude to it until after dinner the next evening, when they were walking through a park at the end of one of the city's wide thoroughfares. She confessed, with a forced, somewhat girlish laugh, that she had been taking an awful lot for granted, expecting him to give up things in New York and come to Connecticut just to help her launch a business. He said that if it was possible, he would be happy to "help a friend along." After the past few days, to be described as "a friend" lightly jolted her.

"I thought we were more than that," she said.

An uncharacteristically suave Elmer responded, "I wouldn't be a gentleman if I thought there was more to it, after such a short acquaintance."

It wasn't until late on Elmer's sixth night in Havana that the word "marriage" was actually mentioned for the first time—by Irene—and while a coy Elmer conceded that it was "a very deep and lasting idea," they still only had known each other for less than a week. Anxious now, she interrogated him about the women in his life, past and present, like a physician trying to identify a dangerous symptom. Elmer mulled over what story to offer. His fierce masculine pride forbade him to claim a Dear John letter received during the war; so instead he contrived a tale of his home-front love dying of pneumonia in 1944 while he was trying to survive combat with the German army in France. A deeply moved Irene rolled close to him under the covers and he held her with his arm. As she told him how painful the world was but that yet two forlorn and lonely people had managed to come together, he was gazing up at the ceiling and its large endlessly revolving black fan, seeing himself as lord of The Champ's Corner, charming the customers, commanding the help, holding court at the bar (possibly wearing a tuxedo), sitting in his private office. She was curiously absent from these reveries.

Days and nights of indulging the variegated

delights of Havana, of sitting in nightclubs and watching the spotlighted rumba dancers, of lavish dinners, of occasional flings in the casinos, and then back to the hotel for another fervent round of lovemaking. And through it all, Elmer continued to congratulate himself on his good luck. Once the idea of marriage had entered Irene's mind, all doors behind it had slammed shut. A friend of hers owned a powerboat that would accommodate some ten or twelve people, and that's where the wedding would take place, on the boat, drifting down the Connecticut River, sometime in July. Elmer agreed. He told her he thought it was terrific, fine. A wonderful idea. Very romantic. He was agreeing to everything, able to do that because he had so far succeeded in distancing both the word and the concept "husband" from everyday thought, because even though many of his friends back in New York were married they were still able to go roistering through the night wifeless and unfettered. If "husband" meant anything to Elmer, it was that flashy restaurant-to-be in Hartford and that attractive seven-room white frame house she had described to him in Middletown, Connecticut. Right now, for Elmer, "husband" had about the same meaning as "reward."

It wasn't until his eighth day in Havana that Elmer began seriously thinking about why he was there. He had been going through Quentin's money with great abandon, and it was the steady thinning of the bankroll that reminded him, coldly, that he did have a purpose in coming to this city, that he in fact had been sent here. His first thought was that the second half of the payout would be nice to have; together with the modest bankroll he had stashed away back in his New York apartment, it would enable him to continue playing the sportsman until after the wedding.

He didn't have to contrive an excuse to be away that night, for Irene had come down with severe stomach cramps and taken to her bed. He told her he was going to step out for a few hours to try his luck at one of the casinos. She told him to wake her when he returned.

Elmer went to his room, picked up the black leather shaving kit that contained the P-38, and left. At the service desk in the lobby he asked to have a rented car sent around and then went outside to wait for it.

Settling himself behind the wheel of the car, he tried to remember what he had learned on his first few days in town, when his purpose had been sharply focused. He had found out where Robinson was staying and had rented a car that first night and driven out to the isolated hotel and parked diagonally across the street and sat there and waited. He was simply there to reconnoiter; he didn't even have the gun with him. At about eight o'clock he saw Robinson emerge from the hotel and depart on a solitary walk through the quiet, sparsely populated streets.

The black man returned about forty minutes later—Elmer had clocked it—and reentered the hotel.

This same routine—Elmer's and Robinson's—was repeated the following night, the ballplayer leaving the hotel at around eight o'clock and walking. To Elmer it was obvious that this was simply a post-dinner stroll, without destination, for Robinson, broad-shouldered and muscular in a yellow polo shirt, was moving with the aimlessness of the casual stroller, hands in pockets, occasionally kicking a stone. On this second night Elmer had waited about fifteen minutes and then had started the car and followed. Within a few minutes his headlights picked up the solitary figure walking slowly and, it seemed, thoughtfully in the quiet night. Elmer had the gun with him this time, in the black leather shaving kit resting next to him on the seat, and as if it had begun an audible ticking he suddenly became stunningly conscious of it. Its proximity filled him with the kind of terrifying self-awareness he used to feel in combat.

He cruised past Robinson without a glance, picking him up in the rearview mirror for a moment. He drove a quarter mile farther, then turned and doubled back along a parallel street, made another turn, and got back onto the street where Robinson was walking. He parked in front of what had probably once been a grocery store—a few faded trade signs were visible between the planks nailed across the windows and door—switched off the headlights, and sat there.

Elmer wasn't sure what he was going to do. And under these circumstances, any indecision at all—even a few moments' worth—was enough to convince him that he wasn't going to shoot anybody that night. And anyway, there was no compelling reason to get it done in a hurry, particularly since it had taken him long enough to finally get to Havana and now that he was here he wanted to enjoy himself. Besides, he felt he ought to get the feel of this business; he had survived months of combat during the war because of a wily sense of self-preservation which had enabled him to outlast the dangers around him. There was only one thought that Elmer had ever taken into combat with him: *I'm not going to get killed.*

He conceded that he had no real plan about any of this, except to get out of the car, shoot the guy, get back into the car, and drive away. Even he had to smile at how ingenuous this all was. It was leaving too much to the chancy and the unknown. All he needed was for some drunken Cuban sleeping it off under a porch to wake up, read the plate number, and remember it. Well, Elmer told himself, when he came to actually pull the trigger he would have figured it out cold, and that would include having removed the license plates and maybe wearing a false mustache and providing other bits of diversion and concealment.

He got out of the car to urinate, making sure to kill the inside light before he opened the door (congratulating himself on that bit of artifice). He peered around at the unstirred darkness with a sense of contempt for those who were in bed inside the jerry-built tin-roofed houses that looked as if they would disintegrate under one good shriek of wind. He stepped into the earthen alleyway formed by the side of the abandoned store and a wooden fence that was sagging under the weight of the shrubbery it had been designed to confine, and there he relieved himself.

He was standing in the alley when he heard the quietly approaching footsteps. He zipped his trousers and pressed himself against the rough plank wall and waited, listening to the footsteps as though trying to weigh and measure their maker. When the man passed, Elmer recognized the yellow polo shirt and the brawny physique. As he listened to the softly cadenced footsteps diminishing, Elmer for one tingling instant thought of getting the P-38 from the car and doing the job right here and now, but then immediately realized it would be foolhardy, for after he gunned the bastard he was going to have to return to the car, probably with lights going on and greaser faces appearing in windows, and maybe even some of them running out in their underwear to see what happened.

A North Americano in a double-breasted suit, with slicked-down black hair, a dented nose . . .

So he compromised by following Robinson for a few minutes, suddenly intrigued by his prey and emboldened by the power he felt he had over him. Then abruptly the moon broke free of its dense cloud cover and spilled faint light over the street. Elmer stopped, watching Robinson cross the street—no question it was he, and the son of a bitch knew he was being followed—and stop and turn around when he got to the other side. About a hundred feet apart, the two men stared intently at each other. Elmer, from his pinnacle of knowing what he knew, smiled listlessly. Then the clouds carried back across that old, old globe of the night and slowly dried up the light. Sure, Elmer thought, turning and walking back toward the car, when you were going to do a job that would last forever there was no point in rushing it and maybe getting it wrong. And besides, he had heard that it was snowing in New York.

So now here he was a week later, back again, parked diagonally across the street from the backwater hotel where the Dodgers were housing the man Quentin Wilson seemed to hate beyond all others. The thought of Quentin made Elmer smirk; with the good fortune that had recently come his way, the ex-middleweight reasoned, he would no longer have to soil himself with the Quentin Wilsons of the world. A

lot of things had been moved aside along with
those years of pain and brawling, of broken
noses and cut eyes, of rope skipping and heavy-
bag punching in fetid airless gymnasiums, of
being jostled aside in grainy shower rooms by
champions and contenders. Getting a whiff of
the glitter now and then, tasting it, knowing it
was there, and then the slow bitter knowledge
that he would never possess it. The dream had
fallen to tattered remnants while he had gone
on in undiminished fullness. And now suddenly
it had been restored; now suddenly it had
turned his way, by luck or chance. Or maybe it
was just him, Elmer Cregar, his toughness and
his perseverance, for after all, he hadn't been
shot to pieces during the war, like so many others he had known. So maybe that was it; endur-
ance, a kind of faith all its own.

He supposed he had known when he left the
hotel tonight what was going to happen—what
was not going to happen. The black leather
shaving kit on the seat next to him was like
some final obligatory gesture to why he had
come to Havana in the first place. He had not
made a conscious decision that he was not
going to shoot anybody; it was as if the decision
had evolved of itself, like something that had
been settled in his absence. To hell with Quentin. He wasn't going to risk all his new good
fortune just to gratify that asshole. And if Quentin whined about the money, Elmer would tell

the bastard that it was a delayed charge for having saved his life over there.

And look at this anyway, Elmer thought as the rain suddenly began pouring down without warning, a torrent from the first drop, rattling on the roof and blurring the windshield. Even if he had wanted to pump some tokens of good luck into the nigger, Elmer thought, he wouldn't have been able to do it tonight.

The thunderstorm accompanied Elmer back to Havana. At times the rain tore earthward in such volume it seemed as if storming ocean waves were flattening against the windshield, and the darting wipers were barely able to maintain visibility. The driving rain was white in the headlights, the exploding thunder reminded him of the war, and the lightning snapping against the teeming sky gave him barbarously swift glimpses of deserted streets, empty parks, balconied buildings, trees slashing in the high wind.

With the near-blinding rain limiting visibility, he believed he must have missed a turn, for he couldn't see any lights. Desperate for some surcease from the maddening storm, if only for a moment, he impetuously pulled the car onto the empty sidewalk and parked under a movie-house marquee, and suddenly the torrential noise stopped beating on the car. He looked out at the street as though at a war zone, ready to swear that the rain was spearing straight through the cobblestoned surface. Then he realized, as several bolts of lightning illuminated the immediate area, that he was only a quarter mile or so from the hotel and that the storm had knocked out the electricity. He realized, too, that his left sleeve was soaking wet, that the window of the rented car didn't close securely. *What shit*, he thought angrily, feeling wildly put upon, cursing Quentin Wilson and Jackie Robinson and the rain and the thunder and the lightning and the darkness. Savagely, he gunned the car and shot back into the street so fast that as it cleared the curb the car for a moment had all four wheels in the air.

A few minutes later he braked in front of his hotel, then had to run a half block through the unabating rain to the revolving door, rushing through it with a fury that left it swinging behind him for several seconds.

Flickering candles made the high-ceilinged lobby look sinister, like a place of rituals. About a dozen people, probably seeking comfort in numbers against the imposed darkness, were sitting on the sofas or standing near the windows watching the storm. In the candlelit bar an entertainer was playing a guitar and singing in Spanish. Soaked to the skin from his dash through the rain, Elmer walked across the carpeted floor to the front desk, the black leather shaving kit in hand. A mustached clerk in jacket and tie—he looked incongruously dry and staid to Elmer—was presiding at the desk as if at an altar, tall, flame-tipped candles in even taller holders on either side of him.

"How long does this last?" Elmer asked.

"Sir?"

"The blackout."

"That cannot be said," the clerk said, smiling and shrugging.

"Is the whole city out?"

"We know only about this area."

"Well, don't knock yourself out. Listen, you got any candles?"

"Every room has candles, sir," the clerk said. "They are in a white box in the bottom drawer of your bureau." He seemed proud of his command of English, enunciating each word carefully, as though he were being rated on it. "You will also find small metal trays to hold the candles."

"In other words," Elmer said, "this is not the first time your lights have gone kablooey."

The clerk smiled politely.

"Will you need help finding your way?" he asked.

"I'll find it," Elmer muttered, turning away.

The staircase to the second floor caught some of the lobby candlelight and Elmer had no problem. The next staircase was in total darkness and he had to ignite his cigarette lighter to find the door to the corridor. Then, guided by the lighter's guttering flame, he managed his way along the corridor to his room. Turning the doorknob as he put the key in the door, he was puzzled to find the door giving before he had turned the key. Jesus, he thought, had he left it unlocked?

"Irene?" he said to the dark, storm-noisy room. "You here?"

Well, if he had forgotten to lock the door, he had also left the windows open, the rush of rain was that loud. As he headed for the windows, where the curtains were flailing in the wind, a crackling snap of lightning silver-lit the room for an instant, and in the shudder of diabolical light he caught sight of someone sitting in a chair against the wall. Elmer stopped in mid-stride.

"Who's that?" he demanded.

"Light a goddamned candle or something."

"Jesus Christ," Elmer said with a mix of surprise and dismay, recognizing the voice. He snapped the lighter and held it above his head, revealing his visitor, who was sitting calmly, legs crossed, arms folded, dressed in a seersucker suit, white shirt, bow tie; slim, self-possessed, emitting as ever those unnerving and irritating signals of condescension.

"Quentin," Elmer said, tossing the shaving kit onto the bed. "What the fuck you doing here?"

21

What was he doing there? How long had he been in Havana? How did he get into the room? Quentin did not answer any of Elmer's questions. It wasn't that Quentin was refusing to answer as much as ignoring, who had questions of his own to be answered.

"Who is the woman?" Quentin asked.

"What woman?"

"Irene. You said 'Irene' when you walked in."

"Oh," Elmer said disparagingly. "Just somebody I picked up."

"She's the one you've been spending my money on."

"Your money?"

"Mine. Until you do something to earn it, it's mine."

Elmer had closed the windows, shutting out the loud immediacy of the rain, which still had not abated. Elmer had found the candles, set two of them on the metal trays and lit them, placing one on a bureau and the other on the bathroom sink. The faint, lurid light did little more than define the room. Elmer, sitting on an uncomfortable straw-seated chair, was not seeing much more than a ghost of a man across the room, like something evoked by a séance, an image heightened by that cultured baritone that Quentin affected and which in this darkness sounded sepulchral.

"It's been more than a week," Quentin said.

"What the hell do you think?" Elmer asked irritably, "that you just walk up to a guy and pop him? Do you think it's that simple?"

"I was just wondering if you've been concentrating all your thoughts and energies on getting it done."

"Well, I did take time out to take a leak now and then," Elmer said sarcastically.

"Between leaks, what have you been doing?"

"Listen, I've been watching the guy every day, every night. Trying to find a pattern in his movements. Also making sure I could get out all right. This is a tricky thing. Otherwise you would have done it yourself, right?" Elmer said insinuatingly.

Quentin never moved, still sitting as when Elmer had first seen him in the brief revelation of the lightning, nor had his voice changed, going on quietly, knowingly, without inflection.

"So you've been hard at work," he said.

"Where do you think I was tonight?" Elmer said. "I might have starched him tonight, except for this fuckin' storm. I was loaded for bear," he said, pointing at the shaving kit, "but then the rain hit and that was that."

"I was afraid you might be losing your nerve."

"No, I haven't lost my goddamned nerve," Elmer said angrily, coming forward in the chair and peering through the candlelight to see Quentin more clearly and be seen more clearly, to convey his irritation, which was increasing by the moment. The rain had soaked through his thin sports jacket, his feet were wet. And he had never liked this son of a bitch anyway, a weird son of a bitch whom he had met only because of a world war, whose face he had always wanted to drive a fist into, who was sitting there now like some goddamned D.A.

"I paid you to come down here to do a job," Quentin said, "not carouse around in bars picking up women."

"You paid me to come down here and murder somebody, that's what you paid me to do. And if you don't like my style, then you can do it yourself."

"You agreed to do something. You took money."

"This is not something you can drag me into court about, is it?" Elmer said, feeling his ire subside for a moment, pleased by his own drollery. It seemed to snare Quentin, who sat wordless for almost a minute; the two of them stared silently at each other through the indefinite light as the rain continued to hurl against the windows and the thunder and lightning came and went, the swift flashes of macabre illumination tightening the tension.

"Then tell me what you're planning," Quentin finally said.

"Sometime in the next three or four days," Elmer said, seeking to deflect him, get rid of him. "I've been working it out in my head. Just leave it to me."

Quentin's silence now seemed thoughtful, almost studious. He broke it by saying, "You've really been giving it a lot of thought, haven't you?" The note of skepticism piqued Elmer.

"That's right, that's right," he said. "If you'll just get the hell on a plane tomorrow morning and go back and leave me alone everything will be all right. I don't need any coaching. I don't want you around fucking it up."

"So it's all carefully planned, is it?"

"I told you it was."

"Then your plan has a hole in it."

"What do you mean?" Elmer asked. He stood up and removed his jacket and tossed it onto the bed. Then he reached behind him to pull his shirt up from his trousers. Then he began to undo the buttons.

"The Dodgers and Montreal are going to Panama in a few days to play a series of exhibition games."

"Is Robinson going?"

Quentin's silence made the answer obvious.

"For how long?" Elmer asked.

"Why do I have to tell you this?"

"Ahhh, don't worry," Elmer said, throwing the shirt onto the bed and heading into the bathroom. "I'll figure it out," he said over his shoulder. In the bathroom he turned on the sink taps, heard a sputtering cough from the pipes and watched a thin stream of water begin trickling out. "Jesus," he said, bending over and cupping his hands to catch some of the wobbly flow, which he splashed against his face, "I'll bet the fuckin' water is going to be out too." He looked at his reflection in the mirror; in the candlelight rising from the side of the sink he appeared almost melodramatically villainous and, perversely, it pleased him. He smiled sardonically at his image. "Where you staying, Quentin?" he asked. There was no answer. He stopped the drain and watched the slow, almost inert water drop into the sink. The flow from the faucet was thin as a thread now. "Jesus," he said, "I wanted to take a shower and clean up. It's been a hell of a night."

The moment Elmer disappeared from view into the bathroom, Quentin rose and picked the shaving kit up from the bed, hefted it for a moment, then slowly zipped it open. He put his hand inside, felt the revolver, and lifted it out. He stared at it for a moment, then looked at the bathroom doorway, where the candlelight seemed to be dying on the floor.

He moved soundlessly across the carpeted floor, the P-38 hanging in his hand against his leg. He first saw Elmer in the mirror, bent over the sink, rubbing water into his eyes. Then he stood facing the doorway, about six feet away, in near darkness.

"The goddamned water's stopped," Elmer said. "I caught about three inches of it." Assuming Quentin was still on the other side of the room, he raised his voice slightly. "I wonder how long this lasts. I wanted to take a goddamned shower. Fuckin' spic hotel, I'll bet this never happens in New York."

A sudden flash of lightning opened the room for a split second. Quentin's eyes dilated as he waited for the following thunder, and as it broke and rolled sonorously he raised the gun, just as Elmer began to turn. What the ex-middleweight saw, if anything, Quentin would never know, as Elmer's eyes squinted as if to express curiosity or wonderment or puzzlement. Quentin fired in unison with the breaking thunder. The bullet tore into Elmer's neck, just below the earlobe, knocking him back and to the floor as a fount of blood sprang and gushed against the mirror and began running.

22

The door was hurled back and the Cuban came running out of the room, one hand holding the side of his head, his buck-toothed face glaring with pain and fear. He was moving too fast ever to be able to get down those stairs and sure enough his furiously accelerated feet were unable to negotiate the staircase and after one stride at the top he went plunging straight out, chest parallel with the lushly carpeted flight, hands held palms out as if to demonstrate that he could perform this stunt without touching. Then he landed and howled and went plowing head first all the way to the bottom, flopping to a halt with his heels raised high behind him, the original pain and fear still contorting his face.

Tinker looked upstairs and saw Allen Johnson storming out of the room recently vacated by the Cuban. The Brooklyn Dodgers' right-hander, wearing only white boxer shorts, was in a state of high fury, which to Tinker and the other writers and players present was hardly uncommon for this brutishly strong and violent Alabaman, who was capable of committing homicide if an infielder booted one behind him or an umpire went the other way on a close call, and when drunk needed no reason whatsoever. Johnson rushed to the banister and with a blast of profanity threw an empty whiskey bottle at two other Cubans in pin-striped suits who were sitting on a divan across the room from Tinker. The bottle went right through a glass-topped coffee table, sending up a shower of silvery splinters. The Cubans shot to their feet as one, women began to scream, the voluptuous madam—known as Belladonna to the Dodgers—came running in from another room, her huge bosom throbbing massively against the low-cut front of her dress. She looked at the Cuban at the foot of the stairs, then at the other two who were screaming in Spanish at Johnson, who, inhumanly large and maniacal from below, was shaking his fist at them.

Belladonna's bouncer ran in, threw aside the girl who had risen from Tinker's lap, and for no good reason except perhaps indiscriminate security landed a solid roundhouse punch on the jaw of a Dodgers infielder, who went sailing back into the arms of an easy chair. The bouncer, an American of indeterminate background, then whirled and punched a writer from the *New York Journal-American* in the stomach so hard the writer's eyes bulged and he scissored over. Tinker took a shot at the bouncer from the side, landing hard on the cheekbone but to little effect.

Allen Johnson was running down the stairs now and the two Cubans were heading up. They met in the middle. With his momentum and his infuriated strength, Johnson bulldozed the Cubans back down the stairs, all three landing in a violent heap on the spot just barely vacated by the first Cuban, who was staggering about holding the side of his head, tiny rivulets of blood beginning to seep through his fingers.

Belladonna was screaming hysterically in Spanish, belying the pose of mannered sophistication she always affected and which Tinker never believed anyway. Then a small mole-faced man stepped into the room, sized the scene up with a rodent's darting eyes and started to withdraw, but Tinker reached out for him, collared him, spun him around, and punched him flush on the jaw. Tinker in turn found himself soundly rocked by the bouncer, who was now wading through the room swinging at whoever he could reach.

Allen Johnson got to his feet at the foot of the stairs, stark naked now—somehow he had lost his boxer shorts in his violent trip down the stairs, and he resembled some terrifying piece of classical statuary come to life—beat down one of the Cubans and began chasing the other, who had to leap over one of the girls, who was on all fours on the floor trying to locate some sort of safety.

Doors were opening upstairs but no one came down, content to stand in the corridor that overlooked the large well-appointed room where the battle was going on, men and women in kimonos or wrapped together in a single blanket, foolishly amused by the scene below.

Belladonna tried to intercept Allen Johnson, who was chasing one of the Cubans but was heading for a direct collision with the bouncer, something the madam desperately wanted to avoid.

"Ahlen! Ahlen!" she yelled.

But Tinker had seen that feral look in that backwoods-violent face and opaque eyes too many times, in saloons along the National League circuit, and knew that, for the moment at least, it was beyond human appeal. The Dodgers pitcher closed his fingers on the front of the madam's dress and tore it free, taking her lace brassiere with it, exposing her thick, large-nippled breasts, then pushing her aside.

A mighty crash of thunder accompanied the exchange of blows between the bouncer and the naked Allen Johnson. The bouncer landed first, but the pitcher landed second, third, and last, the final blow toppling the bouncer backward onto one of Belladonna's divans. Johnson then took hold of the Cuban, the first one, the one whose flight from the pitcher's room had started the whole thing, and with incensed strength and purpose lifted the man into the air and, holding him at collar and crotch, swung him back and then threw him at one of the draped windows, with such fury that the Cuban went hurtling through the glass, riding into the rain-storming night on a yielding ramp of crimson crushed velvet drapery.

"Let's get the fuck out of here," Tinker said to the *Journal-American* man who, still bent forward and clutching his aching midsection, was nonetheless mesmerized by Belladonna's overabounding nakedness.

"Cuban bastards!" Allen Johnson roared as thunder again boomed over Havana and the fusillades of Caribbean rain could be heard through the smashed window. The lights began flickering.

"Come on," Tinker said, pushing the *Journal-American* man ahead of him. They hurried through the garishly lit entranceway. Running ahead of them was the small mole-faced man Tinker had hit. He got to the door first, opened it to the sound of the pounding rain and ran out, followed by the two newspapermen.

"Oh, shit," Tinker said when they hit the street.

From either end of the street police cars were moving in, headlights illuminating the slanting rain.

"Oh, fuck," the *Journal-American* man said. "I'm a married man."

"For the moment," Tinker said.

"It'll take a little while to get it sorted out." This was Horace Glickman, front-office executive of the Brooklyn Dodgers, a Phi Beta Kappa from Columbia whose gray-haired dignity and near-genteel manner were veils over the blunt shrewdness he had acquired while working in the political clubhouses of Tammany Hall before joining the Dodgers. "Between my Spanish and their English and a few American dollars," Horace told Tinker and the *Journal-American* man, "we'll make a deal."

"We weren't doing anything at all," the *Journal-American* man said. "It was your goddamned pitcher who started the whole thing."

"I don't know which is worse," Horace said, "being caught in a cathouse or being caught in a cathouse and saying you weren't doing anything."

"I hope this doesn't get into the papers," the *Journal-American* man said grimly.

"I would say that's up to you," Horace said, "since the only paper in New York that would print it is the one you work for."

They had been in the police station for nearly two hours now. Nobody had been charged, nobody booked. Because several Brooklyn Dodgers were involved, the police knew the club would send someone down to make "arrangements." It had taken this long to locate Horace, who had made "arrangements" several nights before, when a couple of other Dodgers had been hauled in after a brawl at another bordello.

They were all sitting in a large holding room, on wooden benches that closed in the walls like a frame. A rough wooden table and several chairs stood in the middle of the room. A police sergeant sat at the table smoking a cigar. Two policemen were at the door, their hands resting on the heads of clubs jammed into their belts. Her dignity restored, Belladonna was there (a raincoat covering up her torn-away dress) with three of her girls, who were exchanging mischievous smiles with the two policemen. The three Cubans, bruised and disheveled, were sitting in stony, smoldering anger. Several Brooklyn Dodgers, crisp young gazelles on a ball field, were slouched sullenly, arms crossed, legs extended. The mole-faced man, whom Horace had confided to Tinker was a private detective hired to keep tabs on the players, sat alone, his face expressing a general disdain. Absent were the bouncer, left unconscious on the bordello floor, and Allen Johnson, who had been tossed, still naked, into a cell, where he was sleeping it off. It had taken four burly Cuban cops to get him into the wagon and, as Horace told Tinker, it would have taken an army to get a pair of pants on him (Horace had brought a suit of clothes with him to the station). The rain had stopped and the lights had come back on.

"It seems," Horace told Tinker and the *Journal-American* man, "the girl Allen had was the favorite of that Cuban and he went upstairs after her. The guy didn't know he was heading into the lion's den. I suppose it wouldn't have been so bad, except he's the son of a wealthy landowner and is arrogant."

"He's lucky he's alive," Tinker said. "That was Allen at the height of his powers."

"Everybody's lucky they're alive," Horace said. "These rich Cubans sometimes carry guns."

There was a knock on the door and one of the policemen opened it, was told something, then turned and gestured to Horace.

"They've agreed on a price," Horace said, getting up.

"You gonna negotiate, Horace?" Tinker asked whimsically.

"You don't negotiate in enemy territory," the front-office executive said, "especially when the other side has all the guns."

Horace Glickman's financial arrangement with the two senior police officers in the station house included compensation for the damage done to Belladonna's premises (including her dress), which the madam claimed had been caused exclusively by the Dodgers. The Brooklyn National League Baseball Club also apologized formally to the three Cubans, especially the rich one. The transaction's final clause was a request from the police that the Dodgers keep Allen Johnson under control. Horace was able to give them some reassurance on this point: in a few days the team was packing up and going to Panama.

Then everybody filed out of the police station.

The storm had left behind gutters of running water, gurgling sewers, and a night dense with humidity.

Tinker, the *Journal-American* man, and Horace lingered.

"Now what?" Tinker asked.

"I'm going back to my hotel and lock the door behind me," the *Journal-American* man said.

"I've got to get back to Rickey and give him the report," Horace said.

"What's he going to say?" Tinker asked.

"Boys will be boys," Horace said. "Branch may quote the Bible and spear you with Latin apothegms, but he's also a man of the world. He's been around ballplayers for forty years. He'll levy a couple of fines and by May fifteen Allen Johnson will be waived out of the league, though that latter is not for publication."

A police car pulled up to the curb. The doors opened and two uniformed officers emerged and then a plainclothesman and a non-Hispanic woman, around whose shoulders the plainclothesman's arm was placed with great solicitude. The woman was obviously distraught; she had to be helped up the steps into the police station. Horace, in his chancy Spanish, asked one of the officers what it was all about. When he had his answer he turned to the newspapermen.

"Here's something for you newshounds," he said. "American woman. Seems her boyfriend, also an American, was found murdered in his hotel room."

"Not for me," the *Journal-American* man said, raising his hand and whistling down an approaching taxi. "I'm a sportswriter," he added, trotting out into the street. "You coming, Joe?"

"You go ahead," Tinker said. He looked back to Horace. "Who was it? Anybody interesting?"

"Not a ballplayer, thank God," Horace said. "The cop said he looked like he might have been a prizefighter."

After Horace had gone, a curious Tinker went back into the police station. He was soon joined by Oskar Torres, a local newspaperman who had been tipped off about the shooting. The son of a German merchant seaman (who had soon disappeared) and a Cuban woman (whose name he preferred), Oskar had done some stories on Robinson and had subsequently become acquainted with Tinker at the Montreal training camp.

"Her name is Irene Flagler," the bilingual Oskar told Tinker, after being briefly filled in by the plainclothesman. "From Connecticut. The man is—was—from New York. Elmer Cregar."

"Elmer Cregar?" Tinker said with some interest.

"Do you know him?"

"There was a middleweight by that name. Second-rate but tough, a crowd-pleaser."

"They say this fellow looked like a pugilist."

"Fancy word for it, Oskar."

"Does that mean my English is improving?"

"Deteriorating, I'd say. I suppose it's the same Elmer."

"How well did you know him?"

"Professionally, mostly, though I'd see him around here and there."

"Was he still active in the ring?"

"Not as far as I know," Tinker said. "He was mostly prewar. He had a couple of fights when he came out of the army, but that was it. I wonder what he was doing in Havana."

"Getting killed, mostly."

"What were the circumstances?"

"They were staying at the same hotel, the El Toro," Oskar said. "She said Cregar had been showing her around the city. Tonight he went out alone, just before the storm. She went to his room around ten-thirty or so, found the door open, went in and there he was, dead on the bathroom floor. Shot through the neck."

"They have any ideas?"

"Not really," Oskar said. "Not yet. It's possible a thief decided to take advantage of the blackout and broke into the room. That happens during the blackouts."

"And Elmer walked in on him . . ."

"No," Oskar said, dismissing the theory with his hand. "Your friend was not wearing a shirt. So the thief, if it was a thief, came in when your friend was already inside."

"Elmer would be just the type to go after him, gun or no gun. I think he had a screw loose."

"Screw loose?" a puzzled Oskar said.

"Loco," Tinker said, pleased to be able to use one of his few words of Spanish. He lifted his hand and twisted his wrist in a quick half circle. "Just a little bit."

"A small screw was loose," Oskar said, smiling.

"Small but important."

"Is this for you, you think?"

"Well, he was a boxer and I'm a sportswriter," Tinker said. "And it sure is a hell of a lot more interesting than watching Jackie Robinson pick up ground balls."

Assigned, along with a battery of other writers, to "the biggest story in sports," Tinker had been making frequent trips to the Montreal training camp to watch Robinson work himself into shape and get ready for the most momentous debut in big-league history, which everyone knew was inevitable.

Sometimes Tinker sat in the press box (in this case a row of chairs directly behind home plate, with a long wooden table set up for the writers' convenience), while at other times he wandered restlessly through the wooden grandstands, amused by the rapid-fire Spanish which he liked the sound of but did not understand. What he quickly did come to understand, however, was the mystique of Jackie Robinson: the black ballplayer had almost immediately gripped and mesmerized the Cubans, who made it clear that they saw Robinson as the spearhead who would finally make way for dark-skinned Cubans to get to the major leagues. Cheers and shouts and applause greeted Robinson's every move on the diamond, even during the blandness of infield workouts.

The hours burned away under the broiling tropical sun, and Tinker sat there, staring through the mesh screen behind home plate, watching the Montreal players at work, listening to the rhythmic chatter indigenous to every spring camp, his eyes instinctively but uninterestedly watching each fly ball as it was hoisted into the blinding blue sky.

This afternoon, to break the oppressive monotony, he moved from the press section and took a seat behind first base, ostensibly to have a better view of Robinson's work around the bag, but instead of watching Jackie he found himself staring curiously across the field at a man sitting in the last row behind third base. The man was wearing the only suit and tie in the ballpark, a white suit and a white hat, the pristine image broken only by sunglasses and a dark bow tie. Two things about him engaged Tinker's interest: the man was absolutely motionless, as if painted there, gazing steadily toward Robinson, eerily so, for—Tinker made special note of this—he did not even turn his head when one of the batting practice pitches was cracked far into the outfield, but kept his gaze riveted on Robinson. The longer Tinker studied him the more he began feeling there was something disturbingly familiar about him.

Tinker frowned, leaned back, spread his arms along the backs of the empty seats beside him, crossed his legs. *Now who the hell is that?* You met so many people, casually and otherwise. A good reporter was supposed to remember them all. And then lazily Tinker thought *the hell with him* and closed his eyes, thinking with a measure of perverse satisfaction *So I'm not a good reporter*, feeling drowsily detached in the sun's stifling concentration. He thought of a cool shower back at the hotel, maybe a nap, then a few drinks downstairs at the bar and then maybe a few hours of diversion at one of the houses. Some of the Dodgers had told him at the bar of the Nacional last night that he couldn't leave Havana without a visit to Belladonna's on Colon Street.

Tinker smiled, his eyes still closed, arms still extended along the backs of the seats. Return to his typewriter behind home plate, tap out a story about how Jackie was improving around first base, and then put the evening to good use. When he felt himself beginning to doze off he opened his eyes and looked out at the field. Robinson had gone in and somebody else was taking the throws at first base. As Tinker uncrossed his legs and leaned forward to rise, he noticed that the man in the white suit was gone.

23

On the morning after the episode at Belladonna's Tinker was standing on the balcony outside his third-floor hotel room. He hadn't got to sleep until 4 A.M. but nevertheless had risen at 9. The Dodgers were playing the Royals at El Gran Stadium that afternoon, a game Tinker was going to have to cover.

The Dodgers and Royals had already played several games, and Robinson's performances had been electrifying. It was Rickey's idea for the teams to play a series of games at El Gran, a stadium that held thirty-five thousand people, to generate income, to provide competition for the Dodgers, and for another reason—for the Dodgers who were opposed to Jackie to see just how good he was. The Old Man's reasoning was that when the grumblers realized that Jackie could put money in their pockets it would make no difference whether the hand of largesse was black or white or yellow or purple. Tinker, who had listened to the off-the-record comments from some of Robinson's antagonists, didn't think Jackie's talents would buy them off. Bigotry, it seemed, had within its morass certain principles that were not for sale.

Standing on the balcony with its wrought-iron railing, cigarette in hand, Tinker could feel the heat beginning to build. Not the merest oasis of cloud showed in a sky that looked burned into somber emptiness. The streets below were crowded, noisy. The sounds differed from those in New York and Chicago and other cities Tinker had known; here, voices seemed to dominate over engines and machinery. Peddlers and vendors called out the delectability of their wares, some of them ringing silver bells over their boards of sweetmeats and baskets of fresh fruit. One smiling, extravagantly mustached entrepreneur strolled among the crowds with an outstretched arm draped with dozens of colorful bandannas. Loungers at outdoor coffee stands gazed languidly into the milling crowds. Tinker stared into the distance, into the rising heat, sensing the lush, moist greenness of the surrounding suburbs.

Fuck, he thought. He didn't feel like covering a ball game. His cigarette had burned out in his fingers, and he looked at the corner of the balcony where a plant with leaves like cabbage grew from a small rusted tub, flipped the dead cigarette into it, and walked back into his room. He picked up the telephone and after rapping the receiver up and down several times finally raised the operator. He gave her the number of

Oskar Torres's newspaper, reciting the numbers in Spanish. He could count from one to ten in Spanish and was proud of this sliver of learning, refusing to allow it to languish.

"Oskar," Tinker said when the man got on the phone, "have you picked up anything further on that shooting?"

"Only small progress so far," Oskar said. "He was shot by a bullet from a Walther nine-millimeter thirty-eight automatic, a German gun, which I am told is a very powerful weapon."

"That's an odd one, isn't it?"

"The police tell me that a lot of odd ones have turned up since the war. Probably brought back as souvenirs."

"Anybody else been shot by that thing down here that they know of?"

"Not as far as they know," Oskar said. "Your friend has the honor of being the first. Also, it may interest you to know that they do not think this was a bungled robbery. For one thing, the petty thieves that prey upon these hotels generally are not violent; and for another—the clincher, as you might put it—your friend was carrying a considerable amount of money in his pockets."

"How much?"

Oskar laughed. "They wouldn't tell, because by the time this gets into the official reports that sum will have diminished to almost nothing. But from the quality of the innocent looks I got—"

"Innocent looks?" Tinker asked.

"Yes," Oskar said. "The policemen here look especially innocent when they are giving you a cock-and-bull story. From the innocence I saw I would guess the victim must have had on him some good money. Maybe a thousand dollars or more."

"How good are you at deciphering innocence?"

"Deciphering?"

"Figuring out," Tinker said.

"In this instance very good. A policeman that I know, who is an old friend, told me, strictly off the record, that it was around a thousand dollars, maybe a little more. But remember— you never heard that."

"That's some system you've got down here."

"Is it different in New York?"

"I suppose not, except that it's a little harder to look innocent up there. It would make people suspicious. Listen, Oskar," Tinker said, "I've got to go to goddamned Panama tomorrow. I trust you're going to stay on top of this."

"For a few days anyway."

"I may call you from Panama."

"It interests you, eh?"

"An American prizefighter gets shot in his Havana hotel room during a thunderstorm, yes, I'm interested."

"Maybe it was just a jealous husband," Oskar said, adding with a chuckle, "we have been known to have them in Havana."

"No," Tinker said, "I have a feeling there's more to it than that."

"Say, Joe, are you trying to get switched to crime reporting?"

"I'm thinking about it, Oskar old boy," Tinker said. "I am thinking about it."

At two o'clock that afternoon, when he should have been sitting in the press box at El Gran Stadium waiting for the game between the Brooklyn Dodgers and Montreal Royals to begin, Tinker was instead standing in the lobby of the El Toro, waiting for Irene Flagler. She had been neither pleased nor displeased when he called asking to see her, neither interested nor uninterested, agreeing with a note of philosophic resignation in her voice, as though she were somehow obligated. He supposed she had no experience with the press and didn't know how to put off an inquisitive reporter or even if she should. Because these people tended to regard the press as sort of a quasi-official agency and were therefore slightly intimidated, they generally were good interviews. Finessing the press was an art form that required much cultivation.

Irene Flagler still showed signs of the previous night's ordeal. What fading charms she might have possessed were further obscured by the vestiges of shock, sleeplessness, and the vaguely stricken look of suddenly vanished illusions. Her hair and face were plain; she looked rather dowdy, making Tinker wonder what a self-styled sharpie like Elmer had wanted with her.

"We met right over there," Irene said dispassionately, indicating the table near the window. "About ten days ago." She didn't look at the table again for the rest of the conversation.

"I apologize for intruding on your grief," Tinker said.

"Grief?" she said, puzzled.

"Well . . ."

"I hardly knew the man, Mr. Tinker."

"I see. Well, you see, since he was a prizefighter of some modest repute, I felt obligated . . ."

"A *prize*fighter?" she asked.

"You didn't know that?" Tinker asked, and seeing the distaste in her face, said to himself, *I guess not.*

"A prizefighter," she said quietly, without inflection, staring off into space for a moment, looking as though some final, ironic joke had been played on her. "My God."

"What did he tell you?"

"He told me," she said, looking back at him, "that he was a 'sportsman.' "

"Oh."

"He said he had seen lots of combat in the war, that he had been decorated in the Battle of the Bulge."

"That might have been true."

"I doubt it," she said curtly. "The Medal of Honor?"

"He said . . ."

"Yes."

Tinker sighed.

"Do you know what he was doing in Havana?" he asked.

"Preying on lonely women," she said tartly. Then she seemed to relent. "Oh, I suppose it wasn't entirely his fault. I was as much to blame." She lifted her cup of coffee and took several sips. "It was all some romantic fantasy. He was so . . . commanding. He seemed to know everyone. It was all so alluring. I guess the tropical climate does that to you. I'm not ashamed of it." She shrugged indifferently. "A little embarrassed maybe. I'll look back on it someday." She fixed Tinker with a momentary sharp stare. "I'm a widow. A year now. I was lonely."

"I understand. Pardon me for asking, Mrs. Flagler, but are you, shall we say, an affluent woman?"

"You think he was after me for my money?"

"I'm sorry."

"Well," she said, "he was. The illusions are gone and they have to be replaced by something, and I guess that has to be reality. Yes, Mr. Tinker, I am a well-heeled widow and Mr. Cregar was after my money. That's natural, isn't it?"

"A learning experience, Mrs. Flagler."

"That's a way of putting it. But I suppose those things start further back than we realize. I had to gather my courage to make this trip down here. The whole thing was unreal. I think perhaps I was a bit afraid of him. That was part of it. Women generally don't meet men they're afraid of, at least not where I come from. Where I come from everything is just ... so."

"And Elmer wasn't just ... so."

"Oh," she said with a self-mocking laugh, "he was many things, but that wasn't one of them." She drew a deep breath. "And because nothing was real I seemed to allow myself to go along with the unbelievable. When he went out last night—I was ill in bed—I lay there thinking, 'This is ridiculous. I'm not going to marry this man.'"

"Marry?" Tinker asked.

"I just wanted to go home. In fact, when I went to his room last night that's what I was going to tell him: that it had been very nice, et cetera, but that now I was going home. I wasn't looking forward to telling him, but I'd got my courage up."

"You didn't hear the shot?"

"There was a lot of thunder. And anyway, I'd been asleep."

"Was he planning to go back home with you?"

"Oh yes. He had it all worked out. He said something about having to stop off in New York to pick up some money that was going to be owed to him."

"'Was going' to be owed? Is that how he said it?"

"Yes."

"Then it wasn't already owed to him. I mean, he hadn't earned it yet."

"I guess not. It hardly matters now."

"Did he say what it was about, who was involved?"

"No. But I'm sure it was something shady. I really don't care. I just want to go home and remember what I choose to remember."

"You don't know where he went last night, who he was seeing?"

She shut her eyes for a moment and shook her head wearily. "I don't have the slightest idea."

"But you met some of his friends here."

"Oh, characters in casinos and cocktail lounges. I wouldn't say they were friends. He always had to say hello first. But Ernest Hemingway seemed to know him."

"Ernie knows all the ballplayers and fighters."

"'Ernie'?" she asked archly.

"I know him," Tinker said, smiling. "He says hello to a lot of people."

"Apparently," she said dryly.

24

Panama. March 1947.

The following day the Brooklyn Dodgers, the Montreal Royals, and an entourage of newspapermen boarded a plane for Panama, where the two clubs were scheduled to play a series of exhibition games. The Panama leg of Brooklyn's 1947 spring training was another of Branch Rickey's carefully plotted moves to get Jackie Robinson into the major leagues with as little controversy and resistance as possible. So far, most things had gone according to Rickey's hopes and expectations, but not all. For one, Robinson was leaving Havana in a sullen and irritable frame of mind, unhappy at having been segregated in that severely unappealing side-street hotel, and unhappy at being turned into a first baseman. Jackie had not been expecting the not inconsiderable burden of learning a new position to be added to everything else he was having to cope with. In response to a reporter's question about how his first baseman's mitt felt, Jackie had snapped, "I don't know. I've never had one on before, so I have no idea how it's supposed to feel." In addition, Jackie was struggling with stomach problems and a sore back. To some reporters, the player who had come to camp with a look of fierce pride and resolution now bore the mark of the stoic, a man enduring more than he was prevailing. Also to Rickey's disappointment, he had not heard the spontaneous clamor for Jackie's promotion to the team he had hoped would by now be coming from the Dodgers. Regarding Jackie, the big-leaguers had been either guardedly hostile or else noncommittal, a state of affairs that made the Old Man uneasy. Some newspapermen thought Rickey was beginning to lose his nerve, that trying to turn Robinson into a first baseman had all along been Rickey's safety hatch, a reason to say in good conscience that Jackie—who was less than artistic around the bag—had been given a chance and had failed.

But Robinson's reception in Panama was impressive. The Panamanians greeted him as a hero, his picture was on the front pages of the newspapers, large and enthusiastic crowds followed him to and from the ballpark, and when the Dodgers and Royals played separate games against a local team, the Royals and Robinson outdrew the big-leaguers by more than three to one. In Montreal's games against Brooklyn, Robinson, exhorted by Rickey, played spectacularly, hitting the big team's pitching for a better than .500 average, running the bases with a speed and daring that brought the crowds roaring to their feet, and forcing the New York writers to file stories filled with gales of adjectives.

Tinker was sitting alone at the hotel bar, drinking straight whiskeys and staring disapprovingly at his image in the backbar mirror. It was after midnight and the place was empty except for the bartender and two Panamanians who were sitting at a table in total silence. Despite the unfolding Robinson drama, with all its significance and mounting tensions, Tinker found himself brooding on the events in Havana. Another murder, he thought, though not as gripping as the first one, which he had heard so clearly on that November night. This time, however, he had known the victim, after a fashion. He had seen Elmer fight a few times, before the war and after, had watched him work out at Stillman's. Most third-raters were born to look that way, in their demeanor, posture, or facial expressions, and Elmer had been one of them. The cool adulator, the deferential smiler, the envious starer. Top dogs in their own neighborhoods, nothing when they went elsewhere.

There were no Elmer Cregar stories. On the flight from Havana Tinker had asked some of the other writers about the late middleweight and had heard nothing of substance. To one, who had covered the fights for a while, Elmer had been "a potato who became a mashed potato." Elmer's was mostly a prewar name, the definitive burial for mediocrities; the war was now a vast gulf in time and only the truly memorable had been able to leap over it and remain intact in reputation. The only interesting thing about Elmer Cregar seemed to be his violent departure.

A few hours earlier Tinker had reached Oskar Torres in Havana to see what progress had been made in investigating the shooting. There was this: Elmer had rented an automobile on the night of his death. About thirty miles showed on the odometer. Where he had gone no one knew. He had also rented a car about a week or so before, from the same place, and when the police made inquiries an attendant at the garage remembered the Americano asking for directions to the Cristoforo Hotel. This, Oskar said, was a third-rate establishment outside town and was the place, it so happened, where Robinson and the other black players had been staying. No one at the hotel, Oskar added, knew anything about Elmer; as far as anyone could tell, he had never set foot in the place. The police reasoning, Oskar said, was that Elmer had been using it as sort of a landmark, that he was actually going somewhere near there, since the hotel was the only place of any note in that area.

And another thing, Oskar said: the people who had been gathered in the lobby of the El Toro, Elmer's hotel, remembered a man passing through on his way out at approximately the time of the shooting. Because of the blackout and the candlelight, descriptions had been sparse, but it was generally agreed that the man, whom the desk clerk was certain had not been a guest, was thin, of medium height, and had been wearing a white hat, white suit, and, some people said, a dark bow tie. *My man from the ballpark*, Tinker thought as Oskar relayed the description. The man had spoken to no one, but had simply walked quickly through the lobby and out into the thunderstorm. The police were hoping to find him, Oskar said, but so far had had no success. *No*, Tinker thought. *All he has to do is change his suit.*

Tinker left the bar and went outside. The streets were quiet in the warm, balmy night. A few taxis were lined up at the end of the block, the white-shirted drivers collected around the front fender of the lead cab, talking among themselves.

Tinker spotted a familiar figure shambling toward him, hands in pockets, moving almost purposelessly under the palm trees that grew along the street.

"Hey, Joe," he said when he spotted Tinker.

It was Doggy Erwin, one of the Dodgers coaches, a broad-bellied man in his early fifties, stuck with one of those baseball nicknames of long-forgotten origin and unquestioned permanence.

Doggy was a big man, with a spray of close-cropped gray hair and large sad eyes that gave his fleshy, elongated face a wounded, long-suffering look.

"It ain't good, Joey boy," Doggy said, his thumbs hoisting his trousers up over his hard but roundly descending belly.

"What ain't good, Doggy?"

"You ain't heard?" the coach asked. He wiped his face for a moment with one of his enormous hands, a catcher's hands, one who had spent fourteen years in the minor leagues and six weeks in the majors.

"Now what?" Tinker asked with reluctant curiosity.

"This ain't for the papers."

"The good stuff never is."

"Shit," Doggy said, "I've been in baseball more than thirty years and never saw anything like it. Can you imagine, they got up a petition, trying to get guys to sign it."

"A petition for what?"

"To keep Robinson off the team."

"Who's behind it?"

"Ah, shit," Doggy said unhappily. "Walker. Dixie says he won't play with a colored guy."

"Meaning he expects Robinson to make the team."

"Of course Robinson's going to make the team," Doggy said with some emphasis, as if annoyed by Tinker's doubt. "You've seen the guy play ball."

"How many signed the petition?"

"I don't know. I suppose most of the Southern boys. Walker, Casey, Higbe."

"Reese?"

Doggy shook his head. "Pee Wee wouldn't touch it."

"Reiser?"

"Pete told him to stick it up his ass."

"That doesn't sound like too many guys are for it."

"There's others," Doggy said, "but they're afraid to speak out. You know how guys are. So it creates bad blood. Jesus Christ, Joe, is it worth it, to tear a club apart for the sake of one guy?"

"Normally, no," Tinker said. "Except this is no ordinary guy. Come on, you know that."

"I know that, I know that," Doggy said nervously, surveying the empty street. "But this club has a chance to win it all this year."

"And Robinson can help them do it."

"That's what Leo told them."

"Durocher knows?" Tinker asked.

"I'll say he knows," Doggy said. "He just had a meeting. I just come from it. He got everybody out of bed and hauled them into the kitchen behind the mess hall. You should have seen him."

"Leo?"

"In his pajamas and bathrobe. There's the Brooklyn Dodgers, standing around a kitchen in their bathrobes, and Leo letting them have it."

Tinker smiled, envisioning the scene. "What'd he say? Come on, Doggy."

"This ain't for the papers."

"Scout's honor. What'd he say?"

"He told 'em."

"Was Robinson there?"

"No, of course not."

"Rickey?"

"No," Doggy said. "He left it up to Leo. Now you and I know, Joe, that the Old Man can tell you something; but when it comes down to really *telling* you something and having it stay put forever, there's nobody like Leo. He let them know right here and now who's boss, who's managing this team, who's deciding who's playing. 'I don't care if a guy is yellow or black, or if he has stripes like a fuckin' zebra,' Leo says. He tells them again that he's the manager and if he says a guy plays, he plays. Then he tells them that Robinson is a great player and can put money in their pockets. Then he tells them to take their fuckin' petition and wipe their asses with it."

"Any back talk?"

"No back talk. End of meeting."

"What do you think?" Tinker asked.

"I don't know. What do you think?"

"You've got some hard-asses on the team," Tinker said. "They're not going to give up quietly."

"Leo'll get rid of them."

"I don't know. Rickey won't want to break up

the team, Robinson or no Robinson. They'll have to play together."

"You think they can?" Doggy asked hopefully.

"Why not? The guy doesn't have a disease. He's colored, that's all."

"But you know what some of those Southern boys think about that."

"They can think what they want. But if they have to, they'll play. That's my opinion."

"I hope you're right," the worried Doggy said, and sighed.

"You're part of the team, Doggy. What do you think?"

"I don't know," the baggy-looking coach said, shrugging. "I looked for reasons not to like it, but it comes down to I don't care one way or the other. Robinson's not a bad guy, and he can play. If he can help me get a Series share, then . . ."

"You don't care if he has stripes like a fuckin' zebra."

Doggy's sad, seasoned old face broke into a grin that made him look bashful. "Ain't he something, that Leo?"

"Doggy, my old pal of many a long train ride and many an empty bottle," Tinker said, laying a reassuring hand on the coach's shoulder, "it's going to be all right."

"But this ain't for the papers."

"Don't you worry," Tinker said. "I've got other things on my mind. Right now I'm trying to solve a murder."

"Good boy," Doggy said abstractedly. "Leave the serious stuff alone."

At four o'clock in the morning Tinker suddenly sat almost violently upright in bed. He sat there in the darkness, leaning back on his hands. Fifteen miles to the Cristoforo Hotel, fifteen miles back, he thought. Thirty miles on the odometer of Elmer's rented car. The police reasoning was, Oskar said, that Elmer must have been using the hotel as a landmark or reference point for where he was going. No, Tinker thought. He was going to that hotel, where Robinson was staying. Slowly, Tinker lay down again, his head sinking back into its own indentations on the pillow. Why? he asked himself. Why was Elmer going there?

"Howdy, Jack," Tinker said with a mischievous grin.

Robinson looked up from his breakfast in the hotel dining room.

"Can I join you?" Tinker asked, already pulling out a chair. Robinson watched him sit down and half fill a cup from the coffeepot on the table.

"You eaten yet?" Robinson asked.

"This is it," Tinker said, sipping the hot black coffee. "So," he said, putting the cup down. "I heard about the petition."

"Mr. Rickey asked me not to say anything

about it. So I'm not going to say anything about it."

Tinker had learned, in his short acquaintance with the man, that what Jackie said he meant, and that Jackie was too sharp and too tough-minded to be flattered or otherwise persuaded from his ground.

"Well," Tinker said, "I was asked not to write about it, and I'm not going to. Does that make a difference?"

"If you're not going to write about it, then why do you want to talk about it?"

"Just as a friend."

"I appreciate that," Robinson said. "But I think the less said about it the better."

"I can understand that. But this business doesn't make it any easier for you."

"It wasn't everybody."

"I know. I think you've got some friends on the team; they're just afraid to speak out, that's all."

"I'll say this much about it," Robinson said. "What bothered me was not so much those guys signing a petition—shit, I knew how they felt; I would have been surprised if they felt differently—what bothered me was the *fact* of the petition, that they would get it up and pass it around in broad daylight and try to get people to sign it. That they thought it was perfectly acceptable and legitimate. That's not thinking. That's an action without thought. Now—you want to talk baseball, I'll talk baseball."

"Well, in one respect the petition should have cheered you up—this is baseball," Tinker said quickly. "It proves that certain people fully expect you to make the team."

"I hope to make the team," Robinson said, "but that isn't my decision."

Tinker sat silently for several moments, then stared curiously across the table, studying Robinson. "You know, Jack," he said thoughtfully, "it's a hell of a thing. I mean, a petition to keep you out. It's a tough thing for me to understand; how you must feel, I mean."

Robinson showed a flicker of wry amusement.

"Am I being naive?" Tinker asked. "I mean, I've never had to face that."

"Well, Joe," Robinson said, "maybe you just haven't tried to get through the right doors yourself yet."

25

When they heard where he hailed from, the witty folk of the provinces would tell Tinker that New York was a nice place to visit but they wouldn't want to live there. Tinker's variant on this bit of social commentary was that New York was a great place to return to and a fascinating place to live.

"That's the crucial thing," he said, "arrival. That sets the tone. Your arrival has to raise the spirit, stir the imagination, and remind you of all that is noble and mighty."

"My God," Sally said, shaking her head. She was sitting at her dressing table, wearing pink panties and one of Tinker's white shirts. Her long white legs, almost arrogantly sensual, were crossed. She was holding a hand mirror and staring into it with an expression of studious disapproval.

"I'm serious," Tinker said. He was on the bed, his back straight up against the headboard, legs extended before him. He was wearing only his trousers, the ends of his belt lying apart. "The moment the plane touched down in New York I could feel ambition and creativity recharging themselves."

"And lust."

"Oh yes."

"Were you faithful to me in Havana?" she asked casually, bringing the mirror closer to her critically scrutinizing appraisal.

"Could I have done what I just did the past few hours if I hadn't been?"

"I don't know. You're pretty resourceful."

"What do you see in that mirror?"

"Me."

"There's something you should be eternally grateful for," he said.

"Which is?"

"Mirrors don't wear out."

"Are you being snide?" she asked mildly, lifting her chin a bit.

He reached over to the bedside table, shook loose a cigarette from the pack lying there, and put it in his mouth. Physically spent, erotically sated, he sighed, then struck a match and lit the cigarette.

"My parents are beginning to wonder about us," Sally said. "I went home last weekend."

"What did they say?"

"They didn't say anything; it was my kid sister. They'll speak through her. They're very discreet."

"Don't want to soil the conversation with anything sordid, eh?" he said. "So what did they say, through that conduit you call your sister?"

"They're just wondering, that's all." She had put down the mirror and with great delicacy begun applying nail polish.

"Whether we're sleeping together, or planning to get married, or what?" he asked, irritated by his own curiosity.

"Married?" she asked, passing him a glance of the utmost inscrutability.

"I used the word simply as part of my inquiry into your parents' speculations, as filtered through your sister."

"Mr. Tinker, when—if—the word 'marriage' ever seriously enters into one of our conversations I would prefer that it not come obliquely."

"Or discreetly. Or facetiously. Anyway, in my old neighborhood they never used that particular noun. You got 'hitched,' or 'roped,' or 'squandered.' "

"Squandered?"

"As in extravagant or wasteful expenditure of one's primary resource."

"Which is—?"

"His life, I guess," Tinker said with a huge, empty shrug. "I'm only telling you what other people said."

"Because you're a journalist, a person who lives by the principle of reporting without comment or opinion what other people say and do."

He knew she was only bantering, but still he felt constrained to say, "You make me sound like a robot. But I'm not. I've got plenty of comments and opinions." And all of them, it seemed, provoked by recent events. More and more he was understanding how urgent it was for Robinson to succeed, and not for the mundane reason that the team needed a good first baseman—to think *that* would have been sportswriting; to think of Robinson as merely a ballplayer would have been to trivialize and limit what the man was trying to do. And if he ever thought otherwise, Tinker had only to look out the window at that tenement across the street and think about what had not been just another random and meaningless New York City murder.

"It's going to be a hell of an Opening Day at Ebbets," he said.

"Because of Robinson."

"Anything could happen. That's the thing. There's a great unknown about it. The team could blow apart from dissension. Or there could be a violent reaction from a certain segment of the fans. Or it could all go smoothly, and there would be a sizable story in that, too."

"So who said sportswriting doesn't have its own vitality?" she said with a mischievous smile.

"Come on," he said, pointing toward the window, "*there's* the real world: murder on our doorstep. The real world is something that ob-

26

The opening of the 1947 major-league baseball season was just a few days away now and still no announcement had been made concerning the status of Jackie Robinson, though the writers covering the Dodgers were unanimous in their conviction that major-league baseball was soon to introduce its first black player.

The team had returned home and was preparing to play several exhibition games at Ebbets Field, first with Montreal and then with the Yankees, before opening the season on April 15.

Tinker was on the field at Ebbets watching the workout before one of the Montreal games when he received a message to call the paper. He didn't mind leaving the field—it was a raw, blustery day and he had been standing behind the batting cage, hands thrust down into the deep pockets of his trenchcoat, wondering when the happy medium between enervating Caribbean heat and a raw New York spring would descend.

He placed the call from a pay phone in the

runway outside the Dodgers' clubhouse. He asked
for Scott and waited for the editor to come on,
idly watching jacketed players walk to and from
the clubhouse. The door was painted with this
information and injunction:

DODGERS
CLUBHOUSE
KEEP OUT

One of the photographers had asked Robinson, in his Montreal uniform, to pose there,
and Jackie had, with one hand on the knob of
a partially open door. Tinker had appreciated
the picture's double dose of symbolism: the
open door and the KEEP OUT.

"Hello," Tinker said when his boss got on.

"Listen," Scott said, "go talk to somebody,
probably Horace Glickman. See if you can work
up a 'death threat' story. I hear Robinson's been
receiving them. He's been getting a two-man
police escort to and from the ballpark since the
club's been home."

"The team issued a general denial about these
things in Havana."

"I know. Nobody believed it but everybody
went along with it. But if he's still receiving
them—and I hear that he is—then let's find out
about it. See what you can do."

"All right," Tinker said. "I'll call you back."
Then he laughed and added, "Or Rickey will."

"Screw Rickey," Scott said. "He's not running this paper; we are."

" 'We,' Scotty?" Tinker asked chidingly.

"That's right, Joe. You and me." Scott hung up.

Tinker went upstairs, where he found Horace Glickman in a small, cramped office. Gray metal file cabinets stood against one wall, a wooden table covered with newspapers and thick manila folders against another. The wall behind Horace's desk was covered with framed pictures going back to Ebbets Field's opening in 1913. There were shots of the old club owner Charlie Ebbets in a derby and three-piece suit, as well as some of the architects of Brooklyn's baseball history: Nap Rucker, Zack Wheat, Dazzy Vance, Burleigh Grimes, Babe Herman, the longtime manager Wilbert Robinson, Van Lingle Mungo, along with various mayors and borough presidents and other forgotten politicos presenting plaques or scrolls or loving cups to hatless players at home plate with smirking teammates in the background. Leo was there, of course, and so were Whitlow Wyatt and Billy Herman and Dolph Camilli and Dixie Walker and Freddie Fitzsimmons and a 1941 shot of Pete Reiser and Pee Wee Reese looking like a couple of high school seniors.

Horace's jacket was on a hanger hooked onto a coatrack where also hung the homburg he sometimes affected. The Dodgers executive was buttoned snugly into his vest, buds of white shirt showing through. He was signing some papers when Tinker walked in and promptly asked the question that had brought him there.

"What death threats?" Horace asked, putting down his pen and leaning back in his swivel chair.

"Come on, Horace," Tinker said, "don't bull-shit me."

"You look very intimidating, Joe, standing there in your foreign correspondent's coat, collar up, cigarette dangling."

"It's cold out."

"It's going to be just as cold in here."

"We know he's been receiving death threats. How seriously are you taking them?"

"Any death threats would be a police matter."

"But they have been received."

"I'm not at liberty to say."

"Horace," Tinker said patiently, "people know about them."

"Not from me they don't."

"Why is Robinson getting a police escort to and from the ballpark?"

"To keep the autograph-seekers at bay."

"The Old Man has shut the lid on you, has he?"

"What you're asking about," Horace said, "is a police matter. Talk to them."

"And what are they going to tell me?" Tinker asked sarcastically. "That it's a club matter?"

"Joe," Horace said quietly, leaning forward and resting his arms on the desk, "can we talk off the record?"

"Oh, shit, Horace."

"I'm sorry, Joe."

"Horace, you can't bury something like this. Look, you—Rickey—started something with this. You knew it was going to be hot. I know the Old Man's been planning it, mapping it out step by step. But you can't expect us to sit back and let you pick and choose. We've been pretty damned sympathetic and supportive."

"Look, you guys have been writing what you felt, and it just so happens you've been sympathetic and supportive because that's what you've felt."

"That's bullshit, Horace, and you know it. You know how some of the writers really feel. Not many, but a few."

"I know that," Horace said on a note of quiet concession. "But overall there's been a sense of responsibility, if not at ground level then higher up. It's made it easier. We appreciate it."

"We sat on that goddamned petition story, to save your ball club from being torn apart."

"The Old Man was extremely grateful."

"It was different in Havana and Panama, Horace. We were a small group, away from all the noise. But this is New York. We've got editors on our asses, the competition is up again. Every cabdriver and bartender is asking us what's going on. In tropical cathouses nobody gave a shit. But we're back in business now."

"I understand, Joe," Horace said, leaning back again. "Believe me, this isn't adversarial, but you have your job to do and I have mine.

And if I were you, I wouldn't bother the Old Man now; he's under more pressure than you can believe, from the baseball hierarchy to city politicians to Harlem community leaders."

"I don't want to talk to him," Joe said. "He'll singsong me to death."

Horace smiled appreciatively.

"Look, Joe," he said placatingly, "this is a very volatile situation, an unprecedented one. We're trying to keep inflammatory stories out of the papers. That's everybody's best judgment—the Old Man's, the police, the mayor's office. Everybody's. The feeling is there are enough crackpots out there without giving ideas to any more of them. I'm sorry, Joe. Forgive me."

Tinker shook his head. He drew on his cigarette, exhaled, then crushed the stub out in the ashtray on the desk.

"So what do I write?" he asked.

"Whatever it is, you heard nothing from Horace Glickman."

"Christ, if there were death threats against the mayor it would be on every front page."

"I'm sure of that," Horace said.

"So?"

"The mayor," Horace said, "sits in his office all day and comes and goes in a limousine with a police escort."

"And Robinson stands out there every day in front of thousands of people," Tinker said.

Horace gave him a sad smile. "Vulnerability, Joe," he said.

*　　*　　*

"Horace Glickman says he doesn't know anything about any death threats," Tinker, back on the phone in the runway, told Scott.

"He's full of shit," Scott said.

"He says if—*if*—there were any, then it would be a police matter."

"In other words, they don't want it pursued."

"Those are the exact words."

"I'm afraid we can't let it sit, Joe," Scott said.

"They're worried about putting ideas into somebody's head."

"There's always a risk; but if we don't run with it, somebody else will."

"I don't like it," Tinker said, "but I agree with you. Why don't you let me start by going over to the local precinct and see what I can ferret out?"

"That's not your beat, Joe."

"What the fuck do you mean—'not my beat'? My beat is wherever the story leads."

"No, no, no, Joe," Scott said, irritation clearly in his voice. "I'm going to suggest that they put Tony Marino on it."

"Tony Marino?" Tinker shouted. "What the fuck does he know about it?"

"Tony knows how to talk to cops."

"Since when has that become an art form?"

"Joe, Tony's been working the station houses for years. This is right up his alley."

"Yeah, and right up your ass," Tinker said, slamming the phone down.

27

Well, then, the hell with them. This was Tinker's first lucid thought upon waking up after what he knew from the stubble on his chin had been a two-day bender. And he knew too that it evidently hadn't been a pleasant dive into the bottle because the ceiling was much further away—he was lying in blankets on the floor next to the bed, where Sally had undoubtedly pushed or placed him after losing patience with his slovenly boozing or his maudlin self-pity. Nevertheless, he awoke to a sense of the most adamant self-righteousness, lying there with the coarse khaki blanket drawn to his chin like a man stretched out in a barber's chair, so that all that showed of him was his face. He rolled his head on the pillow and morosely eyed the bed from which he had been banished for at least one night and probably two. Well, he would demand an apology for the indignity, he thought. She would come home that evening and glance at him without reprimand, maintaining the aloofness that the well-bred wear like a veil when they have been offended. Waiting for *him* to apologize. The well-bred set great store by apologies; he didn't know why, since generally there was more diplomacy than sincerity in those expressions. Well, shit, he had done nothing wrong except express his frustration and disappointment. People were entitled to do that. And he had—as far as he could remember—done it with style and discretion, getting drunk not in some public place but in the apartment, his home.

He threw off the blanket and sat up. The windup clock on the bureau told him it was noon. His throat was dry but he didn't feel a bit of hangover, which made him feel even more righteous. His head was clear, his stomach solid. Everything was defined: he was going to rise, shower, shave, change his clothes, eat a man-sized breakfast, and tend to his purpose. He wasn't sure he still had a job or a girlfriend, but he did have a purpose.

Captstone was a two-fare neighborhood; from Manhattan you had to take a subway and then a trolley car to get you out to that part of Queens, and since he was pursuing this story on his own and not for the paper, he did not have the luxury of speeding around the city in cabs. He took the IND subway to the Grant Avenue stop in Queens, then rode the Flushing-Ridgewood trolley up a long, almost imperceptible incline to Capstone, where he got off at Grant and Seventy-first Street.

It was a mild April afternoon and he was wearing a corduroy jacket and a white shirt open at the throat. Across the street on his left was a schoolyard demarcated by a high mesh fence, and as he walked along Seventy-first he watched with mild interest the softball game in progress there. He turned away to read the house numbers but then the sound of a well-hit ball compelled him to look back and he saw the ball rising into the air and knew immediately that it was going to clear the fence. The ball bounced once in the middle of the street and Tinker caught it easily on its descent. He never understood why they called them softballs; this oversized sphere—marked CLINCHER between its thick raised seams—was hard as a brick.

With the young players watching him and waiting for the return of the ball, Tinker swung his arm behind him and hurled it back over the fence; it came down near the pitcher's mound, evoking admiring cries of, "Thanks, mister! Nice throw, mister!" *Nice throw, your ass*, Tinker thought. Just a few weeks ago he'd been standing on the sidelines in Panama playing catch with Pete Reiser. Now *there* was an arm.

Just ahead, a letter carrier, big brown leather sack on his back, visored cap on his head, was coming away from one of the one-family houses, each fronted by a growth of hedges, that lined this side of the street. If Brooklyn was the Borough of Churches, Tinker thought, then Queens was the Borough of Hedges. They were to Queens what stone walls were to New England.

"Hey, buddy," Tinker called. The carrier paused. "Do you know where the Wilson house is?"

"Five doors up."

Tinker went on as the carrier turned between the gap in the next row of hedges and went to the front door, picked several from the spray of white envelopes in his hand, and pushed them through the slot.

There was a man standing outside Quentin's house but it certainly was not Quentin. The man was a two-tonner, with the circumference of a barrel. In the bright sunlight his bald head looked polished. He was wearing a plaid shirt that hung straight down; most short, fat men that Tinker knew wore their shirts that way, trying to conceal their girth. The man was at work on the hedges with a large pair of shears. He was smoking a cigar, upon his face what seemed like a permanent expression of abstract satisfaction.

"I'm looking for Quentin Wilson," Tinker said, coming up to him.

The man stopped his work, removed the cigar, and turned to Tinker. He had a slight wheeze.

"He's not home. I'm trimming the hedges for him."

"That's neighborly of you," Tinker said.

"I don't mind. Gives me something to do. I'm retired now. Thirty years I worked for the city."

"Do you know where he is?"

"Saw him go out about an hour ago. He just waved and off he went. You a friend of his?"

"Sort of."

"Well, I don't know when he'll be back. My name's Gustafson," the man said, replacing the cigar in his mouth and extending his hand to Tinker, who allowed its thick fleshy fingers to embrace his. "You want to leave a message?"

"I wanted to talk to him about Harry."

"Harry?" Gustafson asked, squinting the corner of one eye. "Ah, yes, Harry. That was a terrible thing. But policemen run those risks, don't they?"

"Quentin talk about it much?"

"What is there to talk about? It's all over and done with. They got who did it and that's that."

"You're probably right, but my editor sent me out to ask a few questions."

"Editor?"

"I'm a newspaperman, doing what we call a post-story story."

"I get it. What paper you with?"

"The *Mirror*," Tinker said, not knowing why he was lying, except that he wasn't sure if he was still with the *News*, especially when he was supposed to be sitting in Ebbets Field right now, covering the exhibition game with the Yankees.

"*Daily Mirror*, hah?" Gustafson was impressed. "I read the *News* myself," he said with a smile that made his round jowly face look benign. "But I pick up the *Mirror* in the barbershop. I like to read Walter Winchell."

"Me too," Tinker said. "Did you know Harry?"

"I knew the whole family. We've been neighbors since back when. But I didn't know Harry too well. But he was a hell of a guy. So's Quentin. He's a good boy. Brought me back a box of these for keeping an eye on things while he was away," Gustafson said, taking the chewed cigar from his mouth and showing it to Tinker. "Real Havanas. Right from the source."

Tinker maintained his composure.

"How'd he like Havana?" he asked.

"Well enough, I guess. Quentin doesn't say much. You know, bad times in the war, both parents dying while he was over there, then Harry. He's had his share."

"I guess he just needed to get away. Havana's the place for it."

"You been there?"

"Sure. Great place. I hope he took enough time to enjoy it."

"He had about four or five days."

"That'll do it," Tinker said, giving the man a knowing wink.

"I'll bet."

"When did he get back?"

"Oh, ten days or so ago. I wish he'd brought me more of these," Gustafson said, holding up the cigar once more. "I've been rationing them to myself. Nothing like 'em."

"If I go again I'll bring you back some."

"Haha," Gustafson said cheerfully. "You won't."

"So you don't know when he'll be back?"

"No idea," Gustafson said, resuming his work on the hedges, parting the large shears and clipping carefully. "I'll tell him you were by."

As he walked back down the street Tinker felt his mind running with excitement. The moment Gustafson had mentioned Quentin and Havana the image had returned: the man sitting as if painted into the grandstand watching the Montreal workout on that hot afternoon. *I knew I'd seen him before. It was that son of a bitch. What the fuck was he doing there?* And Tinker was already certain that it was the same man who had been seen hurrying through the lobby of the El Toro after Elmer had been shot.

When he reached Grant Avenue Tinker turned left, then left again at the next corner, and began walking along Seventy-second Place, which ran parallel with Seventy-first Street. He walked with slow, measured steps, his mind seeking reasons, connections. A tantalizing, illogical puzzle lay before him: Elmer Cregar had been in Havana, had taken drives (it seemed) to the hotel where Robinson was staying. Quentin had been in Havana and (so it seemed) had shot Elmer. Did it make any sense? No. Was he perhaps fantasizing a bit much? Maybe.

The houses on this side of the street were built backyard to backyard with those on Seventy-first. By looking through the alleys, just wide enough for an automobile, Tinker could see through to the other street and determine how close he was getting to aligning with Quentin's house.

What in God's name, Tinker asked himself, could Quentin Wilson have to do with Elmer Cregar? Perhaps Quentin had met the fighter through Harry, who, as a highly decorated New York City detective (and former star athlete) had gone crossroads with a lot of different people. But what possible reason would Quentin have had for going to Havana and shooting Elmer? Tinker thought of the woman, Irene Flagler. But then, uncharitably, he told himself she was not a woman for whom men would murder. And anyway, in their conversation, she had never mentioned Quentin. But what had she said—something about Elmer going to New York to pick up some money that *was going* to be owed him. By whom and for what? Whatever had happened, and whoever was involved, Elmer had not fulfilled his part of the bargain and for his negligence been given the last salute.

Or am I thinking too much? Tinker asked himself, gazing into each alley as he passed it, watching for the alignment with Quentin's house. When he reached that point he stopped. He was standing in front of a frame house with a small balustraded front porch. He took note of the old wooden building across the street, a onetime public school, according to the "PS 73" carved over the front door, but now the station house of the 112th Precinct. Great, Tinker thought, they won't have far to drag me if I get caught. At least he would have a good story to tell them—that he believed the occupant of the house had murdered a man in Havana and that he, Tinker, was trying to find some evidence to prove it. *Evidence. What a noble and lethal word. Tony Marino got to use it all the time.* But did it excuse breaking and entering?

Shit, Joseph, he admonished himself, you're getting cold feet. Don't be looking for a reason not to do something when there is every reason *to* do it. And if the worst happens, Tinker thought, if that son of a bitch comes in while I'm there, I'll knock him on his ass and take off. And if the hedge-clipper next door tells his story, then let them go looking for me at the *Mirror.*

Still he hesitated. Then he thought: a sportswriter. Stamped and labeled. Launched from a shore to which he could never return. Not allowed to go and talk to the police about death threats. Doomed forever to write about the antics of the toy department. Well, to hell with that. If you are really other than what you seem to be, Tinker told himself, prove it. Now.

He walked into the alley, keeping close to the side of the house. Passing under the kitchen window, which was about a foot above his head, he heard a radio broadcasting a late-afternoon soap opera. Then he was past the house, taking long, full, self-conscious strides across the yard, toward the tall hedge that separated this house from Quentin's. He pushed his way into the hedge, turning his shoulder against the stiff but pliant branches and using his weight. There was some mild, crackling resistance and then he was through to the other side.

Quentin's backyard was empty, with barren patches in the dead brown grass. A pole about the height of an average man stood near the closed garage, a clothesline running from it to a sturdy hook embedded in the wall of the house. The cellar doors, slanted up from the ground, were closed and padlocked. There were two ground-level basement windows. He knelt before one and tried to hoist it, but it wouldn't give. Finding the other also locked, he looked around; except for the upstairs windows of several houses opposite, he was fairly well concealed. He wondered how much noise this was going to make. Removing his handkerchief from his pocket, he wound it around his knuckles and then punched firmly into the glass above the lock, listening to it shatter softly on the basement floor. Then, with some effort, he turned the rusted lock and lifted the window. Going feet first, his hands holding the raised window for balance and support, he eased himself through, flexed his knees to prepare for the brief drop into the darkness, and let go. He landed in a crouch.

Frozen in that position, he waited for several moments, contemplating the silence of a strange house, and as it continued unbroken he slowly stood erect, feeling momentarily the gall of what he was doing, the guilt of transgression, and most of all a flutter of apprehension. *Pack it away*, he told himself, recalling the words of a tough sergeant addressing a small, uneasy patrol he was about to lead into the jungles of Guadalcanal. Tinker struck a match and followed its faint, flaring light through the nearly empty basement toward a narrow rise of steps, which he began mounting as the match went out. One hand on the banister, he moved so softly and soundlessly he felt as though he were floating, his eyes fixed upon the sliver of daylight under the door at the head of the stairs.

When he reached the door he paused for several moments, considering the quality of the silence beyond. There was a sense of pent-up stillness, of closed windows, of noiseless passage from room to room. Then he turned the knob until the door parted from the wall, opening it just far enough to enable him to slip through into the corridor.

Keeping away from the windows, Tinker merely peeped from a distance into the living room, seeing nothing but furniture and carpet. The dining room was similarly unrevealing, merely a table and four neatly arranged high-backed chairs, looking poised and ghost-ridden. A glance into the kitchen told him that here was where meals were taken: a cup and saucer stood on the oilcloth-covered table, unwashed dishes in the sink, a soiled dish towel hanging over the back of a chair.

He returned to the corridor and mounted the staircase to the second floor. Again a leaden stillness pervaded. One bedroom was completely empty of furniture; the other, at the rear of the house, looked lived-in. The bed was unmade. Clothes lay on the floor and on the seat of an upholstered chair. Tinker recognized the face of Harry Wilson in a framed eight-by-ten photograph on the bureau, the haircut and the cut of the suit dating it back at least twenty years. A golf bag was tilted against the wall in one corner, containing not golf clubs but a half dozen baseball bats—they looked brand-new to Tinker—and, looking lethal amid its innocuous neighbors, a rifle, standing barrel up. Fingertips to chin, Tinker stared curiously at the rifle. Then he went to the closet and opened the door.

The first thing he saw in the closet brought a wry smile to his lips: a white Panama hat on the shelf. *Yeah*, he thought. And the white suit was there, too, jacket and trousers on a single hanger, standing out among the darker clothing around it.

He swung the closet door shut and was turning to leave when he saw the pictures on the floor; each one was of Robinson in one pose or another. They had been clipped from newspapers and magazines, and one Tinker recognized from a recent coloroto section of the Sunday *News*. Tinker crouched and studied them, pained revulsion filling his face. Each picture had in one way or another been mutilated, one with what looked like knife cuts to the face. They had been torn, crumpled, slashed, ground underfoot. *What the hell is going on here?*

Tinker pulled open the bureau drawers, found nothing of interest, and eased each shut again. He stared again at the pictures, then again at the golf bag with its incongruous burden of bats and rifle. It wasn't apprehension but a sense of eeriness that made him want to get out of there. He went quickly downstairs, then back to the basement, shutting the door behind him and going carefully down the stairs. He crossed the dark basement and returned to his point of entry. Reaching up and placing his palms on the sill, he thrust himself up through the window and crawled back to daylight, thinking with whimsical satisfaction that the much bulkier Tony Marino wouldn't have been able to manage these modest gymnastics. He glanced around, then pushed down the broken window. With long, stiff-legged strides, looking like a man trying to hurry with decorum from an awkward scene, he crossed the yard, pressed himself through the hedges, and passed along the alley to the street.

Two uniformed policemen were coming down

the tall, broad wooden stairs of the station house across the street. Tinker contemplated them. *I could tell them*, he thought.

There's a guy over there I think is planning to shoot somebody.

How do you know?

I just broke into his house and saw some pretty hot circumstantial evidence.

Sally was sitting in the living room sipping brandy when he walked in.

"Call Scott," she said. "He's already called three times. He sounded edgy."

The phone rang.

"I think he's now called four times," Tinker said, picking up the receiver.

"You're suspended," Scott said bluntly.

"Some salutation," Tinker said. "Why?"

"You know why. You were supposed to be in Ebbets Field this afternoon."

"Oh, shit, Scotty," Tinker said. "So I missed a goddamned exhibition game."

"You also missed something else. In the sixth inning a release was passed around the press box. You want to know what it said, Joe?"

Tinker said nothing.

"I'll read it to you," Scott said. " 'The Brooklyn Dodgers today purchased the contract of Jackie Roosevelt Robinson from the Montreal Royals.' "

28

When the rain finally stopped on that stormy night in Havana, Quentin, who had returned to his hotel and changed out of his soaked white suit, left his room and went downstairs. Ignoring the cabdrivers who began calling to him the moment he emerged from the hotel, he began walking with what he hoped was inconspicuous haste. The humid air felt like a warm, damp cloth. After a few minutes he began perspiring.

The narrow, winding, stone-paved streets kept feeding into plazas, where empty white benches encircled gardens and fountains. Crossing one of the deserted plazas, he found himself being observed by a pair of muscular garrison-capped policemen who were standing, legs apart, on a corner, tapping thick clubs into their palms. He glanced at them and kept moving. The police in this city made him nervous; he had only been here a few days but had taken note of them. After all, he knew something about that profession. He could sense a meanness within these cops, a hostility born out of power, and a barely concealed eagerness to demonstrate it.

Turning a corner, he faded into a narrow side street that was lined with darkened two- and three-story houses with small balconies. The cobblestoned street rose in the middle, as though there were a divide underneath, tilting the few parked cars against the curbs. Where the night seemed darkest he stopped, unbuttoned his suit jacket, and pulled the P-38 from his belt. He raised his chin, the corners of his eyes twitching for a moment. He did not turn around; at the moment his senses were so acute that had anyone been near, he would have known. He dropped the gun against the curb, where thin rivulets of rainwater were running into the sewer. He looked down at the gun for several moments, and then with the toe of his shoe nudged it through the mouth of the sewer and heard it being gulped by the water. Then he turned and began walking back to his hotel.

Quentin returned to New York two days later, feeling cold and dispassionate about what he had realized he was going to do. That first day home he sat upstairs in his bedroom with the yellow window shade drawn to the sill, and when night fell he remained motionless, sitting in the upholstered chair, legs crossed, hands folded over his belt buckle. He could feel the darkness filling up the house as though it were an actual substance emitted by the night. He felt a deep serenity, a transfiguring calm. He believed it had begun taking possession of him almost the moment he left Elmer's room, as though with the discharge of those bullets he had rid himself of all the bitterness and tension of the previous several months, clearing the way for this untroubled and visionary contemplation.

It was as if the plan were being woven in and of the darkness, filtering into him fully shaped, building into its finished design, each feature of which he pondered and then accepted, each given sanction by the almost ceremonial darkness. Occasionally he nodded and allowed a faint, listless smile.

When the subtle arch of dawn began to rise behind the shade, he rose from the chair, removed his shoes and lay down on the bed, and, comforted by the immense calm he felt, fell into deep, dreamless sleep.

The following afternoon he was in a Manhattan gun shop selecting a rifle, for deer, he told the salesman. He came away with a Winchester, the original Model 54, which in 1937 had been slightly modified and renamed Model 70. It was, the salesman said, the best American bolt-action deer-hunting arm. Light and short, it was quickly brought to action—quick as a six-shooter, the salesman said, with a trigger pull of about six pounds. The weapon, Quentin was told, delivered powerful, telling blows. Quentin left the store with the packaged rifle, with bullets, and with the salesman's cheery good wishes for good hunting.

At dawn on a Sunday morning several days later, Quentin left his house carrying the rifle, in its original packaging, and walked to the corner and there in the gray, chill break of day waited for the Flushing-Ridgewood trolley car. Boarding it (he was the only passenger), he dropped a nickel into the fare slot and took his seat. He rode the trolley to the end of the line, the rifle across his knees. At the Ridgewood terminus he got off and boarded the Myrtle Avenue trolley, riding it through Glendale and Richmond Hill, passing through the Sunday-morning emptiness of those tidy working-class neighborhoods.

At the corner of Myrtle Avenue and Woodhaven Boulevard he got off the trolley and headed into the large, heavily wooded expanse of Forest Park, a sprawling 540-acre area of baseball diamonds, ponds, playgrounds, picnic grounds, and hiking paths, and which also included a carousel and wading pool. *Harry took me here*, he thought, remembering his older brother and outings on hot summer days long ago, Harry always so gently protective, the perfect older brother.

He walked deeper into the cool, silent park, dappled by the sharply defined shadows cast by the rising sun. Entering a hollow created by the gentle slope of tree-lined embankments, he went to a young maple and put the rifle down. He drew from his pocket a square of blank paper and several long, thin nails. He nailed the piece of paper to the tree, driving the nails in with a rock, then retreated several hundred feet with the rifle, which he unwrapped and loaded.

He fired six times, absorbing the recoil with comfort, the reports booming out and echoing off through the park. He repackaged the rifle and returned to the tree. He smirked at the sight of five lethal hits, recalling with satisfaction an acerbic platoon sergeant in basic training: *You're not worth shit, Wilson, but you can shoot.* Then he pulled the torn-apart piece of paper from the tree, crumpled it in his fist, and with a contemptuous sideways gesture tossed it away.

The next day, he rode the trolley car to the end of the line in Flushing, where he got off and joined Main Street's throng of afternoon shoppers. He entered a large sporting goods store near the RKO theater. Like many of its kind, the store had opened and begun thriving with the end of the war. The lighting was bright, the shelves filled, the aisles crowded. A chubby, red-cheeked man in shirtsleeves approached Quentin. A plastic card reading "HI I'M BILL" was hooked onto his breast pocket.

"I need a golf bag," Quentin said before the salesman could speak.

"What about clubs?" Hi I'm Bill asked.

"I'll tell you what I need," Quentin said, "when I need it."

What he needed was not golf clubs but a half dozen Louisville Sluggers, and though Hi I'm Bill had several quips in mind for a man who was buying a golf bag and baseball bats, he thought better about delivering them, warned off by his customer's expressionless face.

Burdened now with his cumbersome purchase, Quentin left and went several blocks to another sporting goods store, this one smaller, more specialized. Entering, Quentin headed for the rear of the place, guided by the sign that said "SPORTING APPAREL." Here, on a pipe rack, he found what he was looking for—a Brooklyn Dodgers warm-up jacket, blue, with "DODGERS" in white script across the front. Removing his windbreaker, Quentin tried on one of the jackets, shrugging his shoulders into it as he stood before a full-length mirror. He zipped it up, then groomed himself with his hands. Elastic-cinched at the wrists and waist, the jacket fit well.

"That's what they wear," said a porky, broad-beamed, plaid-shirted salesman, walking over.

"I know," Quentin said, studying himself in the mirror. "You got the cap to go with it?"

"We got everything," the salesman said. "With that jacket and a cap and a ticket you can get into Ebbets Field."

"Save the jokes for the next guy," Quentin said.

The following day he rode first the Grant Avenue trolley and then the De Kalb Avenue and went out to Ebbets Field, where he waited on line at the advance-sale ticket window. Sullenly, he took note of the many blacks who were waiting to buy tickets; he had never seen this many on a ticket line before, and they were laughing and joking. He was offended at how comfortable and at their ease they were. Some of them had large round buttons pinned to their clothing that proclaimed "I'M FOR JACKIE." He could hear some of them, reaching the window, asking the ticket seller if "Jackie" would be playing on Opening Day. It made him compress his lips. *They don't know a goddamned thing about baseball.* They would be coming out here all summer, filling the place up, screaming for the one player. *Killing baseball for the rest of us. Taking it away from us.* If they knew anything, if they read the sports pages with any degree of understanding, they wouldn't have had to ask the question. The stories that came out of Panama had made it a certainty: Robinson was going to be in the Opening Day lineup. The promotion to the Dodgers was now a mere formality, and whatever Rickey thought he was accomplishing by delaying it, he certainly wasn't fooling anybody. *Sure*, Quentin thought, listening to the laughter and the restless excitement around him, *be here on Opening Day. You don't want to miss it.*

When he had his ticket in his pocket, he went to Bedford Avenue and walked along close to the tall, screen-topped structure that was Ebbets Field's right-field wall. He kept his eyes riveted on that wall, and when he finally saw what he wanted to see, he smiled almost lasciviously.

29

Tinker called Robinson at the Hotel McAlpin on the night before Opening Day.

"I'd rather not see anybody tonight, Joe," Robinson said. "Tomorrow is going to be hectic and I'm a bit on edge. I think you can understand."

"This is not about an interview," Tinker said. He was calling from a cigar store just off Herald Square, a few blocks from the McAlpin. "This has got nothing to do with the paper."

"It can't wait?" Robinson asked, sounding both curious and wary.

"No."

"Where are you?"

"I can be there in a few minutes."

"All right," Robinson said, lowering his voice. "I'll meet you in the lobby."

When Tinker came through the McAlpin's front door a few minutes later he found Robinson standing right there, waiting for him, and Jackie picked up the conversation where they had left off as though there had been no hiatus.

"My wife's trying to get the baby settled down," he said. "I don't know what you want, but from the sound of it, it's probably something she's better off not hearing."

They moved to a quiet corner of the lobby and sat on a sofa.

"You said it wasn't newspaper business," Robinson said. He was wearing a sport jacket over a tieless white shirt. There was, as ever, a poised tension in his muscular bulk, a kind of guardedness.

"No," Tinker said, "I don't have any newspaper business at the moment. I've been suspended."

"Why?"

"Because I'm a fuck-up. But listen, I'll tell you why I'm here. I want to know about the threats against you."

Robinson's eyes narrowed. "Why?"

"I want to make sure they're being taken seriously."

Robinson stared at him.

"Look," Tinker said, "don't give me any smoke-screen bullshit about this."

"Do you know something, Joe?"

"I suspect something. I can't prove a god-damned thing. Look, I'm not here to get a story; I'm here because I'm concerned. You've been getting poison-pen letters, haven't you?"

"For a long time."

"And what have you been doing with them?"

"Handing them over to Mr. Rickey, who's

been in very close consultation with the police. It's being taken seriously, I assure you, Joe."

"Will they have enough security out there tomorrow?"

"They had plenty today."

"I'm sorry, Jack," Tinker said. "I hate to alarm you."

"I've been alarmed for a long time," Robinson said, smiling.

"In Havana?"

Robinson frowned. "Why?"

"Just a hunch of mine," Tinker said, trying to read Robinson's face. "You ever feel threatened there? Given your situation, you must have been extremely sensitive to what was going on around you. With strangers, I mean."

Robinson was staring frankly at Tinker, tongue in cheek, apparently in thoughtful recollection.

"Ever see anybody around who you didn't quite trust?" Tinker asked. "Somebody who may have seemed suspicious?"

"I was followed one night," Robinson said. "It was probably nothing."

"But you remember it."

"I'd left the hotel after dinner to take a walk. There was nobody around. We were out in the sticks. But then there was this guy following me."

"You sure?"

"I had the feeling—I remember having the

feeling—that he was following me. There was something strange about it."

"Did you get a look at him?"

"It was dark, just a bit of moonlight. He never really got close."

"But you felt uneasy?"

"Yes."

"Was he a white man?"

"Yes. But I can't tell you anything about him. When I stopped, he stopped. We just stared at each other, maybe a hundred feet or so apart. That's when the moon broke out of the clouds. Then I went on and that was the last of him."

Tinker had been in the *Daily News* morgue that morning, and now he pulled a small glossy from his jacket pocket. It was a prewar photo of middleweight Elmer Cregar, taken just after a weigh-in. The trimly muscled boxer was standing and facing the camera, wearing boxing trunks, arms at his sides. Tinker handed the photo to Robinson, who studied it for several moments.

"My glimpse of the guy isn't much to go on," he said. "I would say there's a definite similarity in build."

"It could possibly be the same man?"

"No more than possibly. Who is he?"

"That's the late Elmer Cregar. He was a so-so club fighter before the war."

"And?"

"He was shot in Havana, a day or so before the teams went to Panama."

"What has that got to do with me?"

"Maybe nothing," Tinker said, returning the picture to his pocket.

"Joe, they've assured me that all possible measures are being taken. I believe them. I trust Mr. Rickey. We've been living with this thing since the first day I signed with Montreal."

"I know," Tinker said. "I know you've come a long way. I just want to make sure they're covering all possibilities."

"I appreciate your concern," Robinson said, getting up. "And the fact that you came around."

Tinker rose and they shook hands.

"Anyway," Tinker said, "good luck out there tomorrow."

"Are you hoping I get some hits or that I simply live through it?"

"Both," Tinker said.

30

They hung the bunting early on the morning of Opening Day, draping the ceremonial worsted decorations on the field-level boxes and along the grandstand façades all around the park, laying on the pomp baseball liked to apply to its grand occasions like the World Series, the All-Star Game, and Opening Day. The white foul lines looked electrically bright as they extended out from their points of origin at home plate and went their eternally separate ways, creating the formal boundaries within which baseball was played. There was a crispness to the green grass of springtime, a venerable serenity to the clean white bases settled at their perfect ninety-foot intervals, a quiet authority within the modest hump of earth that formed the pitcher's mound. It was all up and ready, fresh and unspoiled.

Ebbets Field was festive and noisy, with a running undercurrent of tension and excitement. Over twenty-five thousand fans were there to observe, celebrate, and participate in the most momentous Opening Day in the game's history, an event that was not without an element of the mysterious, for today the noble old game of custom and tradition was receiving into its ranks what seemed almost a new species of player, who was about to force a permanent and significant change.

In the crowded press box the writers were searching for phrases with which to conjoin baseball and history. The photographers had already captured the new man sitting in his Brooklyn uniform in the dugout, signing autographs for youngsters who had crawled across the dugout roof and dangled upside down to get their scorecards to him before the ushers came to pull them back. The new man kept looking up at the young faces hanging down as the boys called to him, and kept getting up and signing and sitting back down again as his bemused and curious teammates looked on, and everyone waited for the game to begin, for the schedule to start running, and for the new man to start making history.

The normal Opening Day chatter and badinage had been absent in the Dodgers' clubhouse as the players dressed and got ready for the game. Some had come over to Robinson and shaken his hand and wished him luck, while others, astir with certain ambiguities, had gone about their preparations with a curious solitude, as if trying to slip out from under the significance of the day. None, whatever his response or nonresponse, was immune to the moment.

They had entered the clubhouse one by one or in twos and threes, and began shedding their jackets and slacks and putting on the uniform that piece by piece transformed them into baseball players. A disparate group of young men from the country wide began slowly to cohere into the pride of a borough, became the Brooklyn Dodgers. As each uniform went on, as each shirtfront was zipped up to unite the word *Dodgers* scripted across it, Jackie Robinson became more and more a part of the team.

Throughout the stands, white-jacketed vendors were selling the ballpark staples—peanuts, hot dogs, ice cream, soft drinks—along with miniature Dodgers pennants attached to thin, limber sticks, and scorecards and stubs of yellow pencil and "I'M FOR JACKIE" buttons that varied in size from a half dollar to a small saucer.

They—the black fans—had begun cheering at Robinson's first appearance and had continued applauding and shouting while Brooklyn's rookie first baseman took batting practice and then infield, snapping the ball back and forth in concert with catcher Bruce Edwards, second baseman Eddie Stanky, shortstop Pee Wee Reese, and third baseman Spider Jorgensen, in a spirited exercise that seemed as much theatrical as it was functional.

Upstairs, in his Ebbets Field office, Branch

Rickey sat alone, the door closed. He was listening to the restive pregame murmur from the crowded grandstands, a sound he knew so well but which today came to him differently, as though it were a hymn gathering toward crescendo. With myriad things to do, with people to talk to, the Old Man had sought out these few reflective, pensive moments to sit alone, puff on his cigar, gaze into the thin air of memories, accept the burdens of time spent, and feel the lonely grandeur of a long journey toward a bright beginning. Branch Rickey had lived too many years and worked too hard not to feel the almost palpable aura of history, of something simple in its nobility working itself into its rightful place. Along with his gratifying sense of accomplishment, Rickey also felt a touch of weariness and concern, for he knew that so much that he had mapped and designed and calculated was today passing from his control, that what he had set in motion was today beginning a life of its own, that the purity of his dream was now being delivered to the whim of events and the actions of other men. The melancholy was understandable, the Old Man knew, and he allowed himself a few peaceful drafts of it before resummoning his strength and resolve, for not even he could know whether the worst was over or yet to come.

Tinker wasn't sure—not of what he was doing, what he was looking for, or what he would do

if he found it. There was no point in going to
the press box, since he wasn't going to be covering the game, nor did he visit the Dodgers'
clubhouse, since that also would have been
pointless. For a time he stood in the rotunda
and watched the fans pouring through the turnstiles and heading up the ramps to their seats.
He stared at faces—there were so many of them
it was dizzying, and they moved by so fast—
telling himself he was looking for some absurd
disguise or some suspicious parcel being carried
into Ebbets Field. He felt maddeningly isolated
amid the swelling excitement of Opening Day
1947 and the debut of Jackie Robinson. He
watched the young and the old, the families, the
well-dressed and the casual, the bright-faced
truants, all of them hurrying past him in a festive tide of humanity.

Later, he roamed the lower stands and the
mezzanine behind first base and then behind
third, trying to scrutinize every face, feeling
more and more frustrated by his helplessness.
Ushers asked him for his ticket and he went on,
up aisles and down aisles, feeling increasingly
thwarted, listening to the crack of batting-
practice line drives and the voices of a swelling
crowd of thousands gathering for the excitement and the innocence of a baseball game.

His anxiety received temporary surcease
when the Dodgers left the field and the visiting
Boston Braves took it over for their pregame
workout. Tinker saw his fellow journalists

standing behind the batting cage talking to the Boston players, getting stories, comments, reactions.

Feeling irritated, hopeless, even foolish, he left the grandstand and made his way down the ramp toward the clubhouses. His press card got him through the guarded wire-mesh door that led to the dirt-surfaced runway below the stands. He frankly didn't know why he was there, what he could find, even what he was looking for. Perhaps he might have a word or two with Robinson, thinking ironically, *Sure, maybe the intended victim can give me some peace of mind.*

That was when he saw the short, baggy-trousered park attendant walking through the cool, shadowed runway, dragging behind him through the dirt the golf bag with several bat handles protruding.

"Hey!" Tinker shouted as the man approached him. "What the hell have you got there?"

The man kept coming, pulling his burden after him by the golf bag's leather strap, stopping when he had come face to face with Tinker.

"Do you believe this?" the man said irritably. "One of our guys found it in one of the shithouses upstairs."

"Who does it belong to?" Tinker demanded.

"Who the hell knows? Can you imagine some damn fool bringing this in and then forgetting it?"

"Oh, shit," Tinker said, lifting out several of the bats and looking into the bag.

"What's the matter?" the man asked. "You know something about it?"

"When did they find it?"

"Why?"

Tinker bunched his fingers on the man's shirt front and jerked him forward.

"When did they find it?"

The man shook free and stepped back, scowling.

"This morning," he said.

"Before the park opened?"

"Yeah, yeah, before the fuckin' park opened."

"Where's Horace Glickman? Have you seen him?"

"He was just outside the clubhouse."

Tinker began running. *He's in the park*, he thought. *Oh Jesus H. Christ, he's in the park*.

Horace was standing at the door of the Dodgers' clubhouse, a sheaf of papers in hand, giving instructions to several front-office people.

"Horace," Tinker said, hurrying to him and taking him by the arm and gently but firmly pulling him aside.

"What's your problem, Joe?" Horace asked impatiently. "I know I've got mine."

"How good is your security?"

"What do you mean?"

"You fuckin' well know what I mean. I think there's a crackpot loose somewhere, probably with a rifle."

"Joe, a guy doesn't just walk into Ebbets Field with a rifle."

"Well, he did."

"How sure are you of this?"

"Pretty goddamned sure. I'm asking you—how good is your security?"

"It's as tight as we can make it."

"Where would he shoot from?"

"I can almost guarantee you nobody will be able to walk around this park with a rifle. Not today."

"Where would he shoot from, Horace?"

"Joe," Horace said, lowering his voice, "we've had the best people in the business in on this, from the NYPD to private consultants. We've got our own specials and we've got plainclothes cops scattered through every section from the boxes to the bleachers. We've got guys on the roof of the park and guys on the rooftops across the street. There's no way, Joe, just no way."

"There's a guy in this park with a rifle."

"How did he get it in?"

Tinker turned and pointed to the man dragging the golf bag, who was now approaching them.

"We found it in one of the men's toilets, Mr. Glickman," the man said.

"This morning," Tinker said. "Before the park opened."

Horace's lips compressed into a thin, straight line.

"He's had all night to position himself," Tinker said.

"I'll tell our people," Horace said. "What more they can do, I don't know." He looked at the golf bag, a pained expression on his face.

"You've got to tell Jackie," Tinker said.

"It won't make any difference."

"He has to be told."

"Oh, he'll be told; but I can assure you, he's going on. You don't think he's going to stop now, do you?"

Horace began heading for the clubhouse.

"No, he can't stop now," Tinker said, feeling a sudden surge of anger, directed not at Horace, not even at Quentin, but at all the twisted and repellent impulses that were driving that demented mind. "He has to go out there," Tinker said, his voice rising. "Tell him that. Tell him"—shouting now at the hurriedly retreating Horace—"that he can't stop now. That he has to go out there. Tell him!"

Quickly Tinker went back up into the afternoon sunshine and began roaming through the grandstands. There were too many faces to look at now, row after row of them. He wanted Horace to be right, that it would be impossible to aim a rifle in this ballpark, that every possible precaution had been taken. You couldn't get away with it, except if it made no difference, if you were fanatic, suicidal. How obsessed was Quentin? Where there was no fear of consequences, there was no sense of risk.

He's here, Tinker thought, looking around with a feeling of despair almost philosophic. Standing in an aisle behind the Dodgers' dugout, he gazed out at the now crowded upper and lower stands in left and center, down the left-field line, then along the right-field line and beyond the high wall and its screen to the rooftops on the other side of Bedford Avenue, where small knots of people were gathering. That was too far, Tinker thought. And anyway, the son of a bitch was here, inside. The golf bag told him that.

Resigned, Tinker became the mute witness. He continued his survey, his reading of faces, but now it was merely obligatory, a sort of loyalty.

The pregame workouts were over. The batting cage had been rolled across the field to its place under the center-field bleachers. The grounds crew had come to rake the infield and affix the white lines of the batter's box. And now the rituals were done, the field was momentarily empty, its green grass yielding to the memories of the old and the dreams of the young.

The electric organ upstairs suddenly struck up a jocular rendition of "Three Blind Mice" as the trio of blue-coated umpires came strolling along the right-field line carrying boxes of brand-new baseballs. And then through the Voice-of-God PA system came the reading of the lineups, first that of the "visiting Boston Braves," then that of the Brooklyn Dodgers, and what vestiges of suspended hope Tinker was still maintaining were quickly dispersed when the amplified voice announced that Robinson was playing first base and batting second. Of course he's playing, Tinker thought; nor was it a matter of courage or bravado or stubbornness: Jackie was there to change something. That's what it was all about: change.

A few minutes later a terrific roar of excitement filled the stadium as the Brooklyn Dodgers, fresh in their home whites, ran from the dugout to take the field.

Nine Brooklyn Dodgers, scattered across Ebbets Field, stood hatless as the National Anthem began. Tinker, who had wandered halfway down the right-field line, kept his eyes riveted on Brooklyn's rookie first baseman. The bigshouldered black man was standing with his head bowed, his first baseman's mitt on his left hand, his cap in his right. *Now*, Tinker thought. *It's going to happen now. He's just standing there.*

Never did "The Star-Spangled Banner" seem so interminable. Tinker kept watching Robinson, waiting. It would have to happen now. There was no better time, with everyone's attention fixed upon the field. A man could stand unseen behind the last row somewhere ... But Tinker, with this thought fixed as definite as a fact in his mind, did not look around. He simply stared at Robinson and waited.

And then the anthem was over and the players were in motion again, the terrible moment had passed, and the fans were yelling and clapping.

"Let's go!"

"Get it started!"

"This is the year!"

Dodgers left-hander Joe Hatten began taking his warm-up pitches as Robinson rolled easy grounders to his infielders. It all looked so orthodox and sanctioned, a tableau Tinker had watched countless times, the enjoyable tension of impending excitement, of a baseball game about to run once more through the old familiar rhythms that were so self-contained in a universe of their own, that had nothing to do with the violent stains of hate and murder. It was as if the game had its own immunity, protected by the innocence of its character.

"Hey, sit down!" someone yelled at Tinker, who was standing in the aisle.

He began moving, slowly, aimlessly, glancing out at Robinson, who was now backing up into his position as Hatten stood on the mound waiting for the Boston lead-off man to set himself in the batter's box. Some late arrivals bumped into Tinker as they hurried to their seats. An ice cream vendor told him to move his ass.

The crowd cheered as Hatten poured his first pitch in for a strike. Tinker, in his reverie, suddenly felt conspicuous as he saw hundreds of faces turning to him, then realized it wasn't he that was attracting them but a foul ball peeled off into the stands just above his head.

He continued to move slowly, glancing out at Robinson, who was now into his game at first base, crouching tensely with each pitch, then straightening after the delivery, punching his glove, shouting a word of encouragement to Hatten. The old familiar motions and gestures made it all seem absurdly normal, imposing on Tinker a deeper and deeper sense of isolation. The shouts of the crowd, coming from all sides, seemed to be carrying him further and further away.

"Way to go!" as the first batter was retired.

"Hey, peanuts!" a vendor cried out.

"What's the count?" someone nearby asked as Hatten worked on the next batter. "The scoreboard ain't got it."

"Come on, Joe, this guy can't hit you!"

"Looked good, Ump!"

"Is it two and two?"

"I don't know, the scoreboard's not working."

"Hey, ice cream!"

"Hey, peanuts!"

"Let's go, Joe, easy pickin's!"

"Don't let him get away, Joe!"

"What's the count?"

"I don't know, the scoreboard's screwed up."

"Already, on Opening Day?"

"The guy must be sleeping in there."

"The scoreboard ain't showing anything."

"What's the count?"

"The scoreboard ..."

"The scoreboard .."

Tinker paused, felt himself turning rigid as he stared with astonishment out at right field and its familiar monument of numbers and information, where, suddenly and incongruously, nothing was happening, where the numbers were not appearing, disappearing, reappearing, where the pitch-by-pitch game report was not happening.

The scoreboard, he thought, feeling as though he'd been struck by an electrifying flash. *He's in the fuckin' scoreboard!*

31

He had never considered himself a religious person, Quentin was thinking; not as a child growing up, not as a teenager, not even as a soldier in combat, when life or death was as chancy as a coin flip. Nor was he a religious man that morning, as he prepared to go to Ebbets Field. But he did possess faith, except that he chose to call it patience. Patience, which he had a lot of, was predicated upon faith, he believed, because its exercise implied a belief that one would achieve or receive what one was being patient about. Quentin realized that there didn't have to be any religiousness in this, that perseverance and self-discipline were secular virtues too, and that patience was sometimes merely a sedative for tension. Nevertheless, he was able to find something soothing and morally excellent in the calm with which he went about his business that morning. This was the way, he was certain, that anything momentous began, with an almost soundless moving about, with an almost lovingly diligent attention to de-tail, with an almost transfiguring sense of serenity, because of the knowledge that later when it was called upon the needed patience would be there, and that it, more than courage or resolve or reason, would provide the final resource. So if he was consciously not a religious man, he still thought enough about it that morning to enable him to feel at his core a perfect stillness that he associated with the presence of faith in its most sublimated form.

A nervous man, he told himself, would be unable to eat, and so, to further establish how well prepared he was, he made himself coffee and several pieces of toast, which he consumed.

After washing the breakfast dishes he went upstairs to his room, where the morning sunlight burned behind the drawn window shade. He removed the Louisville Sluggers and the rifle from the golf bag, then folded up the Brooklyn Dodgers jacket and stuffed it into the bottom of the bag. The cap, he decided, he would wear (it would help him look innocuous), and he put it on his head now. Then he took a length of clothesline that had been in the cellar and this too went into the golf bag. Laying the bag on the bed, he began sliding the bats into it, drawing a peculiar feeling of magic from the touch of each. With the bats inside it, he stood the bag erect on the floor. He picked up the rifle and disconnected stock from barrel and placed them on the bed, after which he lifted one of the pillows, held the corners of the case in his hands and let the pillow drop free. He put the two halves of the rifle into the case and twisted it around and around until it fairly bound the halves and then fixed the wrapping in place with several rubber bands. He pushed the parcel down into the bag among the bats as far as it would go. Into a second pillowcase he placed a long-handled wrench, screwdriver, and hammer, and these also he pushed down into the bag. Finally, after clicking it on and off several times to assure himself that it was working, he added a flashlight to the contents of the golf bag.

When all this was completed, he hefted the bag. It was not terribly heavy, though burdensome. But, he told himself, the more difficult the endeavor, the more satisfying the reward.

He went outside to check the morning mail. The box was empty. It was ten o'clock and he knew that by now the carrier had already passed. He went down the four steps of the brick stoop and stood on the sidewalk in the sunshine, hands on hips, looking first in one direction and then the other, conscious that he did this every morning as if paying obeisance to the day, and now as if paying obeisance to custom. Across the street, school was in session, many of the tall windows pulled down a foot or so from the top. From the fourth-floor music room he could hear a chorus of child voices singing "Down in the Valley." Above the straight line of the school's roof the sky was blue, broken here and there by the stray, solitary white cloud that looked like wanderers from a flock. That was a baseball sky, he thought, and it meant that today they would be playing the game in the schoolyard and on the empty lots of Capstone, and on the side streets under trees, using broomstick handles and pink rubber balls, and on the trimmed diamonds of the public parks: youngsters celebrating the April birth of baseball. And at Ebbets Field the New York Yankees would be playing the Brooklyn Dodgers in the spring's final exhibition game, setting the stage for tomorrow's Opening Day, the beginning of a new season.

With the golf bag strapped over his shoulder, Quentin left the house and walked to the corner, where he waited for the trolley car. Later, as the trolley's heavy iron wheels ground along the tracks of Bedford Avenue, he watched with narrow, sullen eyes as the black people began crowding on. They were noisy and eager and excited, many of them wearing their "I'M FOR JACKIE" buttons. When the car had filled up, the conductor stopped taking on passengers and the trolley skimmed along faster.

Quentin sat with the bag between his legs, swaying lazily with the trolley's motion, from time to time gazing with ironic scrutiny at the faces around him, his gaze so coldly unfathomable that whoever looked into it quickly turned away.

The trolley emptied almost completely at the

Ebbets Field stop. He walked along the ball-park's towering façade on Sullivan Place to the gate indicated on his ticket. To the man at the turnstile who looked curiously at the golf bag, Quentin said cheerfully, "I'm going to get these bats autographed." Tearing the ticket in two, the man shrugged.

He felt comfortable amid the crowds thronging up the long, gradual acclivities of the ramps heading toward the grandstand. No one seemed interested in the fact that a man was attending a baseball game with a golf bag over his shoulder. Once inside a big-league park, people felt a palpitating excitement, awed and transported by the majesty of a secular American temple, focused only on the game that lay ahead, indifferent to those around them. Quentin's blue Dodgers cap marked him a fan, a Brooklyn Dodgers fan, a man in partisan allegiance with the great majority of those around him.

He found his seat upstairs along the third-base line, behind the dugout of the visiting Yankees. He had the fourth seat from the aisle and he sat there with the golf bag standing in front of him. He explained once again, to a curious and garrulous neighbor, that it was his intention to get the bats autographed by Dodger players after the game. Otherwise he sat stolidly through the nine innings, with little interest in what was happening on the field. When the Dodgers were in the field he stared impassively down at the team's newest addition, whose every move around first base was cheered loudly and whose appearances at the plate evoked ovations. *Hello and goodbye*, Quentin thought.

When the game was over he remained in his seat until the departing crowds had thinned. Then he rose, hefted the golf bag onto his shoulder, and headed for the exit ramp. Instead of going all the way to the street, he turned off to one of the refreshment stands on the mezzanine level and bought a soft drink. He stood at the counter and sipped from the paper cup while the crowd continued to leave. Soon he was the only one standing there and the countermen were swiping away with damp cloths, getting ready to close down. Men with long-handled brooms and large, coarse bags were pushing the day's debris into small piles. A few spectators, reluctant to leave the aura of a ballpark, were still wandering aimlessly, holding their rolled-up scorecards, having last, dreamy looks at the field.

Quentin crushed the paper cup in his hand and tossed it into a large metal barrel that was already overflowing with cups, cardboard food containers, mustard-stained napkins, newspapers, scorecards. He crossed the mezzanine to a men's room, pushed the door aside, saw a maintenance man working with mop and pail, and turned and left.

The mezzanine corridor began to curve and

dip toward an exit ramp. Positioned here to face the incoming crowds was a rather jerry-built wooden stand from which scorecards were sold. The vendor stood inside on a platform several feet high and dispensed his wares across a wooden shelf. Quentin looked inside it, then took a careful survey of the immediate area. Seeing no one about, he dragged the structure and placed it against a wall, leaving just enough space for him to slip inside it. He laid the golf bag under the shelf and sat down next to it, drawing his knees up in front of him, staring at the wall. He was pleased with this bit of initiative; it was better than trying to hide in a lavatory or in an Employees Only closet or in some corner of the ballpark.

Dusk began to fall. Calling upon the patience which he believed was the same as faith, he found himself able to sit utterly without moving, without making a sound, infused with the idea that he would soon be in sole possession of the park.

Sounds became fewer. For a time he listened to grandstand seats being banged into upward positions to allow the sweepers to push-broom along the aisles. And then that stopped. And then the voices of men talking or calling to one another became fewer and more distant. Footsteps went past his hiding place, once something on metal wheels. Hours passed and darkness settled and soon he realized that the only sounds he heard were coming from outside the ballpark, the rattle of a passing trolley car or the soft sound of an automobile horn.

His legs ached for a moment as he unfolded them and slowly rose. He stood up inside the structure, a ghostly vendor in a dark and vacated place. He slipped out, then reached back in and pulled out the golf bag. From the bag he removed the Dodgers jacket and put it on over his sweater (the evening was turning chilly, so the jacket would serve a dual function) and then the two pillowcases containing the halves of the rifle and the other things he had brought. He dragged the golf bag with the bats into a nearby lavatory and left it leaning against the wall. *Let them figure it out tomorrow*, he thought.

In the darkness the ballpark and its ramps and girders and tiers of seats seemed endlessly vast. It was a sense both of awe and caution that made him move with self-conscious quiet, the pillowcases in hand.

To be alone was familiar enough; to be alone in the extraordinary silence of so spacious an enclosure, with thousands of empty seats and a forbidden expanse of grass amid the steel and concrete, with the stillness not entombed but poised, was curiously enthralling.

He followed a descending ramp toward the field, emerging from the mezzanine corridor back into the open air, the hugely empty ballpark but faintly visible in the arc of quarter moon that was fixed over the Borough of Brooklyn. He went carefully down the steps, hearing nothing but occasional street sounds from the world beyond the right-field wall. He entered the privileged box seat section behind the first-base dugout and hoisted himself onto the concrete roof and there stood for several moments, holding the pillowcases, surveying the great bowl of darkness in which he stood. Then he set the pillowcases down on the dugout roof, crouched, and jumped, his pocket change ringing softly as his shoes struck the ground.

Taking the pillowcases, he walked toward the outfield, recalling the old intimacy he had once enjoyed here, years ago, in that time now nostalgically embalmed by the phrase *before the war*, when with Harry's help he had obtained a job here and been captivated, like an acolyte in a temple, raking the infield and watering the grass and resodding the outfield, feeling the heartbeat of baseball as he explored the place's every contour and shadow.

He crossed the outfield grass toward the right-field wall—twenty feet high with a seventeen-foot screen on top of it—then walked along the wall past a billboard-sized advertisement for Esquire Boot Polish and another for Gem Razor Blades until he came to the base of the scoreboard.

The scoreboard towered over him, reaching almost to the top of the screen that ran the length of the wall. He paused for a moment and turned and took a long, penetrating look into the darkness, then went to the scoreboard's ground-level door.

Expecting to have to force the door, he was surprised when it swung back under his first pressure. He entered the pitch-black interior, pulling the door shut behind him. Stepping from dark into darker made his surroundings feel the more sinister, as though he had passed into another dimension. He put down the pillowcases and removed the flashlight, but before clicking it on covering the illuminating end with a doubled handkerchief, creating a misty column of light which he moved about prudently (since there were apertures in the scoreboard, the dimmer the light the better, and the sooner the light went out, the better that would be too).

It was surprisingly roomy inside, considering that the grandstand view made the scoreboard look as though it were almost flush with the wall.

He went up several steps to the concrete floor, careful to keep his head from contact with the structural angles. The dim light revealed a wall of large white numbers painted on steel cards that were hanging on pegs, and farther along were the letters of the alphabet, large and clear.

He sat down on a wooden folding chair, placing the burning flashlight at his feet, and emptied the pillowcases, laying out the halves of the rifle, the wrench, the screwdriver, the hammer, the coil of rope. He reassembled the rifle, slid his shells into the breech, closed it, and placed the weapon on the floor.

With his hand muting the light still further, he found some of the peepholes from which the operator followed the game. The openings allowed him ample space to get a decent rest with a clear sighting. The shot would not be difficult, several hundred unobstructed feet, and when he fired the target would be stationary. After selecting what he thought was the best firing position, he retrieved the tools from the floor. He prowled farther into the scoreboard—it was years since he had last been inside it—moving the light slowly along the far wall, wetting his lips as he began feeling the first pangs of anxiety. Then he smiled with relief, for despite the barrier in front of it, the door would cause no great problem. It was covered by a steel-mesh screen that was bolted into the wall at each corner of its square shape. Stepping close and fixing the light, he saw that each bolt protruded about one inch, enough for the jaws of the wrench to take hold. The door itself was padlocked, though the rust-coated lock did not look very formidable.

Intended as an emergency exit in the event of fire, the door had been built into the scoreboard when the then all-wooden structure had originally been raised, in the early 1930s. The door was not large—barely four feet across and around five feet high—and when open created an exit several feet above the Bedford Avenue sidewalk. The scoreboard had undergone modifications just before the war, with concrete floors and walls replacing the old, combustible wood. And so the emergency exit had become unnecessary and had been covered over, though not, as Quentin was relieved to see, irrevocably sealed.

The two upper bolts, against which he could exert the combined strength of his arms, shoulders, and back, yielded more easily than the lower, but these, too, finally began to grind out from their grip in the wall and come loose. With the last bolt dislodged, he took down the screen and confronted the lock, thoughtfully fingering its rough surface.

He took the hammer in hand and closed his fingers around the haft, contemplating the lock, which he already knew was not going to resist him long. Nor did it, as a single well-aimed blow of the hammer broke it apart.

He could see no reason now that the door should not open. Unobstructed, unlocked, it was simply a door, with hinges, a knob, some of its original wood visible through the peeling white paint. Of course it would open, he assured himself, but he would have to try it to be sure, and he could not do that until he was reasonably certain that the street outside was empty. All he wanted was to see the door part just a fraction from the wall; but even for that he would have to wait.

He sat down on the folding chair and shut off

the flashlight. He found the engulfing darkness comforting, as though it were in alliance with him. There were no distractions, nothing to interfere with the patience which he began to concentrate upon, as if it were some element to be swung into action. Limitless patience, he thought, was part of his temperament, something that had been woven into him with the stroke of his heart and the run of his blood. It was part of logic too, he believed; if circumstances dictated that you sit still, do nothing, wait, then a wise man would best do it with willing submission, with patience. The future would not be hurried, not by a single moment.

At two-thirty in the morning he felt the time had come to try the door. He put his hand on the brass knob and began slowly turning, with great care and discretion, like a person entering a bedroom of sleepers. When the knob would turn no farther he pushed gently and the door gave. He allowed it a half dozen inches of sway, caught a brief glimpse of Bedford Avenue, then pulled it shut again.

Tomorrow afternoon, with the Opening Day crowd suddenly on its feet in stunned silence at the sight of a player lying on the ground, that door would open and a man in a Brooklyn Dodgers cap and jacket would drop to the sidewalk holding something wrapped up in a white pillowcase. He would no doubt evoke some curiosity as he slammed the door shut after him, but he would allay that curiosity by walking casually toward Sullivan Place and turn the corner there and head nonchalantly toward the various gates and entrances, by now uninteresting and inconspicuous, and continue on, into the next street, shedding the cap and jacket when it was prudent to do so and stuff them into the pillowcase, and keep going, home, where he would sit and listen to the radio report what he had done, accomplished.

With his arms folded across his chest he sat on the folding chair and allowed himself to nap, knowing that in this position he would not sleep more than an hour or two. When his eyes opened he rose and went to one of the peepholes and peered out, saw Ebbets Field beginning to shape itself in the first somber intimations of dawn, the rooftop lines with their unearthly-looking light towers beginning to appear against the slowly unveiling sky.

Then he sat down and again dwelled within his stolid patience, now in final communion with it.

From his vantage point in the scoreboard he was soon watching the sun lay open the green grass and the tiers of empty seats, and not long after there were noises and movement. He watched the men hang the bunting along the field-level boxes and across the grandstand façades. He watched the grounds crew fuss with the infield and then roll the batting cage in from under the center-field stands. He watched batting practice and infield practice, saw the early arrivals begin appearing in the grandstands and bleachers. And then he saw a short, paunchy man heading along the right-field foul line, a man wearing a Dodgers cap and smoking a cigar and carrying a sheaf of papers. He watched the man cut across the outfield grass and head toward the scoreboard.

Quentin stepped back behind a partition, holding the rifle vertically in front of him. A burst of sunlight that suddenly illuminated the scoreboard's interior told him that the man had entered, and then just as quickly the light vanished. The man flipped a switch near the door that brought to life three bright unshaded bulbs hung at intervals overhead.

Quentin heard the man on the short staircase and stood perfectly still as the man passed the partition, passed Quentin, and when he had gone several steps felt the tip of something at his back and heard a voice say softly, "Right there. Don't turn around."

"Who's that?" the man asked, talking in a growl around his cigar. "How'd you get in here?"

"Do you want to live?"

The cigar dropped from the man's mouth, the papers from his hand. It wasn't that he did not understand what he had just heard, nor the stark import of it; it was simply that he had never had his life measured out for him with such brutal bluntness, with such insulting lack of ceremony. The shock rendered him mute.

"Then be absolutely still and do what I say," Quentin said, holding the rifle steady, its tip indenting the man's white shirt. "Do that and you'll survive."

The implications of that word—*survive*—intensified everything the man was feeling.

"Close your eyes," Quentin said. "Keep them shut. Lie face down and cross your hands behind your back."

The man knelt, then eased himself face down, groaning as his generous paunch flattened in on itself. He groaned again as with some effort he crossed his hands at the wrists behind his back. Quentin quickly knelt, laid aside the rifle, and straddled the prone figure with his knees, and with the length of rope bound the crossed hands together. Then with a handkerchief he blindfolded the man, tying the knot firmly against the bristly gray hairs at the back of the man's head.

"Answer me now," Quentin said, picking up the rifle and stepping back and resuming his erect posture. "Is anyone else coming in here?"

"In the fifth inning," the man said, "a kid comes in to give me a hand."

"Not until the fifth inning?"

"No."

"Good," Quentin said. "He'll be able to untie you then. Now all you have to do is lie there and not say a word. Not a word. Do you have children?"

"Children? Yes."

"Grandchildren?"

"Yes."

"Good. You'll have a story to tell them to-night. As long as you keep still and don't do anything stupid."

Rifle in hand, he took up his position at the peephole. The stands were filled now, murmurous in these final pregame moments. The field was empty, but he could see the players gathering in the opposing dugouts. He watched the umpires come walking down the right-field line. There was a brief meeting at home plate as the umpires and representatives of both teams discussed the ground rules. A few moments later the crowd roared as the Dodgers ran from their dugout and scattered across the field to their positions.

When the public address announcer asked everyone to rise for the playing of the National Anthem, Quentin lifted the rifle, rested the end of the barrel over the edge of the peephole and began sighting Robinson, who had just removed his cap and was standing near the first-base bag. The perfect moment, Quentin thought, as he had considered it when designing this whole bittersweet action; the moment when his target would have to stand absolutely still.

He frowned: the first-base umpire, standing erect, blue cap held over his heart, had positioned himself in a direct line with Robinson, almost obscuring him. *Move*, Quentin muttered. In a brief, wild moment of angry frustration he told himself to take them both. *Now. Do it now. Now. Now.*

He waited. Listening to the anthem, waiting for it to run its course, squinting down the barrel of the rifle and into the sunshine, his finger crooked against the trigger.

When the anthem was over, Robinson began feeding casual grounders to his infielders, moving about, keeping in motion. Quentin made minuscule adjustments each time Robinson moved.

When the game began and Robinson backed up to position himself in the field he continued to be a man in motion, bending forward and straightening up with every pitch, taking a step back or one forward, as his would-be assassin stood concealed several hundred feet away, everything honed down now to millimeters and milliseconds; the assassin now merely the instrument of a reflex, an automaton without thought, poised at the very brink, awaiting his flash of instantaneity.

Robinson's crouch at his position precluded the certainty of a perfect shot, and so Quentin waited. A muttered curse died on his lips. A ground ball to the infield would send his target to cover first base and fix him there for a moment, or a hit to right field would spin him around and freeze him just long enough. *Yes,* Quentin told himself now. *Just hang on for another couple of seconds.* But then a left-handed batter stepped in and Robinson moved over to play closer to the line and in doing so was again partly covered—from Quentin's angle—by the first-base umpire. This time Quentin cursed audibly, then found it necessary to tell himself, *All right. It's all right. In another few seconds . . .*

32

Tinker was in the aisle that separated the lower grandstand from the field boxes when he began running. He was already far down the right-field line, almost parallel with the mound in the Dodgers' bullpen, and did not have a great deal of ground to cover, except that most of it consisted of playing field, with a game in progress; but the spectacular lunacy of dashing across the outfield grass in front of over twenty-five thousand Opening Day customers hardly occurred to Tinker, who was suddenly possessed by the single frantic need to get inside the scoreboard.

He ran down the steps into the box seats, his feet moving so fast they looked as if they were in a violent tap dance, put one hand on top of the low railing and in a motion so swift it seemed as though he had never stopped running vaulted into the air and then down onto the field, landing with feet already—or maybe still—in motion, startling a husky uniformed special cop nearby into freezing with a hot dog and roll in front of his gaping mouth.

Tinker ran in foul territory toward the right-field wall, toward the bench under the Old Gold sign where the Dodgers' bullpen contingent was sitting. Two of them sprang to their feet in preparation for whatever the running man might be up to; but as he neared them Tinker suddenly cut sharply away, running on the field at the base of the right-field wall, hearing one of the players calling him by name. By now the special was in pursuit, having thrown down his hot dog and unlatched one of the field-level gates, lumbering across the grass with reddening face and pumping arms, looking almost comical in his laboring pursuit, like a cop out of an old two-reeler. He, in turn, was quickly followed by a man in a gray fedora and tan raincoat who, as he ran, slid his hand inside his coat and held it there. This man, running fast, was rapidly closing the distance between himself and the out-of-shape special, whose shoulders were heaving, who was panting, who kept calling Tinker a cocksucker and ordering him to come back.

Much of this peculiar chase scene went unobserved by the majority of the crowd, for just as Tinker ran onto the field, the Boston batter hit a towering pop foul behind the plate and almost everyone was watching catcher Bruce Edwards drifting back toward the screen, glove up and face raised skyward, hoping to make the putout.

As he bore down on the scoreboard door, Tinker was prepared to smash through; but to his surprise the door flew back as he twisted the knob. In his excitement, and with his momentum, there was little thought of caution, of danger, of consequences. But the moment he threw the door aside and burst inside and was out of the sunlight and the open air and inside the confined space and saw Quentin standing some fifteen feet away, glaring at him from the elevated working area and swinging the rifle toward him, Tinker felt a shudder of terror. He threw himself over the small staircase and flattened himself as he heard the hard, ugly roar of the rifle.

Several feet behind Tinker, just entering the scoreboard, the special took the shot in the shoulder and spun back against the wall and slowly slid down. Then Tinker heard another shot, this one from behind, this one from a hand gun exploding loudly in the narrow enclosure, and when he heard the rifle clatter to the concrete floor he looked up and saw Quentin staggering back on convulsively collapsing legs, his face insane with blood, and then he fell straight back, his arms cast rigidly upward as if in last, futile supplication.

Tinker drew himself slowly to his knees, gazing in disbelief at Quentin's motionless body, aware of the door behind being slammed shut. Then he noticed the bound and prone scoreboard operator lying just above.

"You all right?" he yelled to the man as the

33

"It's a decision that's been taken," Scott said. "We could ignore it, but I don't think we ought to. I think it's a responsible decision, when you take into consideration what we're dealing with."

Tinker was watching his boss expressionlessly. Scott was obviously uncomfortable. *He doesn't know what I'm going to do*, Tinker thought, taking a perverse pleasure in the moment.

The assistant district attorney, thin, pleasant-faced, prematurely gray, in a three-piece pinstriped suit, was standing in profile at the window, ostensibly watching the traffic below on the evening streets of Brooklyn, but who probably wasn't seeing anything, who was keenly attuned to this conversation, not only to words but inflections, who was waiting for Scott and Tinker to settle the thing between themselves, to see which way it went, before reentering it. The desk lamp was the only light turned on in the assistant D.A.'s office.

"I don't see how you can possibly keep it quiet," Tinker said, standing in the middle of the office, on his feet because he felt defensive. Scott was sitting on a maroon leather sofa against the wall. "One man is dead, another wounded, another was a witness, albeit blindfolded. Is it possible to keep it quiet?"

"Yes, it is," Scott said. "Very simply, if no one says anything, it can be kept quiet."

"But how do you stop people from talking?" Tinker asked.

The assistant D.A. turned from the window. He folded his arms, regarding Tinker with a steady, inquiring stare. *He doesn't know either what I'm going to do.*

"It's a very responsible decision, Joe," Scott said.

"Do I still work for the paper?" Tinker asked.

The assistant D.A. allowed himself a brief, cynical smile.

"Yes," Scott said, a note of weariness in his voice, "you still work for the paper."

"Would you print the story if I wrote it?"

Scott glanced at the assistant D.A., arching a single eyebrow.

"That's not the point, Joe," Scott said. "Whether we would run it or not is irrelevant, because if you write it somebody will print it. So it's really up to you. You know how everyone else feels—me, the publisher, the police, the Dodgers' people, and Mr. Hughson here. If this gets into the papers there is the very real danger of another crackpot getting the same idea. I think you know how volatile this whole situation already is."

"But I repeat," Tinker said, "I'm not the only one who knows. What about the other people involved?"

Hughson unfolded his arms. "In effect, Mr. Tinker," he said, "you *are* the only one who knows. What does the scoreboard operator know? Only that someone came in and overpowered him and tied him up. The man was terrified. He wants to forget the whole thing. The team has also suggested that his job depends upon him forgetting the whole thing."

"He's been threatened," Tinker said.

"No," Hughson said, his expression bland. "He's been promised job security."

"Nice distinction," Tinker said.

"And what does the special cop know?" Hughson said. "Only that someone ran out on the field and that someone else—a maniac— took a shot at him. Does he know what Quentin Wilson was doing in the scoreboard?"

"Has he been promised job security too?" Tinker asked.

"Plus his hospital costs being seen to, and his salary continuing while he convalesces."

"And the cop," Tinker said, "I suppose there's no problem with him."

"He happens to be an exceptionally able and courageous man who is looking forward to a long and distinguished career on the Force."

Tinker smiled whimsically at Scott. "What about me, Scotty?" he asked. "Do I get job security too?"

Scott sighed. "You've been incorrigible without it," he said. "God knows what you'd be like with it."

"But," Tinker said, turning back to Hughson, "twenty-five thousand people saw me and two men run out on the field, run into the scoreboard."

"There's nothing like twenty-five thousand eyewitnesses to prove that nothing happened," Hughson said with a self-satisfied smile that Tinker told himself was lawyerly. "The scoreboard was not functioning and, fine newspaperman that you are, you took it upon yourself to run out there and see why."

"Makes me look like an absolute asshole," Tinker said.

Scott smiled benignly.

"Thanks, Scotty," Tinker muttered.

"You'd had a drink," Hughson said. "Or two. The special injured himself going after you. Nobody knows he suffered a gunshot wound."

"And since Quentin's body wasn't carried out until the park had emptied ..."

"He was never there," Hughson said.

"I won't ask you what you're going to do about him," Tinker said.

"That's right, Joe," Scott said, lifting his hand for a moment. "Don't."

"He has no family," Tinker said. "Nobody to ask any questions."

"That helps," Hughson said.

"And nobody heard gunshots," Tinker said.

"There were no gunshots," Hughson said. "No matter what anyone heard."

"It'll leak out somehow."

"Not necessarily," Hughson said. He eased himself into the swivel chair behind his desk. "And anyway, Joe, think about it: we don't really know what Quentin was doing in that scoreboard, do we?"

"You know damned well."

"We're all entitled to think what we want to think. But you're the only one who claims with absolute certainty to know what he was doing there."

"You think maybe he had taken the injunction 'Kill the umpire' to heart?"

"Joe," Scott said, "we can only appeal to your good judgment."

"For which I've always been noted, huh? Look, you're asking me to bury the story of a lifetime, a story I broke and damned near got killed for. You're a newspaperman, Scotty. What do you think?"

"What I think is," Scott said, "that during the war a lot of good newspapermen sat on a lot of good stories because publication of same might have caused some jeopardy. A lot of very competitive and ambitious correspondents swallowed their egos in the name of common sense."

"The war's over, Scotty," Tinker said.

"So now there's something else. You saw that yourself this afternoon. All it takes is one nut to pick up the idea, say to himself, 'I can do this better.' There's a lot of simmering hatred out there, Joe, a lot of unbalanced people. You don't want to be the one to give one of them a notion."

"It becomes like a sanction," Hughson said. "The very fact that someone tried it makes it seem permissible."

"I need an answer," Tinker said, "to one very critical question: does Robinson know what happened?"

"He was told privately, after the game," Hughson said. "He knows what you did and he's appreciative."

"Does he want the story buried?"

"I discussed it with him," Hughson said. "I told him how we felt, and why. He said, 'You do what you have to do and I'll do what I have to do.' "

"Which is—?"

"He's going ahead, most definitely."

"How can he?" Tinker asked, shaking his head. "How can he possibly take the field every day, under these circumstances, and play a game of ball?"

"I asked him that myself," Hughson said. "I'll give you his answer: 'How can I not?' "

34

Tinker was slouched in the easy chair, legs stretched out in front of him, a tumbler of straight bourbon in his hand. His tieless white shirt was wrinkled, the collar soft and frayed from too many launderings. He looked weary, like a man at journey's end.

Sally was curled in the corner of the sofa, watching him from across the room, looking as though she were gauging his mood or trying to find some entry to his thoughts. It was close to midnight, the random street sounds subdued by the closed windows.

"I'm still not sure," she said, "just how upset you are—or even if you're upset at all—by this."

"By letting the story be killed? I feel a strange indifference to that. What does that tell you about my journalistic integrity? So maybe I'm not such a dedicated newspaperman. There are worse things not to be. And anyway, didn't they tell me that after all there is no story, that since nobody knows for dead certain what Quentin's intentions were, it would all be pure speculation? Maybe they're right," Tinker said tiredly, sipping from his drink. "Who the hell am I to be so presumptuous as to know what a lunatic was thinking?"

"You know damned well what he was thinking, what he was about to do."

"I guess it's the war," he said abstractedly, staring off into space for a moment. "I guess that's what it is. The good old war. You see, I've already been—if you'll pardon the lapse of modesty—a hero, recognized, cited, and bemedaled, and under circumstances more perilous than today's. That lights a little eternal flame under your pride, but at the same time it also burns away a lot of your ego. But if I'm a hero, what is Robinson? Day in and day out, he's going to be on that field. There's an awful lot that's driving that man, I can tell you."

"He believes in something," she said.

"Yes, he does," Tinker said appreciatively. "Should we envy him?"

"In a way. But it isn't always enviable. Most of the time it's something you've been shocked into. I think Robinson knows he's into a striving that may never end, no matter how much he himself may personally accomplish."

"Nobody can do it alone," Tinker said.

"Of course not," she said. "That's where you come in."

"Me?"

"You've got a forum. A couple of million people in this city read you every day. And don't tell me that what you write is simply an account of a baseball game. A sportswriter—a good one, one who is perceptive and can write—has a hell of a lot of scope. It may be baseball games that you're writing about, but those are human beings that are out on the field. What you say about them is going to influence how people are going to feel about them and react to them. This story is just beginning and you have an obligation to see that it's told fully and fairly. What are you grinning at?"

"Nothing," he said. "I'm just glad it was you who made that speech; I don't think I could have brought myself to do it. It would have sounded pompous."

"Pompous? You? Well, probably some day, but not for a while."

He got up and, drink in hand, walked to the window and stood there and looked out.

"Well, well," he said.

"What?" she asked.

"It's been rented again. That apartment."

She frowned for a moment, then said, "Oh. *That* apartment."

"There are lights on. People living there."

"Why shouldn't there be? Life goes on."

"In its way," he said.

AUTHOR'S NOTE

Despite references to actual people and events, this is totally a work of fiction. Consequently, certain liberties with dates and places have been taken.

The words "colored" and "Negro" in referring to blacks are anachronistic today but were common usage at the time this story takes place and are consciously used to better re-create the sense of that time.